D0340516

THE
SEA
OF THE
DEAD

THE
SEA
OF THE
DEAD

Being **VOLUME THREE** *of*
**THE CHRONICLES OF
THE BLACK TULIP**

BARRY WOLVERTON

 WALDEN POND PRESS

An Imprint of HarperCollins*Publishers*

Walden Pond Press is an imprint of HarperCollins Publishers.
Walden Pond Press and the skipping stone logo are trademarks and registered trademarks of
Walden Media, LLC.

The Sea of the Dead
Text copyright © 2017 by Barry Wolverton
Illustrations copyright © 2017 by Dave Stevenson
All rights reserved. Printed in the United States of America.

Library of Congress Control Number: 2017942890
ISBN 978-0-06-222196-4

Typography by Carla Weise
17 18 19 20 21   CG/LSCH   10 9 8 7 6 5 4 3 2 1
❖
First Edition

For Jennifer Rofé
For all these years.

THE
SEA
OF THE
DEAD

And when the childe had come to the Vale of Tears
In place of his fallen master,
For the final battle against the Armies of Dread,
Dread spoke, and said: Fear not, childe;
For today I will show you something
More precious than gold,
Rarer even than the Snow White Ram.
I will show you the Impossible Black Tulip.

—FROM THE FINAL STANZA OF *"THE EPIC OF ARBUTHNOT"*

THE JEWEL
OF CASHMERE

The Minister of Wit fussed with his clothes and beard for an hour before leaving his house, changing his trousers, tying and retying his jama, picking out just the right turban, and grooming his beard with cola nut oil until it shone like a brand-new rupee.

As if he wouldn't be dead before the night was over.

He shrugged on his choga, an expensive, heavily brocaded silk coat that always reminded him of a sofa cushion, and took a good look in the mirror. His wife caught him admiring himself and teased him. "You will make a fine nawab of Cashmere, Mullah," she said. "Everyone knows the primary requirement is vanity."

"Pshaw," said the minister, kissing his wife good night and turning to leave.

"Where are you going, fatso? The front door is that way."

"I'm going out the back," he said, flustered. "I want to check on the garden."

"It's still there," his wife said.

"Yes, yes," he said, hurrying out before she teased the beard right off his face.

The garden was fragrant with spring blooms, jasmine and hyacinth and poppy, and the overwhelming aroma calmed him. He took in every scent and buzz of insect, touched the leathery leaves of a rubber tree, moistened the tips of his fingers with the stray drops of a recent summer rain.

And then, a shock: he opened the garden gate onto the pitiful scene of a young girl slumped against the wall across the alley, petting a rat.

"Urchins!" he said, disgusted. "Be gone from here!"

The girl raised her eyes to him, and he received another shock—they were pale green. Not the irises, but the eyeballs themselves, cupping a pair of huge brown pupils, like an avocado sliced in half. She just stared at him and continued to stroke the rat, and the Minister of Wit felt sure he would lose his nerve and run back inside. But then he thought of having to explain to his wife that he was frightened of a little orphan, and so he stamped his foot in the alley and shouted, "Be gone, I say! Are you deaf?"

The girl turned to set the rat aside and slowly stood up. When she wobbled a few steps toward the garden gate, the minister felt his ample stomach clench. What if she tried to lay hands on him? But to his relief she turned and shuffled up the alley into the darkness.

The minister let out a great gust of air and turned the opposite way, following the alley to Dhari Street and then walking briskly through the heart of Jammu until he saw the sign for the Broken Camel.

The man he knew only as Lord Thursday was waiting for him, his white hair like a boll of cotton and his white eyebrows a pair of billowing clouds. Despite being dressed in a wool jacket and trousers and wearing a tweed cape, he had picked out a spot near the fireplace and apparently made the owner start a fire. That was a Brit for you—always fearing a chill, even in India. And was he drinking hot cider in June?

"Grab a seat, Minister," said Lord Thursday, offering his hand but not bothering to get up. "You're looking splendid as usual. Everything in Cashmere looks splendid, come to think of it. The streets, the gardens, the temples . . ."

"Yes, the great Akbar is quite the aesthete," said the minister, eager to avoid chitchat.

"So what it is you wanted to see me—"

The minister slapped his hand down on the table before Lord Thursday could finish his question. If the Brit was startled, or offended, he didn't show it. The minister peeled his hand away, leaving behind a small piece of paper, neatly folded. "Go ahead, read it."

Thursday picked up the paper, studiously unfolded it, and read. The wind seemed to catch his eyebrows.

"A poem?"

The minister nodded. "They've been left all over Cashmere, allegedly by a woman known only as Habba Khatoon."

"A lady poet?" said Thursday, astonished.

"I'm sure you have lady writers in Britannia," said the minister.

Lord Thursday thought about it for a minute, becoming distracted.

"*Anyway*," said the minister, "the problem is obvious."

"Is it?" said Thursday, marshaling his eyebrows toward the paper again, looking for clues. He mumbled aloud:

Where now is the day's delight?
And where the night's romance?
In garden paths the cobras sleep,
In flowered beds the widows weep
And the nightingale sings of revenge.

Our mourning dress shall be woven air and evening
  dew;
We pluck out our eyes and
Replace them with gemstones.
In henna I have dyed my hands;
In blood I will dye yours.

Thursday's lips kept moving as he read and reread the poem to himself, until the minister realized that the problem was *not* obvious. "Khatoon is known as the nightingale, you see, and the revenge she speaks of is for the Mogul takeover of Cashmere, which many feel was accomplished with deceit."

"Ah, yes," said Thursday, waving a hand at the poem. "The cobras and such."

"'Woven air' and 'evening dew' describe two different kinds of muslin used in Mogul clothing, suggesting that the aggrieved shall mourn by taking back from us."

"And this bit about plucking out their eyes?" said Thursday.

The minister sighed. Was this really a member of British intelligence he was sitting across from? "Akbar's nine ministers, of which I am one, are known as his navaratnas— his nine gems."

Suddenly Lord Thursday's eyebrows leaped upward like a pair of startled cats. "You mean all this talk about a conspiracy to steal the nine gems . . . it's not a jewel heist?"

"No," said the minister. "It's an assassination plot."

All Lord Thursday could do was shake his head. "Dear me, dear me. What can we do?"

"Prevent it?" said the minister. "Just an idea."

"But how?"

The minister stared at Lord Thursday, wondering how much pain he could inflict by plucking out his eyebrows one hair at a time. "The other ministers and I might have dismissed all this as mere poetry, but then I got wind of something called the Lapwing Conspiracy. I have it on good authority that this is the group planning to turn the nightingale's songs of revenge into action."

"Nightingales, lapwings," said Lord Thursday. "Why the preoccupation with small birds?"

"Is that really important?" said the minister, struggling to remain polite.

"Perhaps it's a clue!"

"I assume they take their name from a speech Akbar made a few months ago," the minister explained. "He described the protests against Mogul rule in Cashmere as the screeching of so many lapwings. Regardless," he added quickly, before Lord Thursday could get off track again, "we're all on guard until the identities of these people can be ferreted out. I myself am afraid to show my face in public. Akbar says he can't spare extra security right now, but he's offered the help of the British, per his arrangement with Queen Adeline."

"Well, you're in good hands," said Lord Thursday. "Tell me everything you know, and I can assure you that the Britannic Secret Service will do the rest."

The minister decided not to ask why the BSS didn't *already* know everything, and proceeded to spend the next hour giving Lord Thursday a detailed rundown of the situation. He was so frustrated by the time he left that he marched straight home by the main roads and walked right up to the front of his house, lapwings be damned. He was going to enter *his* house by the front door.

His sudden bravery didn't stop him from stealing glances up and down the street before unlocking the door, or from closing and locking the door behind him as quickly as possible.

"You wouldn't believe the night I've had, Wife," said the minister, shambling back to his bedroom as he unwrapped his choga and tossed his turban aside. "Britannia will forever be stuck in the Middle Ages if this ancient dimwit they sent to me is supposed to be one of the queen's finest."

The minister filled his wash basin with the pitcher of water and washed his face. He looked in the mirror and noticed how quiet the house was. "Where are you, Wife? Shveta?"

"Here I am, Mullah," she said, coming into the bedroom

and wrapping her arms around her husband from behind.

"And what did you get up to tonight?" said the minister.

"I just sat here and thought about how much I worship you," came her reply.

"Funny. Perhaps *you* should be the Minister of Wit."

"Perhaps," she said, moving her hands up his back and gently massaging his shoulders. The minister closed his eyes, the tension from his meeting melting away. "The neck, Wife, the neck. Ah, yes."

Her agile fingers worked her husband's long neck with the skill of one playing a musical instrument. In fact, the minister never realized he was having trouble breathing until he began to feel lightheaded and wobbly, his legs going out from under him. And perhaps, before darkness overtook him, he was able to catch a glimpse of the slight smile on his wife's lips as he collapsed to the floor, sputtering his last words: "Deceitful cow."

The creak of a wooden door made Shveta Do-Piyaza look up.

"Is he dead?" said the girl with the avocado eyes.

"As a doornail," Shveta replied.

PART ONE

THE
LEAGUE
OF BLOOD

CHAPTER

1

BEWARE MONKS
WITH RED SASHES

Anyone who saw the boy tearing down the hill would be forgiven for thinking that he was running for his life. For one thing, there was his reckless, breakneck pace, heedless of the steep slope of the mountain, loose rocks, and the power of gravity. For another, he obviously wasn't from this part of the world, and this was a part of the world that didn't welcome outsiders. And finally, even from a distance you could tell he was spindly—all arms and legs and baggy clothes, like a scarecrow light on the stuffing. It was clear the boy couldn't defend himself; fleeing from trouble was his only option.

He wasn't far down the hill when his feet went out from under him in a shower of rocks and dust, putting him on his backside. But not for long. As soon as his rear end hit the ground and he began sliding, the boy quickly tried to regain his feet, planting his right heel and pushing off with his hands, thrusting himself upright for a few steps before pitching forward and falling hard on his face. He slid down the mountain for at least twenty feet before slowing to a stop with his nose about six inches from a boulder.

Bren didn't try to get up. He just lay there, one cheek in the dirt and his arms spread wide in surrender, and listened to the crunch of boots on gravel coming down from behind him.

"What was it this time?" said Sean, squatting next to him. "Chipmunk? Frog?"

"Rabbit," said Bren, his mouth filling with dust.

"A rabbit," Sean repeated. He stood up, hooking a hand under Bren's arm as he did so and helping him to his feet.

Bren flashed back to his first time on the deck of the *Albatross*, when the rocking boat pitched him off his feet. It was Sean who had helped him up then, too. Bren brushed away the dirt from his trousers and cinched up his tunic, a short brown coat that closed across the front with a yellow sash.

"And what did this rabbit do to send you chasing after it?" Sean asked.

Bren said nothing at first, embarrassed. "There was just something about the way she . . . *it* . . . came near me when I was out getting firewood, like it wasn't afraid of me or anything. Like it *wanted* me to notice it."

"And what did you think when it took off running down the hill?" said Sean. "*Away* from you?"

"I don't know," said Bren, kicking at a loose rock and taking a few steps uphill, away from Sean, who followed him.

"Lad, listen. I'm not going to pretend I understand half of what you told me back in Khotan. About what happened under that tree, and what happened to Mouse. But you sure made it sound like she was gone for good. I know that doesn't stop you missing her something awful. I know I do."

Bren took another few steps up the hill. *What happened under that tree.* He didn't half understand it himself, even though the memory of their last conversation had been replaying in his mind over and over in the weeks since he'd lost her.

There's something you need to know about the girl we found in the cavern, on the Vanishing Island, Mouse had said. *She was never a sorceress, or an heir to anything. She was a pawn of the magician, Anqi Sheng, who sacrificed her to protect the identity of the true heir to the Ancients and their powers. I was the true heir. Anqi Sheng had to keep the white jade far away from everyone until I could find it. His decision fated me not to grow up until I made it to the Vanishing Island. He also needed to buy time— centuries, millennia, whatever it took—for the black jade stone, which had been lost through the ages, to reappear. It's the two stones together where true power lies.*

Mouse had reached up to touch the black stone around Bren's neck, and he tried to remember the way her hands looked before they had turned to dust. She gave him the secret to opening the Dragon's Gate, but told him not to.

That's what Anqi Sheng wanted, to open the gate and release the full power of the Eight Immortals back into the world. But I refuse to honor the prophecy.

She had grabbed Bren's hands, which is when he had noticed that Mouse was aging right before his eyes.

My white stone and your black one. They represent a wound as old as time. They are the key to the gate, Bren, but you mustn't open it!

He could remember the words, but when he tried to remember Mouse—the way she had looked as a child, the sound of her voice, the depth of her black eyes—that's where his perfect memory nevertheless failed him. All he could see was the old woman with the frail skeleton, her skull showing through wisps of grey hair.

The Ancients lost power for a reason, and they are no more deserving than Qin, or Kublai Khan, or the Netherlanders, nor any of the religions that have tried to lay hold of the East. Whoever comes to power, there will no doubt be a prophecy about their downfall.

He had hugged her, tried to hold her so tight she couldn't leave him, but the harder he squeezed, the lighter her frail body felt. And before he knew it, he was grasping at nothing but the wind, and a swirling mass of dried leaves and bare twigs. Mouse was gone.

He kept hearing her last words to him, whispered in his ear: *Those who seek immortality find only death. There are greater rewards elsewhere, if you keep looking.*

She had told him how to open the gate. She also told him he shouldn't. But Bren had to make his own decision, and he had chosen wrong. He had been foolish and selfish and caused terrible destruction. And beyond that, what? His mother—or the ghost of his mother, or a memory of her?—had told him to take back his stone and close the gate *before more damage is done.*

Something told him she wasn't just talking about the earthquake. He reached into his pocket to make sure the black jade stone was still there. If he were to lose it, he would never be able to convince himself that what happened on the mountain had really happened. Even grasping the small, cool stone in his fist, he wasn't entirely sure.

"Bren," Sean called after him. "I know this might not

be the best time to tell you that you're going the wrong way."

Bren, who was near the top of the hill now, turned and looked back at Sean. And then, perhaps out of spite or embarrassment, he continued on to the top and paused before turning around. Sean, trying to catch up, took a false step and fell to his hands and knees. When he looked up, Bren was tearing back down the hill again, right at him.

"Dear God, lad, what is it this time?"

"Men," said Bren, grabbing Sean's arm and helping him up. "Monks with red sashes."

"Red what now?" But Bren was already past him, and Sean, despite a sudden sharp pain in his right ankle, took off running too.

Bren veered toward the Black Jade River, which they had been following from Khotan, as if he might dive right in. But he pulled up short of the river, heading for what appeared to be an upturned skiff along the riverbank.

"Come on!" he said, struggling to turn the boat over by himself. Sean arrived out of breath, his ankle throbbing, and helped Bren flip the boat and push it into the water. Bren got in first.

"Who are those men?" said Sean. "What's wrong with red sashes?"

"I'll tell you after we're safe," said Bren, picking up the

skiff's two oars and handing one to Sean.

"We can't just go around stealing boats," Sean protested, holding his oar across his lap while Bren frantically tried to paddle with his. "This could be someone's livelihood."

"We just need it for a bit," said Bren. "We'll leave a note."

The monks—there were three of them—came to the top of a slope overlooking the river and pointed at them. One of them raised his arm high in the air, as if he were twirling an invisible lasso, and a moment later came the sound of a heavy *thunk* against the side of the skiff. Bren and Sean looked to find a small, three-pointed blade buried in the wood. Another monk's arm went into the air.

"Okay, we'll leave a note," said Sean, putting his oar to water and paddling hard.

The next missile hit the skiff in the stern. The two after that hit the water just behind them.

"Faster!" said Bren. "You know rowing isn't really my strong suit."

"If I row any harder I'll turn us in circles," said Sean.

Bren glanced up long enough to see the three monks running alongside the river after them, and he feared that he and Sean alone wouldn't be able to row fast enough. But the river's current gave them a much-needed boost, and after they turned a bend and put the monks out of sight, they steered the skiff to the far bank and got out on the other side of the river.

"Let's find cover," said Sean, "and then you can tell me why monks are attacking us."

Bren already knew from their travels so far that the mountainous landscape was pocked with caves and eroded sandstone walls where they might be able to hide. And if they couldn't find one soon, he'd just dig one himself. But after climbing up the riverbank and over a rocky ridge, they spotted salvation right away—not just one cave mouth, but dozens of them, as if this part of Asia had been colonized by giant rabbits.

"Thank the Good Lord," said Sean. "They'll never find us, but by dumb luck."

"Don't jinx us!" said Bren, running for one of the caves. "Dumb luck has helped us out a few times."

"Aye," said Sean, following Bren through one of the mouths. They didn't stop until they were deep inside, in total darkness.

"Wonder how far this goes," said Bren, trying to pick up any sense of light or moving air.

"Don't know," said Sean. "Don't know as I want to find out."

"Might be our best way out," said Bren. "We have no idea how long those monks will be after us."

Sean grabbed Bren by the back of his ratty tunic to

keep him from walking farther into the darkness of the cave. "Speaking of that, you were going to tell me why they were chasing us in the first place. And how you knew to be afraid of them."

Bren nodded before realizing that Sean probably couldn't see him. "Yeah, I was coming to that."

THE LEOPARD'S NEST

"It was a monk at the Leopard's Nest who warned me," Bren began, before breaking off. These days he was prone to that, losing his train of thought, not finishing sentences. His mind was constantly taking him elsewhere.

This time it took him back to the highest place he had ever been—the Leopard's Nest monastery in the Kunlun Mountains. Bren and Sean had been walking for a week since leaving the village of Khotan, following the Black Jade River as the old woman of the mountain had instructed. It was the safest and most direct route back to the West, she had explained. Their best chance of getting home to Britannia. They had spent a few days after the earthquake searching for Lady Barrett and Yaozu, without success. They had offered to help the ravaged village, but the locals wanted them gone. Many blamed the outsiders—Bren and Mouse, especially—for the disaster that had visited them.

Wrapped in homespun, hooded vestments to make them anonymous, Bren and Sean had set off with little food and water into a high, arid landscape of changeable moods: hot and blustery by day; at night, distant and frigid.

Their hoods gave them some relief from the sun and wind, and the river was an endless source of freshwater. But neither eased the sores on Bren's feet or took the ache from his bones. At night their garments provided little warmth, but they were able to dig holes in the desert floor to keep from being exposed, and they collected camel dung along the way to burn instead of firewood.

They felt lucky to have the Black Jade River to guide them, and to slake their thirst, but the river attracted other travelers, and animals, until the dark ribbon of water became more like a thread of anxiety constantly being tugged at. This vast region of western China was sparsely populated by a mix of Chinese and Turkic peoples, including Mongols, and though they didn't encounter strangers often, Bren and Sean were forced to wonder each time if they would be welcomed, ignored, or attacked.

Their worst fears were nearly realized one afternoon in a valley in the shadow of the Kunlun, when they stumbled upon a border skirmish between two small groups of men on horseback. They had seen the first group from a distance, watering their horses, when the second group came charging over a hill toward the river, shouting and brandishing scimitars and bows and arrows. Bren and Sean hid until nightfall, and when the sounds of the skirmish finally stopped, Sean suggested that they abandon the river.

"We have a rough map made by one of the villagers in Khotan," he said. "We'll just have to go as the crow flies, over the mountains."

As he said it, they both turned to look at the distant Kunlun range. Despite what they had been through in China on their long march with Yaozu, the Kunlun still seemed impossibly high, even from this distance.

But Bren knew Sean was right. And so, before dawn they set off at an angle to the river, directly toward the mountains. When day broke, Bren couldn't stop himself from turning toward the spot along the river where the fighting had taken place. A handful of men and horses lay still amid swirling motes of dust, as if merely asleep, surrounded by dreams.

"Bren, look."

Sean called his attention away from the dead to the living, a lone horseback rider approaching from the south.

Even from a great distance Bren could tell he was a man of sturdy build, and he appeared to be holding something huge with his right arm.

"Is it one of them?" said Bren. "One of the men who did that?" He nodded toward the carnage by the river.

Sean shook his head. "I don't think so. Why would he be alone? And coming from that direction?"

The two of them just stood there while the man rode toward them. What else could they do? There was nowhere to run, nowhere to hide.

As the rider came closer, Bren, already nauseated by heat, hunger, and the sight of the dead bodies, imagined the man holding up a human head, the trophy of some vanquished foe, the way warriors and executioners do. He almost became sick, until he saw what it really was—a bird. An enormous dark-brown bird of prey.

"Is he a falconer?" said Bren. He knew that Queen Adeline had falconers in her court who joined her on hunts, but they were mostly ceremonial. Prey was captured with conventional weapons.

"He may be a falconer," said Sean, "but that's no falcon. That thing's the size of an eagle."

When at last the lone rider approached, Bren could see that Sean was right. The bird appeared to be a golden eagle, its brown body topped by golden-brown feathers on its head and along the nape of its neck. It was as tall as the man from the waist up, perched on a heavily padded sleeve, which the rider rested along his right thigh. The man stood his horse at a slight angle to Bren and Sean, the eagle's dark-brown eyes fixed fiercely on them.

"What do we do?" said Bren, after almost a minute of silence. No one had moved, no one had said a word. The rider's eyes were as dark and glassy as the eagle's. Bren was sure he hadn't blinked this entire time. He guessed he was Mongolian, or Uighur, or perhaps Tatar, based on where they were and how he was dressed, and the fact that he was on horseback. Aside from his heavily padded sleeve, he wore a brown jacket of sturdy cloth and trousers tucked into knee-length boots of soft leather. His face was a weathered stone, and on his head was a fur-trimmed red hat topped with feathers. Draped across his saddle was a string of wild hares.

"I have no idea," said Sean. "I don't imagine we speak a common tongue. I would suggest not provoking that bird, though."

As if it could tell they were talking about it, the eagle adjusted its grip slightly, its massive talons large enough to crush the man's arm.

And then his arm came up.

Sean flinched. Bren jumped back as the eagle spread its wings, ducked its head, and launched itself straight at them, its feet grazing Bren's head as he dove to the ground.

He cowered there, covering his face, expecting to be ripped apart, when he felt something grab him. Not the eagle, but Sean, helping him to his feet. Again.

"Look at that," said Sean, pointing skyward to where the eagle had already reached soaring altitude. Then he turned to the man on horseback. "He really comes back to you?"

The man didn't answer, of course. But he pointed after the eagle and looked at Bren and Sean. When they didn't appear to understand, he climbed down from his horse and kneeled in the dirt. He drew three figures, two on foot, one on horseback. He sketched a wiggly line that Bren assumed to be the river, and then he drew mountains. Finally he drew the eagle, then pointed from the two men on foot to the eagle and back.

"He wants us to follow it!" said Bren.

He tried to mime what he was saying to the man, and though he did it badly, the man nodded, pointing after the eagle again.

Bren looked at Sean. "Do we have a better option?"

"Aye, no," said Sean. "But we were headed toward the mountains anyway."

"No, I think he means for us to follow the eagle to a specific place. Look."

Bren knelt beside the man's drawing of the mountains and hovered his index finger left and right, until the man understood. He bent over and drew a line from the eagle to a point in the mountains—the highest point, if his drawing were at all to scale.

And that is how Bren and Sean came to find the Leopard's Nest monastery, a small religious fortress tucked away in the crown on the Kunlun range. It took them a week to reach it, and Bren was convinced they never would have found it without the eagle's guidance. Whenever the path they were on forked, or seemed to end, the eagle would appear in the sky like a lodestar, then vanish when they were on the right track again. It was the first time he admitted to Sean that he believed, or wanted to believe, that Mouse might've found a way to help him.

The yellow-robed monks of the Leopard's Nest welcomed them and fed them, and let them sleep in one of their houses, a gold-roofed building that sat like a hat atop a steep mountain peak. It was as if they were used to hosting guests and strangers, which seemed unlikely given how remote their location was.

There were no words exchanged, and not just because of the language barrier. The monks didn't appear to speak to one another unless absolutely necessary. But one monk surprised Bren with an unusual form of communication. Two monks separated Bren and Sean, and Bren's host took him to a remote pavilion and knelt opposite him on a bamboo mat with a low table between them. He produced a small bottle of sand and scattered it on the table, and with a small stylus drew a picture that looked like a cannon.

"I know we came through China," Bren tried to explain, "but I never learned the writing."

The monk erased the cannon, spread the sand again, and drew a rectangle. He added a pole next to it—a flag.

Bren just shook his head.

The monk drew a third image beneath the flag—a ship.

Suddenly Bren knew. "Navy signals!"

The monk nodded, understanding Bren's enthusiasm. He drew two more flags of different shapes. Bren knew the combination immediately: a warning to approaching ships.

"I'm in danger? From whom?"

The monk drew a stick figure—a man, then another.

"There's a whole gang after me?" muttered Bren. "Who are these men?"

The monk stood up. He grabbed the yellow sash around his waist and cinched it tighter.

"Monks? Like you?"

The monk pricked his finger, letting a bright-red drop blossom on the tip. He pointed to his sash again.

"Monks with red sashes," said Bren. "What did I do? How can I stop them?"

Of course, the monk hadn't been able to understand him, other than the tone of panic in Bren's voice, but that's when he left the pavilion and came back with a set of folded clothes, the brown trousers and robe-front tunic Bren was now wearing. Perhaps it's some cloak of protection, Bren had thought idly as the monk helped him into his new clothes. Both Bren and Sean were also given furs, for which they were grateful, with the changing season and the higher elevations they were passing through.

"Where did your monk take you that morning?" said Bren. "I never thought to ask."

"All I got was a silent tour of the monastery's yak farm," said Sean. "For some reason he thought I'd be interested in milking a yak. I grew up on a farm in Eire, and I wanted to tell him I ran away to the sea when I was barely twelve because I didn't want to grab another cow's teat for the rest of my life."

Bren laughed. "Well, you haven't. It was a yak's teat."

Sean laughed, too, and it was if a layer of skin fell from them, making them feel cleaner . . . lighter. That's when they heard voices.

"Where are they coming from?" said Sean.

Bren keened an ear in one direction, then another. The cave tunnel was like an echo chamber. He couldn't tell exactly where any sound was coming from. He had no choice but to guess. "Let's go this way."

They ran deeper into the cave, mostly on blind faith that if the monks with red sashes were pursuing them, they would be coming from behind. The tunnel narrowed and wound deeper into darkness, and to Bren's relief the voices faded. But where were they?

"Over here," said Sean, who was running toward a faint light in the distance. Bren ran after him, blindly guiding himself by slapping at the tunnel walls with his hands, when suddenly he turned a bend and pulled up short, almost running Sean over.

The light was from a small fire, tended by a man who most definitely was not wearing a red sash. But standing in the mouth of the cave opposite them were the three monks who had been chasing them. One of the three monks shouted something; the other two drew daggers from their robes.

"What do we do?" said Bren.

The man tending the fire stood up and turned to Bren. He spoke in English. "I suggest you run or fight."

THE LEAGUE OF BLOOD

Hearing the man speak their language caught both Bren and Sean off guard, which is when the armed monks attacked. One slashed at Bren, who turned in time to avoid a direct hit. The other monk came for Bren too, thrusting his blade at Bren's stomach but missing when Sean knocked his arm aside with a piece of firewood.

The third monk—the leader, Bren assumed—started toward him, plunging his hands into his robe and drawing out small curved blades in each hand. *What did I do?* Bren wondered, as it was becoming apparent to him that he alone was the target. Sean was just in the way—literally. He stepped in front of the leader, holding the piece of firewood like a club. The leader stopped until the other two were ready to strike again. Bren reached into his trouser pockets, but he had nothing. The folding knife Mr. Tybert had given him was long gone. But then he felt the stone. . . .

It all happened in a flash. Bren remembered how the muggers in Map had attacked him and how his mother's stone had saved him. How it had saved everyone on the *Albatross* when they had been ambushed by Iberian warships. Could it save him again?

Sean was outmanned and outarmed. Bren did the only thing he could do—jump in front of his friend as all three monks attacked.

He heard Sean scream. Or maybe it was his own screams, he couldn't tell. He felt the burning sensation as three blades entered his body, setting his insides on fire. He coughed up blood.

He had never heard anyone describe to him what it was like to die. How could they? But as Bren fell to the ground, all he could feel was a sense of relief. The pain subsided, replaced by numbness. It was as if he were drowning in a warm bath. No one came to his aid. All Bren could do was close his eyes and wonder, before it all slipped away, why his mother hadn't saved his life this time.

He woke up in total darkness. The air was cold and dry, which he took as a good sign, until he smelled the acrid odor of smoldering fire. Or was that brimstone? Demons were poking at his sides; the pain was unbearable.

"Be still, lad," said one. "He's trying to save you."

"Sean?" said Bren, still unable to see.

"Aye, it's me. It's dark out, and we had to snuff the fire in case any more of those bloody monks are looking for us."

Bren tried to sit up, but a set of hands he didn't recognize gently stopped him. "Lie still," said the stranger. "Your wounds are quite serious."

Bren realized his tunic was undone, and he felt for the places where the blades had entered his body. Two were already stitched shut; the man was working on the third.

"What happened?" said Bren.

"Our new friend here saved my life, and he's trying to save yours, if you'll let him," said Sean. "Quit talking. You're wasting your strength."

What strength? thought Bren, who let his head fall back against something soft. He was soon out cold.

▲▲▲

The next time he opened his eyes, it was daytime. Natural light filled the entrance to the cave, and Sean and the stranger were sitting around a small fire, sharing a meal. The stranger was thin and had a full grey beard. He wore a white turban and a dark green robe that looked like it hadn't been cleaned in a very long time.

"Ah, Bren is awake!" said the man.

"How do you feel?" Sean asked.

Bren wasn't sure how to answer. He was alive, and when he sat up, he felt stiff and sore, but his pain was numbed. He looked down at his stomach and sides and admired the neat surgical work and tidy stitches.

"Meet Ali-Shir," said Sean. "Warrior poet and surgeon."

Ali-Shir laughed. "Your friend is being funny. I know a few things."

It was Sean's turn to laugh. "A few things? You singlehandedly disarmed all three of those monks and sent them running for their lives! And then you performed some combination of witchcraft and surgery to keep Bren from bleeding to death!"

"So the three monks are still out there?" said Bren.

"I'm afraid so," said Ali-Shir. "Proof that your friend exaggerates. A real warrior would have killed them, I suppose."

"Aren't you afraid they'll come back? With friends?"

Sean smiled. "We moved. While you were asleep, lad."

Bren looked around. He never would have known he was in a different cave. "How do you know English?" he said. "I guess you've already explained that while I was out."

"I don't mind telling my story twice," said Ali-Shir. "I

—33—

am a linguist. I grew up on the eastern frontier of the Persian Empire; my parents were Turkic. As a child, I learned several of the central Asian languages as well as Persian. I received an invitation to study at the House of Wisdom, in Baghdad, but I was expelled for heresy."

"Heresy?" said Bren.

"I asserted that the Turkic language was superior to all others for the purposes of literature. The Persian elite did not fancy that. So I came back home, and then began traveling east, to learn and study the Himalayan and Chinese languages. I picked up English in Baghdad because of the Church of the East there."

"And you picked up medicine and martial arts as well?" said Sean.

Ali-Shir shrugged. "I am a poet," he said. "I will admit to that. In fact, while you were recovering, Bren, I was composing a few lines about your bravery."

"Bravery?" said Bren.

"I was as shocked as you are by the use of the word," said Sean. "What you did was plain foolishness."

Bren tried to activate his memory, recalling the events of however many days ago that was. He had thrown himself in front of Sean, right in the path of the three blades, because . . . because he thought the black jade would protect him. Instinctively he reached for his pocket, to make sure the stone was still there. It was, but why hadn't it worked?

"Why were they trying to kill us?" said Bren.

"Not *us*," said Ali-Shir. "You! The leader referred to Bren as *the Knowledge Thief*."

"What does that mean?" said Bren. It sounded like something Mr. Black would have called him back when Bren used to sneak books out of the old man's store.

"Well, did you steal something from them?" said Ali-Shir.

"I don't even know who they are!" said Bren.

"Ah, I see," said Ali-Shir. "Judging by their dress, I'd say they were part of the League of Blood."

"Bloody terrific," said Sean.

"The League of Blood is not traditionally a violent group," said Ali-Shir.

"You could've fooled me!" said Bren, holding open his tunic to show off his three stitched wounds.

"What I mean is, their name doesn't mean what it sounds like. At least, not in translation. The League of Blood believes certain people were born to control the knowledge of the world. Or perhaps the knowledge *in* the world is more accurate."

"You mean, *blood* like family?" said Sean.

"Precisely. This select group of heirs is called the Nine Unknown. They supposedly guard nine sacred books of knowledge that would be dangerous if they fell into the wrong hands." Ali-Shir turned to Bren. "These monks must believe you have stolen one, or something connected to them."

Bren couldn't believe he almost *died* over something so absurd. "Why in heaven's name do they think that?" he said.

"Wait a second," said Sean. "You said the monk at the Leopard's Nest warned you about men in red sashes. Why would he have done that, given what Ali-Shir just told us?"

Bren just shook his head. "I don't know, honestly! I didn't steal anything from the Leopard's Nest."

"Are you sure?" said Ali-Shir.

"Of course I'm sure!"

Ali-Shir thought for a moment, then snapped his fingers. "What about a gift? Did one of the monks give you something? Something that perhaps wasn't his to give?"

"No," said Bren. "They gave us food and shelter. And the clothes I'm wearing. The ones I had been traveling in were falling apart."

"They didn't give me a new outfit," said Sean.

Ali-Shir came over to Bren. "May I?" he said, motioning for Bren to take off his tunic. Bren handed it to him, and Ali-Shir turned it inside out, looking at it backward and forward. Finally he spread it out along the ground and began picking at the stitching along the inside of the collar. After he'd worked at it for several minutes, Bren could see what he was up to.

"There's something sewn into the back?"

"You're pulling my leg," said Sean.

But all Ali-Shir was pulling was a large square of fabric from inside Bren's tunic, carefully working loose the threads so as not to damage the fabric itself. When he was done, he turned the loose piece over and laid it on the ground for all of them to see. It was an incredibly detailed painting, an ornate geometric pattern of circles and squares, with figures of gods or people and cosmological images. The innermost circle had a background of sky blue and appeared to show three mountains thrust out of snow or ice, the sun rising behind the one in the center.

"I don't believe it," said Bren.

"I'll be damned," said Sean.

"We may all be damned," said Ali-Shir. "If this is worth killing for, then the League will not stop pursuing you."

Bren wanted to curl up in a ball and cry. Why him?

"Do you have any notion of what this is?" Sean asked.

"In a literal sense, yes," said Ali-Shir. "It looks like a tangka. It's a style of Tibetan art, a painting on cloth. Often used as teaching tools because they typically depict religious stories or historical events."

"Sort of like a book?" said Bren.

Ali-Shir thought about it. "Yes, I suppose you could consider them booklike in a way."

"So you're saying this small painting might be one of

the nine books of sacred knowledge," said Sean.

"I did not say that," said Ali-Shir. "I said it appeared to be a tangka. Your conclusions beyond that are as good as mine."

"I should just leave it here," said Bren. "That way if anyone catches us, I can prove I didn't steal anything."

"Perhaps," said Ali-Shir. "Assuming they believe you. Then again, perhaps you were given this for a reason, and are meant to use it."

"How?" said Bren, not meaning to raise his voice. "I'm sorry. I'm just . . . this is too much."

Ali-Shir gently laid a hand on his shoulder. "I think I should put your tunic back together for you. And then I believe I can get both of you out of here safely, headed west. There are caravans that pass north of here, not too far, traveling one of the old Silk Roads to Cashmere, India, and Persia."

"You're not coming with us?" said Bren.

Ali-Shir shook his head. "No, my young friend. Sean explained to me that your ultimate goal is to reach home. Your home. My home, and destiny, lie here."

FUGITIVES

A man who might have been a cadaver dressed up for a prank sat propped at the end of the church bench, clutching a Bible. It was no ordinary Bible, either. It looked to weigh half as much as the man himself, bound in thick brown leather and held closed with two brass-buckled leather straps. The man held it as if it were his last worldly possession, which in fact it was.

It was hot in the church. It was hot everywhere in India, and the thin man nestled into the blanketing heat and fell asleep.

He had a strange dream. He was sitting at a long wooden table in a candlelit hall, with a ledger opened before him, filled with names and notations. With one hand he held a large quill pen, and with the other he touched the end of his nose, which extended far in front of his face and curved to a narrow point. He thought that was odd, so he reached into his robes for a looking glass (*How did he know he would find one?*) and looked at his reflection. He was Thoth, the ibis-headed Egyptian god of writing, the scribe for the gods.

He replaced the looking glass and looked up from his ledger to find he was not alone in the long hall. In the middle of the floor was a large set of scales, being operated by a jackal-headed man—Anubis. Waiting hungrily alongside was Ammit, the god with the body of a lion and the head of a crocodile. Anubis had placed the Feather of Truth on one side, and on the other, he prepared to set a fresh heart that Thoth recognized. It belonged to Emily Owen, mother of Brendan Owen. The scribe felt the blood run cold through his ibis heart. He tried to put the quill pen aside, but found he couldn't. He was compelled to record the results of judgment, whether Emily Owen would be allowed to pass into the Afterlife or be devoured by Ammit.

Anubis lifted the beating heart in both hands and moved it toward the scale as the crocodile god opened his mouth, his teeth stained with the dried blood and tissue of unworthy hearts.

Thoth felt his hand shake as Anubis set the heart upon the scale, and the breath caught in his narrow throat as the heart began to descend while the Feather of Truth slowly rose from the ground.

When the heart and the feather were level, the scales came to rest. Ammit closed his mouth in disappointment and stalked away; Thoth, his hand still shaking, recorded the result in his ledger.

But he wasn't done. It was the scribe's duty to record the spells Emily Owen would need to pass through the Afterlife—to write her Book of the Dead.

He was alone in the hall now. The ledger was gone and before him was a long, blank scroll of papyrus. The man dutifully began to write the necessary hieroglyphs across the page, somehow knowing them without knowing. He wondered if he would get to see Emily Owen in person, but instinctively he knew his purpose was to guide her to another—her son. It would be a long book, a difficult one to finish, and as he paused to contemplate the difficulty, someone began trying to take the book away from him, tugging at it from behind. Someone he couldn't see, but he cried out, "No! I have to finish! It's a matter of life and death!"

Archibald, wake up! Archibald!

Archibald Black woke with a start, clutching at the Bible in his arms. Sitting next to him was David Owen, one hand on Black's shoulder and the other on the Bible.

"Don't worry, Archibald," said David. "I'm not trying to steal your Bible. I was just afraid the bloody huge thing would crush you."

Black tried to sit up, but the Gutenberg Bible was in fact so heavy that it more or less had him pinned against the edge of the church bench. When David Owen held his hands out again, Black nodded and let him take the Bible and help him sit upright.

"Did you know you fell asleep?" said David.

"Of course I did!" said Black, checking the corners of his mouth for drool. "I'm exhausted, as I'm sure you are."

David nodded. "Speaking of exhausted, I'm afraid I may have exhausted our options for getting out of here. Apparently Jammu becomes the winter capital for Cashmere. Everyone's coming in; no one's going out."

"That's preposterous," said Black, stretching his rather lengthy back and arms to restore his circulation. Church pews apparently were universally uncomfortable, to prevent the wicked from dozing off. Black was no ordinary sinner, though. He and David Owen had come to India on false pretenses, as part of Britannia's Indian Royal Survey in the service of Mogul emperor Akbar, and now were unofficially fugitives, having used the distraction of an earthquake in northern India to escape the emperor's army and flee to Cashmere. David Owen claimed this was a disputed territory, but they had discovered that wasn't exactly true. In

Emperor Akbar's mind, there was no dispute who ruled Cashmere.

Now they were trying to escape again. By David Owen's reckoning as a professional mapmaker, they were due east from Baghdad, which had been their original destination—the House of Wisdom. But they were nearly two thousand miles away. Black had joked that there was an old saying: "A journey of a thousand miles begins with a single step." But there were two of them, so everything was double.

David Owen hadn't found the joke funny. After all, making it to the House of Wisdom was never much of a plan. It didn't necessarily bring them any closer to finding his son, Bren. In fact, it might be taking them farther from him.

"Obviously people are going to be traveling out of Jammu, David," said Black. "And we haven't exhausted all our options. That's why I'm here." He indicated the sanctuary of the church, which remained empty but for the two of them.

"What sort of church is this?" David wondered. "Doesn't seem to fit here."

"It's one established by the disciples of Prester John," Black explained. "Supposedly the last Christian king of the East. It's almost a cult, really, with pockets of true believers sprinkled across the Orient and India."

"Are we seeking sanctuary here?" said David.

"No," said Black. "Deliverance. Ah, here comes our man now."

A creaking door slammed shut, and David Owen saw the stooped older man shuffling across the altar and up the aisle toward them. "You're Black?" he said when he was still a few steps away.

Archibald pushed himself to standing while David remained seated, holding the enormous Bible. "You must be Prester Thaddeus," said Black. The two shook hands, and the stooped man sat down, motioning for Black to do the same.

"Now, as I understand it, you're a long way from home," said Prester Thaddeus, in a cheerful voice that David Owen thought had a hint of avarice in it. *Here were two wayward travelers, he must be thinking, and he is going to take advantage of them.*

"Fortunately, we don't need to get home," said Black. "Just to Persia."

"Still a world away," said Prester Thaddeus. "How do you imagine I can help?"

Black arched a scolding eyebrow at the minister. "I don't *imagine* anything. I was told by the person who set up this meeting that you could arrange for my friend and me to join a delegation to the Church of the East, leaving in a few days."

The minister clucked his tongue. "Ah, you heard correctly. We are sending a delegation westward, but those pilgrims were carefully selected. Each has something special, you might say, to offer."

I was right! thought David triumphantly, and he elbowed Black in the ribs.

"Ow! What the devil did you do that for?" Rubbing his side, Black turned back to Prester Thaddeus. "And might you have a suggestion for what we could offer? To make us worthy pilgrims?"

The minister's eyes went directly to the Bible in David Owen's arms. Black arched the other eyebrow.

"You must be joking," said Black. "This is a Gutenberg Bible. Do you have any idea how rare it is?"

David laughed. *Of course he does, you twit!* Prester Thaddeus just smiled.

"Christian Bibles are hard to come by in India. Such an important example of the Word of God would be invaluable to our ministry here."

"No doubt," said Black. "But I simply can't part with this. We need it for a much more vital purpose."

Prester Thaddeus merely shrugged and stood up, his stooped figure seeming to lunge at them. "Very well, perhaps there is another way." He motioned for his guests to stand and follow him.

Black turned smugly to Owen. "You just have to be

firm with people sometimes. Show some backbone."

"He gave up awfully easy," said David. "Although I must say, these days it's easier than ever to see your backbone."

They followed the minister through the creaking door at the back of the church, along a hallway, and through another door that opened onto a blinding light. For a moment David Owen thought the odd little minister had delivered them directly to salvation, until he realized they were just outside.

"Where on earth are you taking us?" Black demanded, shielding his eyes from the sun.

Prester Thaddeus didn't answer but kept walking until they entered a narrow alleyway that led to an unmarked door.

"What is this?" said Black, more confused than commanding now.

"The key to everything," said Prester Thaddeus, and he knocked twice. Nothing happened for a moment or two, until Black and Owen heard a lock being turned, and slowly the door opened inward. A light from within was just bright enough to see that it was a girl who had answered the door. And even in the dim light Black could tell that she had the strangest green eyes he had ever seen.

CHAPTER
5

THE BLACK
GRAVEL PASS

Bren had never seen yak before. More important, he had never smelled yak before. Although to be fair, the foul odor he was inhaling could very well have been coming from the dozen or so unwashed humans he was traveling with, not the half-dozen shaggy oxen.

Ali-Shir's parting gift to Bren and Sean was to arrange for them to join a caravan traveling west toward India, to a place called Leh, the capital of the Himalayan kingdom of Ladakh. The king there was building a new palace for his family, and all summer caravans of supplies and men and women looking for work had been traveling there. Bren and

Sean had been lucky—the weather would soon make the route impassible until the following spring. This was their chance to leave China undetected and escape the League of Blood. At least, they hoped it was.

Yaks were the most extraordinary beasts of burden Bren had ever seen. And they needed to be. Once the caravan crossed the Kunlun Mountains, the possibility of foraging became remote. They were entering a vast, high-altitude desert, unpopulated and scarce of life. South of the Black Jade River were nothing but soda lakes, where in a pinch they might be able to feed on algae blooms or briny shrimp. North of their route were bandits and warlords. In short, the yaks had to carry a month's supply of food for them, in addition to all their goods for trade.

It reminded Bren of being on the *Albatross,* and how the Far East traders had to carry months' or even a year's worth of supplies with them. One difference was that the yaks weren't carrying water. Instead, they drank milk from their three cows. Yak's milk proved to be golden in color, almost like butter and nearly as thick. Bren was reluctant, but the milk was sweet, with a hint of almond flavor.

The herdsmen used the milk to make other food, too—butter, a creamy food they called yogurt, cheese, and something called kashk, where they let the yogurt or milk go sour and harden, then rolled it into ball or broke it off into chunks. Bren never acquired a taste for it, but he never turned it down, for it was filling, if nothing else.

Among the supplies they were carrying to Leh were Chinese silk and spices, as well as works of art, paintings and sculpture that the king of Ladakh wanted for his new palace. But their most important cargo was a sled of timber known as huanghuali, considered the finest wood in Asia and the one used exclusively for furniture by many of the great dynasties. It came exclusively from the island of the Pearl Cliffs, Ali-Shir had told them, and thus was exceedingly rare.

"The Pearl Cliffs?" Bren and Sean had said at once, before proceeding to astonish Ali-Shir by explaining that they had been there, when their guide, Yaozu, had led them through a secret tunnel to mainland China.

When they had first joined the caravan, one of the women reminded Bren of Lady Barrett in a way. It was the old crone who cooked for them at night, using dried yak dung she had collected along the way for fuel since there was no wood. The connection made absolutely no sense. The woman must've been a hundred years old, with a face like tanned leather, and she walked with such a pronounced stoop that it looked as if she were constantly searching for something she had dropped. But once, while she was hunched over her kettle, something like a fox sneaked up on her, hoping to snatch a morsel for its own dinner, and the woman grabbed her walking stick and, in one surprisingly graceful motion, swung it behind her to bop the fox right between the eyes, sending it off dazed and hungry.

That was it, just that one gesture. It brought to Bren's mind the way Lady Barrett had so skillfully wielded her sword, the Tamer of Beasts.

Consider that unlucky fox tamed, the old-fashioned way.

The rest of the caravan were considerably younger and more able-bodied. Most were, after all, planning to stay in Leh and help build the king's palace. Ali-Shir had explained to Bren that traders like these led a difficult life, making long trips often to be deprived of their wares by bandits. The king of Ladakh had promised good wages and housing for the duration of the build. Ali-Shir also expressed some doubt that those promises would meet the caravaners' expectations. From what Bren had come to know of powerful men, he suspected Ali-Shir was right.

One night around their dung-fire, one of the men began telling a tale, starting off in solemn, hushed tones, but gradually becoming more animated, at one point pantomiming an attacking animal, or perhaps a monster. The horrified faces of the others made Bren assume he and Sean had just missed out on a good ghost story. Later, after the others had bedded down, the old cook came to them and explained what had happened—in English.

"He was warning us about the Beast of the Black Gravel Pass," she croaked.

"Warning us?" said Bren. "You mean, it wasn't just a story?"

The cook's mouth crinkled a little. "Not to them."

"Why are you telling us this?" Sean wanted to know. "*How* are you telling us this? We didn't think anyone here spoke English."

Bren too was wondering why the woman had never spoken to them before now. Then again, these were people who seemed to operate solely on the basis of necessity. Perhaps that applied to conversation as well.

"I'm telling you to be careful," the cook continued, ignoring Sean's follow-up question.

"So you believe in this beast too?" said Bren.

"I believe the beast is an invention," she said. "Meant to scare travelers, possibly even enemies. I've no doubt a pilgrim or two has been attacked and killed by a large animal up here in the mountains, but no, I don't believe some legendary creature guards the pass, like a dragon guarding a hoard."

Sean scratched his head. "So what are you warning us about then?"

The cook lowered her voice even more. "I overheard the man who told the story talking to another, a few nights back. I believe they mean to rob you. The beast is their cover story."

Bren couldn't help himself—he laughed. "Rob us of what? We have nothing!"

"That's not what they think," she said. "I didn't make out exactly what they were saying, but they believe you have something quite valuable." She looked squarely at Bren. "You, in particular."

He didn't laugh this time. He shuddered. Was one or both of these men in the League of Blood? How could they have known about the tangka? He could tell Sean was thinking the same thing.

"Should we sneak off during the night?" Sean asked.

"Where would you go?" the cook replied, which was a good question. "Just be on your guard. We're only a few days from the pass. You have the advantage of knowing who means you harm and where they mean to do it."

Bren felt sick. Their position felt anything but advantageous to him. His black jade stone was apparently worthless now, and he didn't see how he and Sean could defeat a pair of trained assassins, if that's what they were.

Over the next few days, Bren felt as if he were carrying as much weight as one of the yaks. These mountains, despite their altitude, were free of summer snow, but only because of the high winds that seemed to beat directly against you no matter which direction you turned. Bren had never felt colder in his life, despite the caravan supplying him and Sean with animal pelts to wrap themselves in. And Bren was still struggling with breathing normally this high up. He seemed to tire before everyone else, even the ancient cook.

The only blessing was that the road was not terribly steep. When you were already near the top of the world, how much higher could you go?

The toll of this barren route on pack animals became obvious as well. Bren began to notice the bleached and dusty bones littering the path. At least, he assumed they were animal bones. Who's to say some of them weren't human? For that matter, had it been the arduous journey that felled them, or was there really a beast lying in wait?

Sean seemed to sense Bren's concerns, and the day before they were to reach the pass, he led him over to some of the stray bones and picked one up.

"Look at this, lad. What do you see?"

"A bone," said Bren, feeling ridiculous for stating the obvious.

"Anything else?" Sean asked.

"A leg bone?"

Sean laughed. "No, I mean, do you see any damage to the bone? Any cuts or teeth marks?"

Bren looked more closely. He shook his head, and Sean picked up several more.

"What about these?"

Again Bren didn't see anything but bare bone.

"I've been keeping an eye out ever since the old woman told us that story," said Sean. "When I was a kid in Eire and we'd find remains of sheep that'd been taken off by wolves, you'd see teeth marks all over the bones. 'Course the buzzards would pick at the bones, too, but you could tell the difference. If a man or an animal's been killed with a blade, same thing. You'll often find cuts along the bone where the blade has gone all the way through flesh and tendon."

Bren felt his muscles twitch.

"There doesn't appear to be much evidence that our path is terrorized by some unholy beast or bandits," Sean continued. "Just a lot of death by natural causes. Exposure, exhaustion, starvation."

"Men can die of all those things, too," said Bren.

Sean nodded. "True enough. But in dire situations, the caravan will take care of themselves at the expense of the beasts."

"But what do you think of the cook's warning?" Bren wanted to know. "Do you think we're in danger?"

Sean didn't answer right away, but finally he nodded again. "I think it's best to assume we are."

That did it. Bren decided he wouldn't dare close his eyes during their last night before reaching the pass. Nor would he lie down, for fear his body would give in to exhaustion. Finally Sean convinced him they shouldn't behave out of the ordinary, which might arouse suspicion, but instead should take turns watching each other through-out the night.

Bren underestimated just how exhausted his body was. He dozed off an hour into his first watch.

What woke him wasn't a beast, or a treacherous traveling companion, but a bird. A tiny bird, trying to burrow under his pelt and into the tunic beneath his robe.

"Are you cold?" Bren whispered, cupping the bird in his hands. He tried to tuck it back inside his shirt, but the bird darted away into the night.

Bren rubbed the sleep out of his eyes and stood up to go relieve himself just off the road. When he turned to come back, he saw a shadow moving toward where he had been sleeping—where Sean *was* still sleeping.

"Sean! Sean!"

Bren's screams stopped the men in their tracks. There were two of them, and their hesitation gave Sean time to get to his feet. In the moonlight Bren could see that Sean had in his hand the short dagger he had carried with him since they first met on the *Albatross*. Unfortunately, the two men each carried butterfly swords—wide blades about the length of a man's forearm.

Bren took a step in their direction when something stopped him. He panicked before realizing his trousers were caught on something, and the moment he reached down to pull them loose, something leaped at him.

He was on his back in a flash, pinned down by two massive paws. He could feel claws pressing through his clothes into his shoulders, and he looked up with horror into a gaping mouth ringed with sharp teeth. He heard others in the caravan screaming in panic, and Bren wanted to join them, but he couldn't breathe.

And then the big cat closed its mouth and turned its head to the side. Its yellow eyes were fixed on something, and Bren, still pinned to the ground, turned his head to look, too. The old cook was standing there, pointing something at the cat. Not her walking stick, but a sword. For a moment, the gold sword with the scarlet hilt flashed across Bren's mind . . . the Tamer of Beasts. But no, that magical sword had disappeared along with Lady Barrett. This was just a dull-colored steel blade, but it did have this beast's full attention.

The cat retracted its claws from Bren's shoulders and stepped away from him. He could just make out the old cook's crinkled mouth mumbling something, as if she were baiting the cat, or perhaps casting a spell. She said something aloud, in her own language, and the two men with the butterfly swords reluctantly left Sean and cautiously approached. Others in the caravan produced small weapons, various kinds of knives mostly, or picked up pots and pans if they had nothing else. They were slowly surrounding the wary cat.

The men with butterfly swords attacked first, and when they did, the cook slipped behind one and slashed at his ankles with her sword. He cried out and crumpled to the ground, and as soon as he did, the big cat pounced, clamping its mouth on the back of his neck and dragging him off toward the darkness. The other, unsure whether to save his friend or defend himself, stood momentarily stunned, and the cook thrust her sword right through his stomach. He fell to his knees.

The cook drew out her sword, now red from tip to hilt, and watched the man fall face-forward to the ground. She picked up his sword with her free hand and said something to the rest of the caravan before turning to Bren and Sean. "I told them we're taking two of the yaks and going on ahead."

"We?" Sean replied.

"Gather your things quickly," she continued. "I don't believe anyone else was in on the plot to rob you, but the farther ahead we get, the better."

Bren obeyed and Sean did too, eventually. They didn't have much, and before long they were leading two of the yaks along the road in the moonlight with a bitter wind in their faces. They walked the rest of the night, and when day broke, Bren could see a narrow saddle between two mountains in the distance.

"The Black Gravel Pass," said the cook. "I'm sure you're as tired as I am, but let's keep going until nightfall, if you can."

What could Bren say? If a hundred-year-old woman could keep going, who were they to argue?

"Where did you learn to fight like that?" he asked.

The cook just looked at him with small bright-blue eyes. "Next time we camp, I'll build us a fire and explain everything."

CHAPTER

6

THE LADY VANISHES

They camped just before nightfall, on the other side of the Black Gravel Pass in a flat area of scrubby vegetation off the main road. Sean and Bren set to work stacking the dried yak dung and sparking a flame with the cook's flint and stone.

Once the fire was going strong, the cook sat cross-legged before it and leaned in toward the flames, close enough that Bren could see her flinch from the heat. He wondered if she was a conjurer or fortune-teller and this was some sort of—what was the word?—*pyromancy*. Fortune-telling by fire, the word Lady Barrett had used to describe what Mouse had done when she read the oracle bones.

But something else happened. The woman's face began to melt. Bren glanced at Sean to see if he was seeing the same thing, and Sean's glassy-eyed expression told Bren he was. He looked back at the cook, whose eyelids were now drooping at the corners, and whose wrinkles were deepening along her cheeks. She put her hands to her face and tugged at the loose skin, and to Bren's horror, the skin peeled away in strips of flesh, which the woman cast into the fire.

Bren didn't fully grasp what was happening until the woman pulled off her tangle of grey hair, and Lady Jean Barrett smiled at him from behind blotches of stray makeup.

"Dear Lord," Sean muttered.

"I thought," Bren stammered. "I thought you went through the gate. We looked for you after the earthquake. You and Yaozu."

He had never actually seen Lady Barrett or Yaozu go through the Dragon's Gate. The ground had begun to tremble once he placed the white and black jade stones in the river, and suddenly Bren had been alone. Until he saw his mother sitting there. Or the ghost of his mother, or a figment of his imagination. Except he had touched her, hadn't he? Felt his hand in hers? Didn't he have the black jade stone to prove it?

"If you weren't—aren't—dead," said Bren, "where did you go?"

Lady Barrett pulled a rag from her robes and began to wipe away the remains of her disguise. Bren wondered how he hadn't noticed her hands before, how they weren't covered with fake skin. Maybe it was just a trick of the mind, that once he saw the stooped figure and the aged face, he made the rest of her old, too. Or maybe it was just that even though her hands were those of a young woman, they were dirty and calloused from all her adventures.

"That's a difficult question to answer, Bren," she said, her voice still raspy from croaking as the old cook. "Remember when you tried to tell me about what had happened to you and Mouse on the Vanishing Island? How difficult it was to explain?"

"Because I didn't half understand it myself," said Bren. She nodded. "Exactly."

"What about Yaozu?" said Sean. "I watched the two of you walk through a hole in the mountain."

"Through to what?" said Bren.

"That's just it," said Lady Barrett. "I'm not sure. I don't know what I was expecting—a bright light, Heaven, Hell—but it wasn't all that different from where we had been standing. Except you two weren't there. I called to Yaozu, and he answered me, but I couldn't see him. I called again, and he was gone. It was as if we had each gone through our own version of the gate."

Bren understood what she was trying to describe. He had seen his mother sitting there in that rock-strewn landscape. Not in some afterlife or other world.

"Did you feel like you were being given a second chance—to change your mind?" Bren asked, remembering how his mother implored him to turn back.

"Yes!" said Lady Barrett. "It did feel like that, at first. But I kept walking, trying to figure out what was happening. I almost turned back. In fact, I did turn around, but I saw nothing like the opening I'd come through. Then the ground began to tremble, and in the distance I thought I saw a light, so I ran toward it. I never reached it, and the next thing I knew it seemed I'd been walking for days and had no idea where I was."

"Where did you end up?" said Bren.

"In the borderlands to the north. I was wandering in the desert. I don't know why I kept going the direction I was going, but eventually I saw a caravan in the distance. I followed them to a gate with five bright-white arches and a wall inlaid with bricks of many colors. It was beautiful. I feared that I would immediately be identified as an outsider, unwelcome, but this city—Shule, they called it—was a tapestry of every culture in this part of the world. Chinese, Turkic, Mongol . . . even Indian and Himalayan."

"So why did you feel the need to disguise yourself?" said Bren.

"Besides the fact that I enjoy playing dress-up?" said Lady Barrett, smiling. Suddenly Bren realized how much he'd missed her. He wondered, laughing to himself, if Sean felt the same way. "The truth is, I soon learned that two groups known as the Black and White Mountaineers were fighting for control of the city. By far the safest people were the merchants and traders. After all, they are the ones that give Shule its life. So I decided to join one of the cara-vans. I figured that was also my best bet for getting out of there. A built-in excuse to leave, if you will."

"So what happened to the Tamer of Beasts?" said Bren.

Lady Barrett reached for the dull grey blade she had been carrying. She picked up one of the stones ringing the fire and began smacking it against the blade. After a few good hits, a hint of gold shone through.

"Hard to look like a local merchant with a gold and scarlet sword," she said.

"Isn't it against some supernatural law to deface a magi-cal artifact?" said Sean.

Lady Barrett laughed. "Possibly. But the thing is, I'm not sure it's magical anymore."

Bren nearly jumped out of his seat. "It doesn't work anymore?" He thought back to their recent leopard attack. "You didn't use it to keep the beast from killing me?"

"No," she said. "You're lucky to be alive. We all are."

Bren dug around in his pocket until he produced the black jade stone. "Mine doesn't work anymore, either!" He looked at Sean. "That's why I jumped in front of you back in the cave. I thought I could protect all of us because of *this*."

They all fell silent for a while, considering everything they just told one another. Finally Bren said, "It must have something to do with the Dragon's Gate. Mouse didn't want me to open it because it would supposedly release the full power of the Eight Immortals back into the world. But maybe . . ."

"Maybe once the artifacts were back on the other side, the Immortals kept them there?" said Lady Barrett. "The power that animated them, anyway?"

Bren nodded. "Maybe. Yaozu did talk about how the Ancients had abused their power. The Emperors of Heaven and Hell had given them real magic—natural magic—and the Ancients had created the artifacts instead to make magic easier to use. Our stones—mine and Mouse's—supposedly had the divided spirit of one of the Immortals himself. Perhaps opening the gate was his chance to return to his real body, and the Immortals' chance to undo their mistake."

"You should hear yourselves," said Sean, still determined to be skeptical, despite all he had been through with Bren.

"I just know my stone seems to be worthless," said

Bren. "And so does Lady Barrett's sword. We have no idea about Yaozu's jade tablet, because no one knows what happened to him, or it."

"Why don't we discuss all the magic in the world, or lack thereof, on a full stomach," said Lady Barrett, rattling through her things for a dinner pot.

"I didn't know you could cook!" said Bren, whose admiration of the dashing adventurer, antiquary, and magician was coming back in full force.

"What's to know?" said Sean. "It's yak's milk ten different ways!"

Lady Barrett laughed. "I did miss you too, Mr. Graham."

"Why didn't you tell us who you were sooner?" said Bren.

"I wanted to tell you as soon as I saw you," she said. "I wanted to run right up to you and throw my arms around you. You too, Mr. Graham."

Sean blushed.

"But if I had done that, the rest of the caravan would have wondered who I really was, and then we all would have been under suspicion. I could have told you privately, but in my experience, the fewer people to know a secret, the better."

"What did you know about the two men who attacked us?" Sean wondered.

"Not much," Lady Barrett admitted. "They had signed

on not long before you. Maybe now's as good a time as any to tell me why they thought you had something worth stealing?"

Bren hesitated before answering. He wasn't sure how to begin. "Lady Barrett, have you heard of the League of Blood?"

"No," she said, smiling broadly, "but it sounds deliciously sinister. Tell me *more!*"

Bren explained about their trip from Khotan to the Leopard's Nest, and the men in red sashes, and what Ali-Shir had told them about the League of Blood. He didn't want to remove his tunic, because even by the fire it was cold at night, so he sketched, from memory, a rough drawing of the tangka in his journal, the one thing he had managed to hang on to since Khotan, for Lady Barrett.

"You say this is sewn into your shirt?"

"Yeah," said Bren. "I had no idea until the monks with red sashes caught up to us."

"It's interesting, but I'm afraid I've no idea what it is or what it means. I bet Archibald would know," she added with a wink. Bren immediately felt heart-sore for his old friend.

"Something just occurred to me," said Sean. "You explained how the monk warned you by using pictures of navy signal flags. How on bloody earth did a monk living in the mountains nowhere near the sea know navy signals?"

Bren thought about it for a second. "I don't know." He looked to Lady Barrett, who just shrugged.

"Oh well," said Sean, who began preparing his bedding for the night. "So now what? Do we still travel to Leh? Or do you have another plan?"

"I think we should proceed to Leh," said Lady Barrett. "The road is well established, and it goes in the right direction—toward home. We can make a new plan from there. Plus we could send a letter from there to Bren's father, and Archibald, with decent hope that it will reach them."

Bren and Lady Barrett prepared for bed as well. As he lay down, Bren couldn't help but think about the Dragon's Gate, and his experience compared to what Lady Barrett had told them.

"Lady Barrett, did you see anyone on the other side of the gate? Someone you knew, perhaps?"

"What do you mean, Bren?"

Now that he'd brought it up, he wasn't sure how much he really wanted to talk about it. He decided to change the subject. "Never mind. You don't really believe there's a Beast of the Black Gravel Pass, do you?"

"I'm going to be the Beast of the Black Gravel Pass if I don't get some shuteye," said Sean. "Pipe down, both of you. We have long days ahead of us."

Lady Barrett, whose bedding was close to Bren's,

whispered, "I'll let him pretend to be in charge just this once."

"Good plan," he whispered back, suppressing a laugh. Then, feeling guilty, he added, "I really don't know what I would have done without him since we all split up."

In the darkness he felt Lady Barrett reach out and squeeze his arm. "We're together again," she said. "Everything's going to be all right."

He immediately felt better, and was soon asleep.

THE QUEEN
OF CASHMERE

Archibald Black stared at the girl with the uncom-
monly green eyes, and she in turn stared back at him.
They were sitting face-to-face in an ornate, vaulted room
that completely defied Black's expectations. He and David
Owen had been led by Prester Thaddeus down a dark alley
to an unmarked door, and when the girl let them in, they
had passed through a crumbling corridor that reeked of
garbage and twitched with rats.

The girl had led them down several corridors, and
then up a flight of stairs, and just before passing through

an unremarkable door into this remarkable room, Prester Thaddeus had taken David away.

"Do you mind if I ask where we are?" said Black. "Where is my friend?"

"Which question do you want answered?" the girl replied.

Black thought about it. "Both. In that order."

"You are in Cashmere. Your friend is elsewhere," said the girl, and she got up and left.

"I suppose I asked for that," Black mumbled to himself. He stood up from the sofa he was sitting on and walked to the door where the girl had exited. It was locked. There were no other doors or windows in the room. He sat back down and looked more closely at the decorative motifs along the walls. They appeared to be murals of a sort, depicting Indian kings or gods, elephants, monkeys, cobras, and more than a few scenes of men and women that made Black feel flush.

Before long, he heard the lock turn and the door opened again. The girl came in, followed by a strikingly tall woman who seemed to glide across the floor. She wore a soft gold embroidered blouse, and a pale pink-and-white skirt that flowed past her feet. She wore pearl bracelets on both wrists and pearl earrings, multiple strands of precious stones around her neck, and a jeweled headpiece that featured a large ruby that lay across her forehead.

She was so striking Black almost failed to notice the two armed men who followed her into the room. They each carried monstrous swords whose blades got wider from the hilt, and they took positions on either side of the sofa while the woman and the girl stood in front of Black.

"Have I done something wrong?" said Black.

"You tell me," said the woman.

Black glanced at the two armed men before answering. "No?"

"How long have you been a spy?"

"A spy?" said Black, and he burst out laughing. "Wait, are you serious?"

"Quite," said the woman.

Black thought about it for a moment. He had hoped Emperor Akbar would presume him and David dead after the earthquake. But if he knew they were alive, and came to the conclusion that the whole reason for the Royal Survey was to spy on the Moguls, then he and David quite possibly might have triggered an international incident.

"I can see how it looks," said Black, squirming now. "But I can assure Emperor Akbar that we have absolutely no intention of spying on him."

The woman furrowed her lustrous black eyebrows. "Spying *on* him? No, my dear, I am accusing you of spying *for* him."

Black was stunned. "Who are you exactly?"

The woman's casual, friendly demeanor vanished, replaced by a fierce look that made Black scooch back on his sofa cushion. "I am Shveta, the only living descendant of Queen Kota Rani, the last legitimate ruler of Cashmere. And I intend to restore her line."

Black's prominent Adam's apple bobbed up and down his long neck as he swallowed hard. "Very well. But . . . I am not a spy."

"Prove it," said Shveta.

"How?"

"That's your problem, bub."

The armed men laughed, and Black started calculating his chances of getting past all of them and making it out the door. Assuming it wasn't currently locked. He glanced at the green-eyed girl, and he could have sworn that she shook her head, just barely, as if she could read his mind and was warning him not to do anything stupid.

"Ani, go get the other one," said Shveta, "and bring the book."

The girl left. *Ani*, thought Black. *And at least David is alive.* While they waited, Black tapped his foot nervously while Shveta continued to lord over him, folding her arms across her stomach with her hands hidden up the sleeves of her blouse. He couldn't look at her, so he turned to the bodyguard on his right.

"And what is your name, my good man?"

The guard held the gruesome sword in front of Black's face. "This is my name."

To Black's relief, Ani returned with David, clutching Black's Bible. She sat him on the couch. "Nice to see you again," said Black. "Did they accuse you of being a spy as well?"

David nodded. Shveta glided over and gently removed the Bible from his arms. One of the armed men fetched a small, low table, which he set in front of the sofa, and the other retrieved a chair for Shveta.

"What is this?" she said.

"I told you—" David started to say, but she held her hand up to his face. She wanted Black to answer.

"It's one of the original Gutenberg Bibles," said Black. "The first book produced with movable type. It's a technique whereby—"

"I'm aware of movable type," said Shveta. "I just don't believe you." She opened the book to a random page. "What is this language? Latin?"

"Naturally," said Black. "It was printed from the Vulgate, the officially recognized version of the Bible, which is written in Latin."

Shveta flipped through more pages, seemingly with no purpose in mind but to stall for time. "Latin isn't one of the languages I speak. In fact, I don't know anyone who reads or speaks it. Which of course makes it the perfect language for you to record your espionage."

This was getting to be too much for Black. "If I were keeping secret notes, why on earth would I record them in a gigantic tome that I have to lug around like a pack animal?"

"You're right, it's a silly idea," Shveta agreed, and then narrowed her eyes. "Which is why no one would suspect you." Before Black could protest, she added, "Also, I've had some of my people look into this, after your friend here gave us his story. This is not what the binding of these so-called Gutenberg Bibles looked like. And they were bound in two volumes, not one."

Black was indignant. "I'll have you know that my family was an early investor in Mr. Gutenberg's project. My great-grandfather requested one complete volume, and this binding was created specifically to accommodate the larger book."

Shveta started to reply, but this time it was Black who cut *her* off. "And if you have people who can research all that, you expect me to believe you can't find someone who can read Latin and tell you that this is, in fact, a Bible and not a spy journal?"

Shveta, who had folded her arms again, hiding her hands, slowly drew them out of her sleeves, showing Black a set of razor-sharp, inhuman claws. And then they were gone again. Black felt David grab his arm.

"Honestly, we're not spies," said Black.

Shveta tilted her head to one side. "Well, spies or not, perhaps there is a way for you to win your release."

"Anything!" David blurted.

"You landed at Bombay Island, yes?" Shveta began. "And traveled with Akbar's men through central and northern India?"

Black nodded cautiously.

"That's a very long time to eavesdrop on careless soldiers talking about their emperor's plans, yes?"

Black drew in a deep breath. "I'm afraid you've terribly overestimated our usefulness. David and I spent most of our time trying to figure out how to get free of the army."

"We may have overheard a few things," David put in.

"Go on," she said.

"Akbar and Queen Adeline had some sort of arrangement for Britannia to help the Moguls take over the south, below the Deccan Plateau."

Shveta waved her arm like she was shooing a fly. To Black's relief—no claws this time. An illusion, perhaps? "Everyone knows that," said Shveta. "So why did he take you north instead? Where were you headed before you supposedly *escaped*?"

David shrugged. "I'm not sure. Archibald was telling you the truth."

"Archibald!" one of the armed men blurted, rubbing

the top of Black's mostly bald head.

"I think you know more than you think," said Shveta. "You are surveyors, yes?"

"Not really," said Black.

"I'm actually a mapmaker," said David. "For Rand McNally."

"Ah, you see, I am learning more and more about you by the minute. So you have traveled these many miles with Akbar's men, with your trained mapmaker's eye surveying the land as you go."

"We didn't actually survey anything," said Black. "Not until we reached Agra, anyway. We never understood what was going on. We were just trying to get to Persia. David's son is missing. It's a rather long story."

"And a delightful one, I'm sure," said Shveta. "But you do understand this, don't you? That you're not going anywhere until I get what I want?"

"We're not spies," Black said again.

"We may never agree on that," said Shveta. "But what I do believe is that you and your mapmaker friend here could give me a great deal of useful information about our enemies. I want you to draw an accurate map of what you've seen and heard, the terrain and positions of Akbar's army, along with any other intelligence you shall recall when you try hard enough."

Black was beginning to suspect that Shveta never

thought they were spies. That it was all just an elaborate setup to pressure them into this. And he had to hand it to her, it was working. "And when we present this map, then what?" he said.

Shveta smiled. "Do you always ask so many questions, bub? Let's see what you come up with first. Then we'll talk."

A PRINCELY RESCUE

"Do people ever ride their yaks?" Bren asked, thinking about how nice it might be not to walk all the time. He put his hand along the broad back of the bull he was walking beside, as if measuring it for a saddle.

"They do," said Lady Barrett, who was leading the cow. "But merchants on long caravans consider the yaks' backs more valuable for carrying goods than people. I don't know if these two have ever been ridden."

They were so slow and sturdy, thought Bren, and their curved horns were practically like handles. He didn't weigh much more than a bundle of silk cloth anyway.

"I suggest we just keep walking," said Lady Barrett, to Bren's disappointment. "I know it won't be easy, but who'd have thought we'd make it this far, all things considered?"

"You did, remember?" said Sean. "When you convinced Bren and Mouse to detour through China with you?"

For once Lady Barrett didn't have a snappy response. The mention of Mouse brought down a curtain of silence around them for some time to come as they marched onward.

What eventually broke their silence was an obstacle none of them saw coming, one that made the decision to walk or ride a moot point. They had scaled the final ridge of the mountain they were on, and found themselves staring down into a wide valley. Between them and the valley, though—and stretching for miles, it seemed—was a glacier that cascaded down the entire side of the mountain like some vast sheet of glass. The valley itself was frozen, too, though whether it was a frozen river or ground, Bren couldn't tell.

"It's extraordinary how the weather patterns can change between these mountain ranges," said Lady Barrett.

"This can't be normal," said Sean. "We're still on the caravan route, aren't we?"

"As far as I know," said Lady Barrett. "But the merchants and traders who have been doing this for centuries know the routes are seasonal. Perhaps we missed a turn to a preferable path. Or maybe there isn't one. Many a caravan has met its demise over a long, arduous journey."

"Well that's comforting," said Sean.

"I'm all for positive thinking," said Lady Barrett, "but we have to face facts. We need a way down or a way around."

"Maybe we could just wait until it melts," said Bren.

"Aye," said Sean. "We'll just sit up here until next spring."

Lady Barrett stroked her chin and looked back the way they had come. "I really don't remember missing a turn. Granted, we're at summer's end, but our former companions obviously thought the way would still be passable."

"Maybe we should let them catch back up to us," said Bren. "We could go back toward the Black Gravel Pass, where we know for sure they were headed."

"Might be too late," said Sean. "They may have gone another way already."

"Perhaps," said Lady Barrett. "Still, it may be our only option."

Just then, the female yak began to inch forward. Before they could stop her, she had stepped onto the edge of the glacier, her front hooves skid-scraping onto the frosty surface, churning up a froth of icy particles, which roughened the surface and seemed to help give her purchase. She gingerly brought her rear feet onto the glacier as well, taking a step or two before stopping. She managed to stand still, apparently sure-footed, at a slight angle to the slope of the mountain.

"Do you really think she can walk all the way down?"

"Yaks can handle most anything," said Lady Barrett. "It's why they use them in these parts."

"Even if she can," said Sean, "what about us?"

The yak looked slowly back over her shoulder at the bull, as if to say, *Here's our chance to get away from these people.*

"Think the yaks could carry us all the way down?" said Bren.

"There's only one way to find out," said Lady Barrett. "Obviously, the braver of the two adults should try first."

At that, both she and Sean stepped toward the cow. Both lost their footing as soon as they stepped onto the glacier, sliding forward until they hit the yak broadside. The impact put them on their rear ends and stopped their momentum, but it knocked the startled beast off-balance, and as Bren watched helplessly, the yak lost grip with all four hooves and began to slide.

At first it was a slow but frantic descent, the yak flailing her legs in a futile attempt to regain her footing on the steep slope. And then all four legs went out from under her, splayed in four different directions, until she was sledding down the mountainside on her belly with ever-increasing speed, bellowing so loudly that her voice echoed across the chasm.

There was nothing to do but watch, and what a sight it turned out to be. After a seemingly endless descent, the yak hit a part of the mountain where the descent became more gradual and began to slow, until she coasted off the relatively flat end of the glacier onto the snow-covered valley and spun slowly to a stop like a sprung clock.

"Is she okay?" said Bren.

The yak gingerly got to her feet, ice and snow beading up all around her shaggy body and bearded face, and turned to look back up the mountain, as if to ask what was taking the rest of them so long.

"Now what?" said Sean, just before Bren launched himself forward, sliding between the two of them and grabbing both by the arms, pulling all three feetfirst down the glacier.

The spray of ice from their shoes was so painful, Bren had to shut his eyes, so his only sensations for what felt like the next hour were of brittle cold striking his face and the deafening pressure of wind whipping by his ears. Oh, and his rear end somehow feeling both on fire and numbingly cold.

At last Bren felt everything start to slow down, his body feeling less like it had fallen through a trapdoor and more like he was coasting down one of the gentle hills of Britannia's countryside. And suddenly whatever was holding up his backside went from cold and hard to cold and soft as they all came to a slushy stop in the snowy valley.

When Bren opened his eyes again, the first thing he saw was the yak, just standing there. Was that a smile? No, he was just imagining things. A rapid change in altitude like that was bound to scramble your brains.

"Everyone okay?" Sean asked feebly. His hair and eyebrows were covered in frost and his pale nose was beet red, so he looked a bit like a snowman.

"That was fun, wasn't it?" said Lady Barrett, popping to her feet. "We'd never have gotten down the mountain that fast if not for the glacier. What a stroke of good fortune!"

"Aye, I've never felt luckier," said Sean, staggering up out of the snow, looking as if he might puke.

"What about him?" said Bren, looking back up at the bull, still standing at the crest of the ridge. He turned around and slowly walked the other way.

"I guess we're down to one yak," said Lady Barrett.

"Probably should've thought of that beforehand," said Sean. "We may bloody well need him."

He was right. "Sorry," said Bren. "I didn't think."

He was dusting the snow from his pants and looking around the frozen valley. Or was it a river? Either way, it wasn't obvious which way they should go. Up or down the valley or across the next mountain ridge? Sean was thinking the same thing.

"Which way does the famed Silk Road go?" he asked Lady Barrett. "I thought there'd be more signs."

"Trouble is, there was more than one Silk Road," she said. "Which direction looks best to you two?"

Bren looked back up the mountain, as if his gut was telling him to retreat. Near the top he saw a group of people that he at first assumed to be the rest of the caravan they had left behind. But this group was farther north along the edge of the glacier than he and Sean and Lady Barrett had been.

"Lady Barrett, do you still have your pocket spyglass?" He pointed up. "I don't think that's the caravan."

Lady Barrett found her spyglass and took a look. "You're right, it's not. Six men. Mongols, I'm guessing."

"Are they following us?" Sean asked.

The spyglass still fixed to her eye, Lady Barrett shook her head. "They appear to be looking north of us." She turned her gaze up the valley. "More men. Many more. On horseback. Not Mongols, I don't think."

"An army?" said Bren.

"Could be," said Lady Barrett. She inspected the people atop the mountain again. "They're rigging something up. Can't quite tell . . . oh boy."

"What is it?" said Bren.

"I think it's explosives."

"They're going to try to blow the glacier," said Sean. "Ice avalanche. We need to get the bloody hell out of this valley."

"What about them?" said Bren, pointing toward the cavalry. "Shouldn't we warn them?"

"We don't know who they are," said Sean. "Maybe they're the bad guys."

"Maybe they're the good guys," Bren retorted.

Sean let out a great sigh and turned to Lady Barrett. "You're so keen on being the leader. *You* decide."

She was turning and turning the spyglass in her hands, staring into the distance. Finally she said, "We don't know who's good or bad in this context, or who deserves what. We do know that one group is about to try to kill the other, and that we could prevent the carnage. Morality dictates that we do so."

Sean rolled his eyes. "Thank you, Professor."

"You told her to make the decision," said Bren. "Let's go."

Bren turned and started half running up the valley, followed by Lady Barrett. Sean, who had to put his slack jaw back in place, was last. They forgot all about the yak, but when she noticed she was being left, she ran after them at a pace Bren didn't think possible for an animal that size.

"Hey!" screamed Bren, when he got close enough that he thought the men on horseback could hear him. "Hey!"

He resorted to frantic arm waving, and when they were perhaps a hundred yards from the men, one of them pointed their way. Now that he had their attention, he pointed up to the men with explosives. "Up there!"

A few of the men did look, and seconds later one of them was barking orders at the others, who sprang into action and began to gallop off down the valley in the direction from which Bren had come.

Just then, there was a concussive blast, and for a moment Bren wasn't sure if it was the sudden thunder of hooves or the explosives going off. It didn't take him long to figure out which. He saw Lady Barrett and Sean looking up at the towering plume of black smoke, and they all stood frozen as a long horizontal crack began to open along the top of the glacier.

A commanding voice said, "We need to move. Get on."

Bren looked up to see the man he took to be the group's leader, holding out his arm to Bren. Two other mounted men went to Lady Barrett and Sean.

"I said, get on!" the man repeated, and Bren and Sean took the hands that were offered to them and climbed up. Lady Barrett, who seemed incapable of doing anything except in the most improbable way, instead jumped on the back of their surprised yak, grabbed her thick coat, and spurred her into action.

"We're not going to make it," said Bren, who had barely attached himself to his rescuer's horse before it took off galloping down the valley.

"No future king of Ladakh is going to be buried by a bunch of filthy gold miners," the man shouted over the deafening noise of galloping horses and a piece of the massive glacier grinding down the mountainside. Even as he said it, his horse seemed to speed up.

So our rescuer is a prince? thought Bren as he buried his face in the man's thick fur tunic and held on to a pair of leather straps attached to the horse's saddle. He tried to stay down, but when he heard another explosion followed by a cracking sound, he couldn't resist looking back.

The glacier had torn across the roughest part of the mountainside, and in doing so had begun to come apart in the middle. The end farthest from them fell with sudden speed, crashing into the valley. When it did so, Bren finally learned that they were galloping across a frozen river, as the calved glacier plunged through the surface, bringing up an eruption of water and ice. The realization of how fast the glacier could fall seized Bren with panic—there was no way their horses, and a yak, could outrun the other half.

It was the mountain itself, however, that saved them. The remaining part, freed of half its weight, ground to a halt along the rocky ridge.

The cavalry slowed their pace when they realized what had happened, and eventually they came to rest near a tall, narrow pass in another mountain range, several hundred yards past where Bren, Sean, and Lady Barrett had come down the mountain.

Bren sat up on the back of his horse. When he turned the leather straps loose, his arms and hands ached. He must've had them in a death grip. He realized his whole body was damp with sweat, despite the freezing temperatures.

"How are you, young man?" his rescuer asked.

"Okay, I think," said Bren. "How are you?"

The man laughed out loud with gusto. "Me? I am grateful to you and your friends, that's how I am. I don't think it's giving you too much credit to say you saved our lives."

"Oh, well, it seemed like the right thing to do," Bren stammered, leaving out the part where they debated whether to help or not.

"I should think my father would like to thank you," said the man.

"Your father?" said Bren.

"Jamyang Namgyal, the King of Ladakh. I am his firstborn, Sengge."

"I'm Bren Owen," said Bren. "Firstborn of David Owen." He felt stupid as soon as he said it.

"Well, Bren Owen," said Sengge, "please come with us through the pass. Let us show you our kingdom and offer you rest and food."

Bren didn't know what to expect, or whether they had anything to fear. All he knew was that he was bone weary and starving. All three of them were. They eagerly agreed, and soon they were off again, though a wondrous natural gate to the other side of the mountain.

ENEMIES
OF THE BLUE SKY

Remarkably, the other side of the mountain was almost free of snow and ice, and nestled in the valley was a cluster of small white buildings, surrounded by a handful of larger buildings high above that seemed to have grown right from the rock faces. The largest structure wasn't even complete yet—Bren realized it must be the king's new palace that brought caravans like theirs to Leh.

Sengge noticed Bren admiring the work in progress. "We hope to complete as much of the new palace as we can before winter, when the caravans can no longer come through, and then finish the job next summer."

"We started out with a caravan carrying loads of wood for the palace," Bren explained. "We got separated when two men tried to rob us."

Sengge frowned. "There aren't many passable roads through these mountains," he said. "If these bandits come to town you must point them out. We will cut off their hands."

"Oh, they won't," said Bren. "Lady Barrett already took care of them."

"Her?" Sengge turned in the direction of Lady Barrett, who appeared to be arguing with Sean about something.

"Trust me," said Bren. "Don't underestimate her."

Sengge let out a great laugh. "Duly noted!"

They continued down the path toward the city, which to Bren's surprise wasn't gated. He supposed the mountain walls served as protection—along with what appeared to be Ladakh's considerable army—but his argument with Sean and Lady Barrett about who were really the "good guys" and "bad guys" kept bothering him.

"Sengge, why were those men trying to kill you?"

The prince's horse took half a dozen strides before he answered. "These mountains are full of natural resources. Gold in particular. Suffice it to say we dispute each other's claims."

"But who are they?"

"Mongols," Sengge replied bitterly. "Blue Sky worshippers."

Bren had no idea what that meant, but Sengge didn't elaborate. All he said was, "We are Buddhist, trying to build a peaceful kingdom. Yes, we have a large army, but that's because to our north and east are Mongols, who are conquerors, and to our west and south are the Moguls, adding more and more land to their empire. We have no choice but to push back."

Bren nodded but remained silent. What Sengge said might be true, but he had heard enough wicked people justify their actions to know he should guard his trust closely.

Sengge led them through the most crowded part of the city, sort of a merchants' quarter where Bren saw huge bins filled with salt, various grains, odd-looking plants and peppers, and silk, which he recognized at once.

"I briefly got to wear silk when I was in China," said Bren.

"You were in China?" said Sengge. "You were far from home, weren't you?"

"Still am," said Bren. "But I'm trying to get back."

Sengge nudged his horse over to a merchant who was folding a different sort of cloth and motioned for the woman to hand him a piece. He held it out to Bren. "Feel this."

"What is this?" said Bren, greedily clutching the soft fabric. Soft wasn't even the right word. He felt like he was holding a pillowy cloud.

"Cashmere," said Sengge. "Comes from a smelly old goat. Can you believe it?"

Bren was secretly praying the prince would make a gift of it, but he took the piece back and returned it to the merchant.

"We get the finest of everything here," boasted Sengge. "Four major routes of the Silk Road converge in Ladakh."

"I would rename it the Cashmere Road," said Bren, and the prince laughed.

From the city Sengge led Bren, Sean, and Lady Barrett up a narrow mountain road to a group of fortresslike white buildings perched atop a series of foothills. They passed through a wooden door of golden timbers into a courtyard lush with grass, potted plants, and caged birds that were chirping and singing nonstop.

"Wait here," Sengge instructed. "Enjoy the view. I will go find my father, and we will see about your accommodations."

They were higher up than when they had come down into town through the mountain pass, and from here Bren could see a complete map of the town and the mountains that ringed it. A golden eagle dropped from the clouds and soared over the palace.

"From here the word *kingdom* seems to fit," said Lady Barrett.

"It did seem less than impressive from the ground," said Sean. "But this is nigh majestic."

"The mountains are full of gold and other resources, according to the prince," said Bren. "He claims that was why those men were trying to kill his army."

"You sound skeptical," said Lady Barrett.

Bren shrugged. "Look at this view. It's a shame people want to blow holes in the mountains to get what's inside." And yet he was the one who felt ashamed saying it. Didn't he do the same thing when he opened the Dragon's Gate?

"You sound like that loony old Netherlander back in his so-called Paradise," said Sean, laughing. "Do you want to strut around nekkid, too?"

Bren was saved from having to respond when Sengge reappeared. "Sorry for the delay. My father insisted on taking you directly to a midday feast. The kitchen has been scrambling."

Bren and the others were led into a dining room where a long table was overflowing with food. He almost cried he was so happy to see something besides yak milk or yak yogurt. King Jamyang entered, greeted them warmly, and invited them to sit down and dig in. They enjoyed savory noodle bowls and dumplings filled with meat, nutty bread and butter, and for dessert a baked dish made of sweet red fruit.

When dinner was done, the king gave them a tour of his current home, and then he offered to show them the grander, nine-story palace still under construction. This required climbing higher up the mountain, and after a feast this was harder than Bren would have imagined.

"It was my son's idea," said King Jamyang, with an arch look at Sengge. "He pretends to honor me, but of course this will all be his."

Sengge smiled. "A prosperous kingdom will honor you and your legacy, Father. The palaces and the monasteries honor our religion."

Bren could see what he meant as soon as they entered one of the completed floors of the new palace. Front and center was a large statue of a gilded woman, inlaid with turquoise and coral, posed not as some earth mother or fertility goddess, but as a warrior. She wore a hat the size of a steeple on her head, and fanning out from her back were two stylized wings shaped like battle-ax blades.

"Who is that?" Bren asked.

"The Goddess of the White Parasol," said King Jamyang. "Protector against supernatural danger. The Buddha charged her with cutting asunder all malignant demons and their spells, to turn aside all enemies and dangers and hatred."

On the floor above was another statue, this one of a man that the king and his son explained was a representation of the "Future Buddha," which Bren in his mind likened to the Second Coming of the Christian Lord.

"Not everyone adheres to our beliefs," said Sengge.

"The Mongols you saved us from . . . they have joined forces with a sect of Buddhism that wishes to destroy us and take our land and temples."

"The Blue Sky worshippers?" said Bren. Sengge nodded. That explained why all the religious buildings were built like fortresses. While the palace itself was sturdily built of stone, wood, mud bricks, and plaster, the completed floors were richly decorated with not just statues but tapestries and other wall art. Bren pulled up short when he noticed a large painting on silk, similar to the one that he had unknowingly smuggled out of the Leopard's Nest.

"You are admiring one of our tangka," the king noticed, seeming pleased. "Most are not so large because of the intricacy involved in the design and the work. I'm quite proud of this one."

Bren stole a glance at Sean and Lady Barrett. Lady Barrett gave an almost imperceptible shake of her head. They wanted to know the meaning of Bren's painting, but they didn't know if they could trust Sengge or his father. "I've heard of tangka" is all Bren said for now.

When their tour was over, King Jamyang left his guests in his son's care, and Sengge took them to another building perched atop another hill where he conducted most of his business affairs. Here the religious imagery was spare, replaced by tactical maps used by his army, shelves of books, military clothing, and weaponry. Sengge brought them to a table and spread out a map of the central Asian region.

"Where is it you wanted to go exactly?" he asked.

"I know the Silk Road we were on passes into Cashmere," Lady Barrett answered. "It's a disputed region, so I thought perhaps we could find sanctuary there until we figure out how to make it back home."

Sengge laughed. "Disputed by whom? Certainly not the Moguls. And you are a long, long way from home."

Those words made Bren ache inside. All he wanted to do was to get home, and Sengge made it seem like an impossible dream.

"It's not as hopeless as you think," said Lady Barrett, speaking to Sengge but seeming to read Bren's mind as well. "All three of us are from Britannia, and I happen to know the Britannic government is forging a relationship with Emperor Akbar to help both countries consolidate territory."

Sengge reacted with surprise. "That's a brave thing to tell me, as you well know by now that we don't consider the Moslems our friends."

"And you needn't consider us your enemy," Lady Barrett assured him. "We just want to take any advantage to get us across safely."

Sengge nodded and leaned on the table with both hands, studying the map. "I may be able to give you another advantage or two," he said. "Look here." They all gathered round. "There's a pass through the Ladakh Range to our west that will lead you down to the Indus River. You cross that into Cashmere proper. You can see how mountainous it is," he said, running his finger westward along the map. "Fortunately the trade road avoids the highest elevations. I will make a copy of this map for you before you leave."

"Thank you," said Lady Barrett.

"It's no trouble," the prince assured them. "Though, in return, I hope you don't object if I ask a small favor of you."

Bren suddenly felt like they were being led into a trap. Sengge went to a small cabinet behind his desk and opened a drawer. He came back with a pair of sealed letters. "There is a woman in Cashmere leading an underground resistance to the Mogul invasion. They call it the Lapwing Conspiracy. Her name is Shveta Do-Piyaza, former wife of Emperor Akbar's former Minister of Wit."

"That's a lot of *formers*," said Sean. "What happened to him?"

"She murdered him, naturally," said Sengge. "Although I assure you the deed was both just and necessary."

"I'll bet," said Lady Barrett. "Don't get me wrong. I'm all for women seizing power."

Sengge laughed. "Shveta seized it by the neck, I'm told! Nevertheless, she's not in power by any means. But she is dangerous if she doesn't know you. Brits, especially, are suspect, since your country is known to be in alliance with Akbar. That's where our mutually beneficial arrangement comes in."

"Can't we just avoid her?" said Sean. "How dangerous can she be? She's just one woman."

Lady Barrett burst out laughing. "Coming from the man I put on the ground with one punch!"

Sean's face reddened. "You didn't put me down!"

"The side of the ship saved you," Lady Barrett retorted.

Sengge turned to Bren. "Are these two married?"

It was Bren's turn to burst out laughing.

"You're going to travel from Leh to Srinagar, the summer capital of Cashmere," Sengge continued. "Even as we speak the government is moving its operations to the winter capital of Jammu. With the murder of Shveta's husband, the Moguls are on high alert, so Shveta is moving her operations the opposite way, from Jammu to Srinagar. And good thing for you, too. It's much closer. Perhaps two hundred, two hundred fifty miles due west of here."

Bren sighed. He wondered if he would ever get to stop walking.

"The first envelope is a letter for Shveta," Sengge continued. "We have a common goal—resistance to the Moslems—and have been working together for some time. No one will suspect you three are my emissaries. Of course, you won't know how to find her, for good reason. You'll take the letter to a drop box the resistance has been using."

The prince handed them a scrap of paper with what looked like an address written on it. "Can you remember this?"

"Yes," said Bren.

Sengge took back the scrap of paper and threw it away. "The second letter is for an emergency only." He opened it and showed them a bronze disk the size of a medallion. Bren recognized it immediately.

"A paiza!" said Bren. "But I thought they were only used by Kublai Khan and his heirs."

"The Ming Dynasty has continued to use them," Sengge explained. "I have managed to forge a number of them. They won't guarantee you protection from bandits, but they will help. And they will certainly give credence to your cover story of being Silk Road traders."

"Thank you," said Lady Barrett, taking the paiza.

"And how about I trade you three horses for your yak?" said Sengge. "You must be tired of walking."

"Yes!" Bren almost shouted. Although he felt a sudden tinge of regret at losing the yak. He had come to like the shaggy, ice-skating beast.

And so the three of them retired early and left at daybreak, with Lady Barrett in possession of the letter for the rebel leader. Bren wondered if she had been tempted during the night to break the seal and read it. He knew he would have. It would be risky, of course, especially considering that Sengge had described this woman as dangerous. But it was also dangerous not having any idea what you were getting into. Bren would have preferred to know for sure, and watching Lady Barrett ride confidently with one hand on the hilt of her sword, he suspected she would agree with him.

DECAMPING

The first time they stopped to make camp, Bren asked Lady Barrett if he could see the paiza. When she handed it to him, he spun the back side of the bronze medallion toward the setting sun.

"What are you doing?" she asked.

"Just a hunch," said Bren, wondering if this paiza held a secret message, like the one given to him by the dying sailor all those months ago back in Map. But when he caught the sun's rays and reflected them against a nearby boulder . . . nothing. "Never mind," he said, handing the paiza back.

But then he asked, "So what did the letter say?"

Lady Barrett had been unloading her saddlebag. She momentarily stopped, as if she had been caught off guard. "What letter?"

"You don't mean this letter, do you?" said Sean, digging through his clothes with both hands until his face turned bright red. "Where the bloody hell is it?"

"Are you looking for this?" said Lady Barrett, holding up the parchment envelope with the bright-red wax seal of the king of Ladakh.

"I took that from you last night so you wouldn't try to open it!" Sean fumed. "I know how you are, and I also know how it looks when you deliver a sealed letter unsealed!"

Lady Barrett sidled her horse next to Sean's and held out the envelope. He snatched it and inspected the seal, which appeared to be undisturbed.

"I saw you take it," she scoffed. "I sleep like a bird. Take it back if you're so worried I'm going to snoop."

"Never mind." Sean handed it back, outfoxed again.

Bren smiled. "So what did the letter say?"

Lady Barrett carefully placed the letter back inside her jacket. "For the most part, what our new friend said was true," she began. "About this conspiracy and their common goal to resist Mogul rule."

"Wait—you *did* read the letter?" Sean gasped. "What

the—I just examined that seal myself! How the bloody hell . . ."

"I'm a magician, remember?" said Lady Barrett.

Sean gave up trying to argue. "Okay, then. Anything important he *didn't* tell us? That could get us into hot water?"

"Plenty," said Lady Barrett.

▲▲▲

A man who might have been a turtle in another life sat hunched over a large table, one of his stubby-fingered hands holding a quill pen while the other kept a large sheet of parchment from curling back up off the table. The pen hovered above the parchment, a globe of ink swollen and dangling from its nib like a drop of dew.

"I can't work with you staring at me like that," said David Owen.

Ani was sitting opposite him, at a table that looked to be something out of an apothecary shop. There were several powders, potions, and vials, along with seeds, peppers, plants, and a mortar and pestle. She tilted her head to one side, and her long dark hair fell over her slender right shoulder. David guessed she was about Bren's age or a bit older.

Bren's age. He had been gone more than a year now. He'd had a birthday.

A blob of ink splattered on the parchment, leaving a purply-black starburst. "Bloody mess," said David, frantically blotting the ink with his dirty shirtsleeve.

"The Nightingale doesn't care for foul language," said Ani. "She says it is unpoetic."

David looked up at her. It was hard to look Ani in the eyes, not because her odd condition was grotesque in any way, but because it was somehow . . . otherworldly. It was as if something far more powerful than a young girl inhabited her body.

"The Nightingale?" David asked.

Ani lifted her hand above her head, to indicate a tall person.

"Shveta?" said David. "You call her the Nightingale?"

Ani nodded. "It's her secret identity."

"Then why are you telling me?" said David.

Ani narrowed her eyes. "You'll never live to tell anyone!"

David Owen dropped his pen in alarm. It landed on the ink smudge and rolled off the table, leaving a black streak in its wake. "She's going to kill us?"

The door to the room swung open, and Shveta and her two bodyguards marched in. "No one is killing anyone," said Shveta. David couldn't help but notice that her armed escorts seemed disappointed by the news. "What have you got for me?"

"I'm afraid I have to start over," he said, indicating the large smudge and streak of ink. "Ani startled me."

The bodyguards laughed. Shveta was not amused, and

neither was Ani. She marched over to the apothecary table, found a small bottle of white powder, came over to David's map and sprinkled the powder all over the spilled ink. Then she tipped the parchment, dumping the excess powder into David's lap.

"Hey, how did you do that?" he said, noticing that the spilled ink was almost completely gone.

"Quit stalling for time," said Shveta, pointing to David's work.

"Fine. My understanding when I signed up for the Royal Survey was that we were to cover the south, below the Deccan," he said, indicating the southern tip of the Indian subcontinent. "When we arrived, we were whisked north, from Bombay Island to Agra, through the jungle during the rainy season."

"What did you do along the way?" said Shveta.

"Got wet, mostly," said David. "The survey equipment never came out of our cases until we got far enough north and east that I was able to actually think about escaping to Cashmere."

"And Akbar's troops? How many were you traveling with?"

"A thousand or so? I'm not entirely sure."

"So not a full division," said one of the armed men.

"But was your group to rendezvous with others?" said Shveta.

David lowered his eyes. "I may have picked up some

notion of that." He indicated on the map where he would place the other troops he had heard about.

Shveta nodded and looked at Ani. "Go get the string bean."

When Ani returned with Black, she was walking behind him and his hands were raised. He looked indignantly at Shveta. "Arming children! Have you no shame?"

Ani came out from behind him, revealing that she had been threatening him with a long eggplant. She smiled.

"For pity's sake," muttered Black, dropping his arms. "David, are you okay?"

"He's fine," said Shveta. "Everyone's fine until I say otherwise. Now, come take a look at your friend's map and answer me a few questions."

Black did as he was told, and Shveta quizzed him the same way she had David, altering a question or two or subtly changing the way she asked them. When Black was done she seemed satisfied that his and David's stories lined up.

"I knew it," she said, folding her arms so her hands disappeared beneath her silk sleeves and pacing slowly around the room. "Akbar's not truly worried about securing the south—there's not much left there to resist him. He's making much grander plans, gobbling up western China, perhaps even moving into Persia."

"Persia?" said Black, astonished. "That would be madness!"

"Would it?" said Shveta. "No empire lasts forever.

Else we'd all be Sumerian."

Black opened his mouth to argue before realizing she had a point. So instead he asked, "So what now? Are we free to go?"

Shveta laughed. "What's your hurry, bub? Aren't you wanted by Akbar? How do you envision worming your way to Persia from here without being caught?"

"Well, I thought . . . I mean, we were just going to . . . okay, we hadn't figured that out yet, to be quite honest."

"No kidding," said Shveta. "Besides, I never promised to let you go."

David Owen could almost hear Black's teeth grinding. He wasn't used to losing so many arguments.

"What is it you really want from us?" Black demanded.

"I want you to come with us," said Shveta.

"You're leaving?" said David.

"Well I have to," said Shveta. "I murdered my husband."

Black glanced up at the bodyguard nearest him, as if to ask whether she was kidding or not. The guard nodded, making a choking motion with his hands.

"So you're a fugitive, too," said Black.

"Not exactly . . . not yet," said Shveta. "Ani and I took great pains to make it look like he had been stabbed to death in an alley near the Broken Camel, the last place he was seen. There had been not-so-veiled threats made against Akbar's ministers, of whom my husband was one. Veiled threats orchestrated by me, of course, but they don't know that either. Right now Akbar is more interested in keeping the rest of the ministers alive than finding out who killed Mullah Do-Piyaza."

"Won't it look suspicious if you leave town?" said Black.

"They want to burn her," said Ani.

David and Black both turned to her, somewhat shocked. "They burn murderer suspects here?"

"No, they burn wives," said Shveta, her voice hardening. "You're expected to throw yourself on the funeral pyre of your beloved husband. An ancient and barbaric tradition, which I intend to put an end to when I'm in charge around here." She folded her arms and let her anger subside. "Besides, I have work to do if I am to put things right. How would it sound to you if I told you I could get you safely to Persia—and from there, home? Wasn't that where you wanted to go?"

Black tried not to react with too much eagerness. He was afraid there was a catch. "You're not doing this out of the goodness of your heart," he said, "nor because you value our companionship. You want something."

Shveta smiled. "You catch on quick, bub."

THE VALE
OF CASHMERE

There was a road that led north from Jammu, Cashmere's winter capital, over the Pir Panjal range, to
Srinagar, its summer one. The distance was just short
of two hundred miles, but once one crossed through the
mountains there was a gentle descent into a wide valley fed
by the Vyath River. This was Shveta's initial destination,
the place that would put them on the cusp of being out
of India and beyond the official boundaries of the Mogul
Empire.

The problem was, this was the only road from Jammu

to Srinagar. Whether you were a fugitive from secular law or religious custom, it was still dangerous to take the only road out of town.

"Have you never heard of hiding in plain sight?" Shveta asked Black.

In fact, he had. He had explained the idea to Bren long ago when they were considering the safest place to hide the bronze medallion—the paiza—given to Bren by the mysterious dying stranger. Black had settled on a false book with a hidden compartment, shelved right at the front of Black's store. It would have been a clever idea if it hadn't been Bren himself who came to steal it.

But in fact, they weren't being so bold. For one thing, they all rode donkeys. These were the beasts of burden for the lower classes, and the group was dressed accordingly. Shveta had ditched her jewels and colorful silk clothes for rags, and her bodyguards (who, it turned out, were brothers named Aadesh and Aadarsh) and Ani wore sackcloth robes. Of course, for Black and David, no special clothing was necessary. They already looked impoverished. Shveta had even forbidden anyone to bring a weapon, in case they were searched.

"What about bandits?" David had asked.

"You've made it this far, despite everything," Shveta had replied. "You must be able to handle yourself pretty well." Which was probably the nicest thing anyone had ever said to David Owen. He practically beamed from the back of his donkey.

Rainy season was two months gone, but when they began to descend into the valley, they saw lakes and wetlands brimming with life. Along one silvery shore, Black noticed hundreds, maybe thousands, of small green-backed birds, skittering along the water's edge, dabbling their narrow bills in the water before stretching their wings just enough to coast low over the shore to another location, repeating these movements over and over with shrill cries.

"What are those birds?" he asked. "Do you know?"

"Lapwings," Shveta replied.

"They cause a fuss, don't they?" said David.

"Do they ever," said Shveta.

"In the light they look like green sapphires," said Black, staring at the congregation of small birds.

"You have an eye for stones?"

Black's narrow throat suddenly dried up. He thought about the black jade stone Bren used to wear, the one his mother had given him. Emily had brought it by his store when she returned from the lake country with it, before she had given it to Bren. She had wanted Black's opinion on whether Bren would like it, or if a boy his age would be embarrassed to wear jewelry given to him by his mother. It occurred to him in that moment that he had never told David Owen about that.

"No," he managed to say in answer to Shveta. "They're just pretty, is all I meant."

Shveta laughed. "Some people don't care for them at all."

Ani and the two bodyguards began laughing as well, and Black and David just looked at each other, wondering if they had been left out of an inside joke.

When they made camp, Black was surprised to see the bodyguards pull out a small, foldable chessboard and two small sacks of black and white pieces. "You play?" Black asked.

They looked at him like it was a stupid question. "Everyone in India plays chess," said Aadesh. "The game was invented here."

"May I play the winner?" said Black. He hadn't realized how much he missed it. Aadarsh stood up and motioned for Black to take his place.

"Be my guest," he said. "I hate chess. I only play to make my brother happy."

Black eagerly took his seat. He was playing white, and he made his first move. An hour after the others had gone to bed, they were still playing, until finally Black realized that Aadesh had a winning position. He resigned.

"Good game," he said, holding out his hand. Aadesh shook it but gave Black a wry grin.

"I was toying with you," he said. "I wasn't ready for bed yet."

Black took that as a challenge, but in the week it took them to travel from Jammu to a few miles outside Srinagar, he and Aadesh played every night, and Black only managed one draw to six losses.

"You stink," said Aadarsh, watching one of their games. "I don't even like to play and I give Aadesh better games."

"I toy with you as well," said Aadesh, winking at Black.

Other than the challenge of climbing through the Pir Panjal, their journey had been remarkably uneventful. It was on their last day's ride, when they had brought their donkeys to drink alongside the Vyath River, that something caught their eye. Approaching from the east at a gallop were three mounted horses bearing down on them.

Shveta, Ani, and the two bodyguards didn't move, but David went right for his donkey. "I told you we should've been armed!" he said, laying his hands on the donkey's back and lifting his left foot for the stirrup. Unfortunately, his donkey had other ideas—perhaps to drink a while longer—and sidled away, causing David to hoist himself against a moving object. He landed hard, facedown, in a thicket of river sedge.

Shveta briefly turned to look at him and then back to the three horsemen. "Did dum-dum really think we weren't armed?" she said, and Aadesh and Aadarsh promptly pulled a pair of spade-handled daggers from their robes, holding them up like a pair of panthers showing off their retractable claws.

To Black's surprise, Ani was armed, too, and with more than an eggplant this time. From inside her sleeves she pulled out what looked like small darts and moved one to her left hand while holding the others with her right.

More surprising still, Shveta didn't draw a weapon at all. Black didn't believe for a second, however, that she was defenseless. He looked back at the horsemen as their collision of hooves grew louder.

"Actually, I don't think our supposed attackers are armed," said Black. "At least, they don't seem to have drawn any weapons."

"Too bad for them," said Shveta, and with a sweep of her arm her bodyguards and Ani fanned out to meet them. Ani took the lead, raising her left arm up and flinging her hand forward, and though Black was unable to follow the dart, he quickly saw the results—the lead horse suddenly reared up, nearly throwing its rider, who managed to hold on while spinning the horse sideways.

"Hold fire! Hold fire!" cried one of the other two riders—in English. He and the other rider had slowed their horses when their leader had been attacked.

"Seems like a poor strategy," said Shveta, and Ani flung another missile, this time at the smallest of three, who a moment later cried out. It was a voice that seemed eerily familiar to Black, and in that moment his already wobbly legs turned to sauce.

"Stop! Stop! Stop!" he yelled as Ani armed herself again and Aadesh and Aadarsh ran forward to stab the wounded riders. Black shoved Ani to the ground and tried to grab one of the dagger-wielding brothers by the arm, but he might as well have thrown a lasso over a charging bull.

Shveta wasn't pleased. "Kill him, too, if you have to."

Aadesh stood over Black, one of the daggers raised, seeming unsure whether he really wanted to kill his chess partner. His hesitation cost him. Black heard a violent buzz and then saw the deadly quick strike of a sword just as it knocked the raised dagger from Aadesh's hand.

Stunned, he raised his left-side dagger to the swordsman, only to have that one knocked out too by the backswing.

Everything stopped. Aadesh stood face-to-face with the point of the sword, its bearer still sitting cockily astride her horse. Black might've recognized her, but he was staring at Bren. He couldn't believe it was him . . . but it was, it was Bren, kneeling on the ground next to his horse, blood seeping through the clothes around his left shoulder. He held Ani's bloody missile in his right hand.

"Mr. Black!" he sputtered. "I knew it was you, even from a mile away, even though it didn't make any sense. . . ."

He tried to finish but choked up.

Shveta was in disbelief. "You two know each other?"

On cue, Black ran toward Bren, who never even had to get up. Black dropped to his knees and hugged Bren as hard as his bony arms would let him. They both began to sob with joy.

Lady Barrett moved her sword from Aadesh's nose and pointed it in Shveta's direction. "You must be the leader of this group, since you're not doing anything."

Shveta's eyes glittered like one of her jewels. "I am."

"Then you should know we're friends, not foes," said Lady Barrett. "At least, friends to this man, and, I assume, that man over there."

Black had completely forgotten about David, who had hit the ground harder than anyone realized and was out cold for several minutes. He relaxed his hug and turned to see David staggering forward out of the tall river grass. It was obvious he had seen Bren, but still he moved slowly . . . cautiously. Black felt Bren tense under his arms. And suddenly, he felt . . . awkward . . . this wasn't right. Fighting every urge to hug Bren tight again, he stood up and moved aside, gently nudging Bren forward as he did so, and finally father and son ran toward each other and embraced, the first time they had hugged each other in years.

Black stood next to Lady Barrett's horse. "I can't believe I didn't recognize you," he said.

"Thank heavens you're as recognizable as a beanstalk in a cornfield," she said, laughing.

Sean just sat there, his eyes darting from Bren and his father to the huge man still standing in front of him, still with both daggers drawn. Aadarsh finally seemed to grasp what was happening and put his daggers away. Ani went back to Shveta's side.

Shveta merely folded her arms across her chest in resignation. "Fantastic," she said. "More hostages."

PART TWO

THE ENDS OF THE EARTH

THE IMITATION
MANDALA

"Hostages?" said Lady Barrett. "What do you mean, hostages?"

"Just like it sounds, chakka," said Shveta.

Lady Barrett narrowed her eyes. "Tell me what that word means right now."

"I learned your language," Shveta retorted. "Maybe you should learn mine."

"Why do so many of your people speak English?" Black interrupted. "I've been wondering about that for weeks."

"You worry about the strangest things, Archibald," said Lady Barrett. Upon hearing his name, Shveta's bodyguards started laughing again.

"Prester John's church was once a pretty big deal in these parts," said Shveta. "As he was an enemy to Moslems and Mongols, many Hindus and Buddhists learned his tongue."

"Fascinating," said Black.

"Shall we continue with our history of the Asian subcontinent or get on with it?" said Shveta.

"Get on with whatever you wish," said Lady Barrett, sitting up straight on her horse and resting one palm on the pommel of her sword. "Your so-called hostages are coming with us."

"Draw that sword again and we'll fight for real this time," said Shveta. "The vultures will be picking your eyeballs out of your skull while wild dogs feed on your rotting corpse."

Bren watched this confrontation with awe. Lady Barrett was never one to back down from a fight, whether physical or verbal, but this time she seemed uncertain.

"Who is that?" whispered David Owen to his son.

"Who is *that?*" Bren whispered back to his father.

Neither had a chance to answer. Black was waving his long arms frantically as if he were trying to signal a distant ship.

"No one's fighting anyone!" he shouted. "Lady Jean Barrett, Shveta Do-Piyaza. Shveta, Lady Barrett. I think I can clear a few things up."

"Shveta?" Bren interjected. "Shveta Do-Piyaza?"

"You've heard of me?"

"We have a letter for you!" As soon as he said it, he regretted it, and the look on Lady Barrett's face told him he was right. They could have used the letter as leverage. Also, there was probably a reason Sengge told them Shveta was dangerous.

"Well, I'm waiting," said Shveta, her palm upturned. Lady Barrett reluctantly handed over the sealed envelope.

"We came through the kingdom of Ladakh," Lady Barrett explained. "Prince Sengge told us who you were, and we were supposed to leave that in a safe location in Srinagar."

As Shveta broke the seal and began to read, Lady Barrett kept talking. "*Shway-tha,*" she said, in a long, drawn-out breath. "That's lovely. I've often found it regrettable that my parents chose to give me such an abrupt, one-syllable name as *Jean.*"

"Multiple syllables aren't the end all, be all," said Black, quickly turning on Aadesh and Aadarsh to say, "Not a peep out of you two!" They smiled.

When Shveta had finished reading, she glanced up at Lady Barrett, as if she immediately suspected that her new nemesis might have read it. But she said nothing.

"Anyway," said Black, "we aren't hostages . . . not exactly. I mean, we were, but I think the simplest way to explain it is, we've come to a mutually beneficial arrangement."

He turned to Shveta as if to ask, *Is that a fair explanation?* "You're doing okay, bub," she said. "Keep going."

"The upshot is, Shveta is traveling to Persia. That's where we want to go. She can get us there safely, in a roundabout sort of way."

"So can I," said Lady Barrett.

Black sighed. "I've no doubt. But . . . let's just try cooperating for a while, shall we?"

Lady Barrett shrugged, and before they set off, Shveta insisted that Bren let her ride his horse. A donkey was more fit for a boy, wasn't it? Bren agreed, and Shveta mounted the horse and brought it aside Lady Barrett's for a brief moment before spurring it on ahead, taking the lead. Lady Barrett was quick to correct that situation, and on it went like that, the two of them yo-yoing back and forth at the front.

All Sean could do was smile. "I'm really going to enjoy this," he said to Bren.

▲▲▲

Srinagar was by far the largest city Bren had yet seen in Asia, and it was as stunning as it was large. A river flowed through it and fed several large lakes, whose shores were dotted with houseboats. Behind them were the snow-covered mountains they had crossed, but here in the valley, which was still warm, everything was green and brightly colored by flowers and hanging gardens. Among the crowded homes were bright-white mosques and stone Hindu temples with their tall, flat-topped towers.

Shveta took them to the servants' entrance of a large building that could have been either a government building or wealthy home, Bren wasn't sure. Either way it didn't seem very inconspicuous, except for the fact that it was unoccupied. All the furniture had been covered and everything put away for the winter.

"You'll find rooms down here, and a kitchen and pantry," said Shveta as she, Ani, Aadesh, and Aadarsh headed for a set of stairs going up. "You'll have to fend for yourself tonight."

"You're leaving us alone?" said Lady Barrett.

"Don't get any ideas," said Shveta.

Finding food in the pantry was the easy part, and Bren and Sean already knew Lady Barrett could cook just about anything. The problem was when they all sat down around the table to eat. Bren had never had an easy time talking to his father, and being apart for more than a year didn't make things any easier. Bren had experienced half-a-lifetime's worth of adventure, but the fact that he had betrayed his father—and Black—to get there made him reluctant to talk about it, even if the fact that his father was here meant that he was likely forgiven.

Black tried to break the tension by catching up with Lady Barrett. "I'd forgotten how skilled you were with a sword," he said. "The look on Aadesh's face when you disarmed him was priceless."

"I was actually trying to lop off his hand, but I missed," she said with a grin.

"She's better with her fists," said Sean, winking at Bren.

Bren and Lady Barrett laughed, and with everyone loosening up, David Owen chimed in, asking Bren, "Did you make any other friends besides Sean?"

The laughter abruptly stopped.

"One," Bren said finally. "A girl named Mouse. She's not with us anymore."

Bren's father dropped his eyes and pretended to eat. Everyone did, for a minute or two, until Lady Barrett said, "Archibald, why don't you explain this mutually beneficial arrangement to me. I have a feeling it's a bit more than having someone to trade conversation with on the way to Persia."

"What makes you think that?" said Black.

"Because," said Lady Barrett, "I read that letter Bren handed her."

"What did it say?" Black asked.

"I have a feeling you know, or at least have an inkling," Lady Barrett replied. "But I'll play along. Prince Sengge, future king of Ladakh, is importing more than wood from China. He's assembling an army of mercenaries. And he thought this information would be helpful to one Shveta Do-Piyaza on her mission to the Church of the East in Persia, to—how shall I put this?—launch a Crusade."

"And she won't be successful," said Black. "But we'll all get to go home."

"I showed our cards," said Lady Barrett. "Your turn."

Black drummed his fingers on the table before finally answering. "David and I agreed to vouch for her claim that she has Christian allies already. That we were in fact spying on the Mogul Empire."

"She had me draw maps," said David. "Archibald and I saw and heard a lot on our trek across India, and she intends to make a gift of these maps showing Akbar's positions and his weaknesses."

"Not to mention my Gutenberg Bible," said Black with disgust. "More of a symbolic gift than anything, but a show of good faith. Although it corrupts the word *faith* to use it in this context."

"What does all this mean?" said Bren.

"Nothing," said Black. "Shveta is Hindu. She's not going to convince Christendom to go to war with the

Mogul Empire because she thinks she's entitled to be queen of Cashmere."

"I hope you're right, Archibald," said Lady Barrett. "But don't underestimate Christendom's fear of Moslems. No matter how cozy things seem with Akbar right now."

▲▲▲

Before they had turned in for the evening, Ani had brought down fresh linens and silk sleeping clothes. Bren had never been so happy to get out of the clothes he was wearing and sleep in something clean and comfortable, and in a real bed. He wished he'd been kidnapped sooner.

The next morning, Shveta led her entourage downstairs, dressed more like the queen she aspired to be rather than in her peddler's disguise. Her bright clothes flowed around her as if she were wearing the light itself, and her jewels pulsed—especially the large red ruby that lay across her forehead.

Bren and company were sitting around their table, having breakfast, and he could tell by the look on Lady Barrett's face that she would love to disguise herself as Indian royalty.

"Good, everyone's up," said Shveta. "Come with me."

She didn't give them time to dress. Instead she led them back upstairs, through several heavy curtains to another part of the house, a large room ornately decorated with gilded furniture and wall-sized paintings. While the others sat down at a table, Shveta went and stood before one of the paintings, staring at it as if she were noticing it for the first time. It was a naked, muscular man holding a trident, riding a lobster-footed horse across a wild sea. Clouds roiled in a red-orange sky.

"Poseidon?" Bren asked, almost to himself. He noticed two lines of writing at the bottom. Latin? But the words were too faded for him to translate.

"I love this room most of all," said Shveta, still gazing at the painting. "What do you think of this?"

No one answered at first. Finally, David Owen said feebly, "It's lovely."

Shveta folded her arms and tapped her feet three times before spinning in David's direction. "It's camel dung."

"Oh, well . . . ," David said.

"No, she's right," said Lady Barrett. "It's a complete rip-off. I've seen the original in Amsterdam, right down to the Latin inscription."

"It's not even a good rip-off," said Shveta. "And you'll see below the Latin there, a Persian inscription by the painter saying that this is his work."

"Well, technically, even a copy of another work of art is his work," said Lady Barrett. "If you want to debate the finer points of forgery."

"I don't," said Shveta. "To me, this painting is symbolic of empire . . . any empire . . . the way they take from others what they want, discard what they don't."

"That fairly well describes the general creep of civilization," said Black.

"Why are we here?" said Lady Barrett. "You aren't really interested in discussing art."

"Oh, but I am," said Shveta, and she snapped her fingers at Ani, who produced Bren's tunic, the one the monk at the Leopard's Nest had given him. She tossed the tunic back to Bren, but on the table she spread out the tangka that had been sewn inside it.

"Hey! That's mine!" said Bren. "You snuck downstairs and took it?"

"Yes," said Ani matter-of-factly as she spread the tangka out on the table.

"You were hiding this from me," said Shveta.

Black and his father both looked at Bren, wondering why he had been hiding it from them, too.

"Not exactly," said Bren. "I don't even know what it is. A monk who gave me the tunic had hidden it inside. I didn't know anything about it until later."

"And what did you learn *later*?" Shveta asked.

"That it might be a tangka," said Bren. "Some traditional form of Tibetan painting done on cloth."

Shveta folded her arms across her stomach, inside the sleeves of her bright-orange blouse. "That's it?"

Bren hesitated. "Yes."

Shveta stared at him with the most penetrating dark-brown eyes Bren had ever seen. He tried to blink, but he couldn't. Finally, she unfolded her arms and leaned over the table, studying the painting again.

"Shall I tell you what this looks like to me?" she said. "It looks to me like a mandala."

"A mandala?" said Bren.

"A picture of the universe," said Shveta. "A symbol of balance and completeness, or the wish for it. Although mandalas have meant different things and served different purposes through the ages."

"What's wrong?" said Lady Barrett.

Shveta was slowly shaking her head, still staring intently at the painting. "Something's not right, but I can't put my finger on it. This seems . . . incomplete."

David Owen was now resting both elbows on the table, leaning in for a closer look.

"It also looks like some of the first European world maps made," he said. "Not terribly accurate, mind you. More representational. They frequently showed the world as a circle, with a *T* inside, representing the only three continents we knew—Europe, Asia, and Africa. And in the corners and around the edges would be all sorts of additional information and flourishes, a portrait of the mapmaker, pictures of angels . . . planetary and celestial bodies . . . winds. Sorry," he mumbled, pushing back from the table. "After drawing maps for twenty years, everything looks like a map to me."

Shveta wagged a finger at him, but not in a scolding way. "No, you may be on to something."

"It's a map?" said Bren, wondering how many different hidden maps a boy could uncover in one lifetime. The paiza, the oracle bones, Qin's tomb . . .

"Not a map, exactly," said Shveta. "But it may be a painting of a place. Or places. When I said it seemed incomplete, I was looking at this . . ."

She pointed to the sky-blue center, at what Bren had thought looked like three mountains, or parts of them.

"I have to agree," said David. "This looks less like a map than an actual landscape, one being viewed through a lens."

"Or a spyglass!" said Bren, thinking of how often sea-farers first sighted land through their small telescopes.

"So what are we spying at?" said Black.

David Owen shook his head. "Good question, Archibald. Unlike a map, our painting here seems to lack notations or legends of any kind."

"Perfect," said Sean. "So we know nothing."

Lady Barrett laughed. "You should be used to it by now."

THE ROAD
TO SAMARKAND

S ean and Bren finished packing their things and loading their horses, along with one camel Lady Barrett had haggled for with a Cashmere livestock dealer. She claimed she had raced camels once when she was on an antiquities dig in northern Africa, disguised as a Bedouin. But the others were skeptical of her story when she tried to mount the camel like a horse.

"You have to make him kneel first," said Shveta, her voice a syrup of condescension.

Lady Barrett, embarrassed at first, quickly recovered.

"Unlike you, I don't try to make everyone bow to me and my alleged royal lineage."

The barb almost got to the unflappable Shveta. Despite her dark skin, Bren could see tiny blooms of anger on both cheeks. He noticed that Ani was smiling. He was curious about her relationship to Shveta, and made a note to try and get to know her better as they went.

"What's our next stop to be?" David asked.

"Samarkand," Shveta replied. "The road is mostly flat across steppe land, and the territory is controlled by a remnant satrap of the old Persian Empire—the pre-Moslem empire, I should say. From there we travel to the Caspian Sea. The Volga traders will be all over the ports there, most going back north, but some resupplying to go south, to Baghdad. We'll join one of their trains."

"*That's* the most direct route to Baghdad?" David asked.

"I understand how eager you all must be to return to Britannia, after all you've been through," said Shveta. "Unfortunately, we're not birds. Mountains and rivers and seas and, more important, people who might wish us harm stand in our way. Rather than the most direct route, I've opted for the safest. Okay with you, bub?"

"Of course," said David.

"Besides," Shveta continued, "you've finally found your son, against improbable odds. Enjoy some quality time together."

"How long must we actually travel as a group?" said Black.

"What's the matter, string bean? You don't like our company?"

Black looked in Aadesh's direction. "I do enjoy our chess matches. I think I'm getting better."

"You're not," said Aadesh.

They were on the road an hour after sunrise after a breakfast of chewy dates and some sort of porridge softened by milk that Bren just assumed was from a camel or a yak or maybe a giraffe. Srinagar was near the border of the Mogul line of control, guarded mainly by the fierce Rajput soldiers the Moguls had hired. But as the Rajput were Hindu, Shveta wasn't concerned about being arrested, even if she was recognized.

"Money talks with mercenaries," she said, rattling a bag of coins.

They crossed the unofficial border of the Mogul Empire without incident, but Shveta had neglected to tell them that the Hindu Kush mountain range stood between them and the flat steppe land. At least they were on horses this time, thought Bren, and as it turned out, there was a well-worn road through the mountains that kept them away from the highest, snow-covered peaks. It was the steppe land that proved the most difficult. It was flat, yes, but also nearly treeless. They walked under a scorching sun all day; at night they ate and slept exposed to cold winds.

One evening after a supper of dried camel meat and more dates, Shveta told them a story about the city they were traveling to.

"They say Samarkand is the city where all modern magic began."

"*Modern* magic?" said Bren.

"Artificery magic," said Shveta. "Magic performed with devices . . . crystal balls and wands and jewelry, to name a few of the more clichéd examples. And when I say *modern*, of course I'm being relative. Artificery magic is the only magic people have known for millennia now. And even that is almost gone, thanks to laziness, neglect, and misuse."

"What do you mean?" said Bren, thinking of Yaozu's stories of the Eight Immortals . . . how they had come to be and then come to be abused.

"Long ago . . . *loooong* ago," Shveta began, "men and women knew the true language of magic. The first language there was, perhaps. The true names for things, and their meaning. *Natural* magic. It still had to be learned, and practiced, but once it was not unusual for a person to be able to call the wind and rain, or to heal . . . and destroy."

Shveta stoked their small fire as the wind picked up.

"Natural magic, despite the name, is difficult. It requires discipline, patience, and above all, *humility*. Three things that ninety-nine percent of all humans lack. It was in Samarkand that an alternative was created. *Summoning.* Making a demon or a demigod or a djinn from the Other Side do the work for you."

Bren instinctively touched the black jade stone in his pocket. The worthless black jade stone. Except that it was the only thing he had left that had come from his mother—twice. And it reminded him of Mouse.

He glanced at Lady Barrett to see if she, too, was thinking what he was. She was resting the palm of her right hand on the pommel of her now-powerless sword.

"A powerful magician," Shveta continued, "discovered not only how to summon a djinn, but how to trap it in our world, using a device. In this case, an amulet."

"The Amulet of Samarkand!" said Lady Barrett. "A legendary artifact in my field. And by legendary, I mean no one believes it's real."

"Believe what you want," said Shveta. "True, the amulet hasn't been seen or heard from in centuries, but I know what I know."

"What did it do?" said Bren eagerly, ignoring Lady Barrett.

Shveta smiled. She seemed to love an admiring audience. "This magician trapped one of the most powerful djinn from the Other Side, and then he himself became the most powerful magician in the known world."

"Merlin?" said Bren.

Shveta scoffed. "*Merlin?* Please, boy. Get your nose out of storybooks."

"Hey!" said Black. "I make a good living convincing people to bury their noses in books."

It was David Owen's turn to laugh out loud. "Archibald, your store hasn't turned a profit once, I'd wager. You live off the magic of inheritance."

Black stiffened and opened his mouth to argue, but a convincing argument seemed to elude him.

"*Anyway,*" said Shveta, drawing the attention back to herself, "you wouldn't have heard of this magician, but you would certainly know him by his labors—namely, enslaving djinn to perform magic for the so-called magicians of this world. Big surprise, the djinn didn't care for this arrangement, fighting it from the beginning, and for the most part, winning. Now humans have lost the true language of magic."

"Do you know the story of the Eight Immortals?" Bren asked.

"Tell me," said Shveta.

He fumbled for the right place to start. "Before the world began . . ." No, that sounded like it would take too long. "In the time of the Ancients . . ." Ugh, now he sounded like he was trying to be a wise old man.

"You see this sword?" Lady Barrett interjected, removing the scabbard from her waist and holding it at Shveta's eye level. "It's one of the Eight Immortals. Or at least it was."

"You ruined it?" said Ani.

"Not exactly," said Lady Barrett. "It was possessed with the power of a demigod the Chinese believed helped rule Heaven, Hell, and Earth at the beginning of time. There were eight of them—the Three Sovereigns and Five Emperors, and they eventually ceded control of Earth to people the Chinese now refer to as the Ancients. These Ancients were given the gift of magic—natural magic, as you call it. But they betrayed this gift by creating eight magical artifacts instead, one for each of the demigods' gifts."

"The Eight Immortals," said Shveta.

"You catch on quick," said Lady Barrett with a smirk.

"So if you didn't ruin it, what happened?"

"She took it through the Dragon's Gate, and it came back normal," said Bren.

"The what now?" said Shveta. Black and David Owen looked at Bren questioningly as well.

Bren let out a deep breath. "The Dragon's Gate. The place in China where Mouse wanted to go."

"Who?" said three or four people at once.

How to explain Mouse? Was she a girl? An old woman? A spirit? "She was my friend," said Bren. "I mentioned her before. We met on the *Albatross.* We found a sort of map on this island where we shipwrecked, and it took us to this mountain that looked like a dragon. But we had to rob a tomb first . . ."

Lady Barrett jumped in when she saw the shock on David Owens's face. "The Dragon's Gate was a portal, I guess you'd call it. To another world."

"What other world?" said Black.

"The spirit world?" said Lady Barrett. "An alternate universe? This *Other Side* Shveta refers to? I guess it depends on how you think about these things. I was there and I'm still not sure. All I know is, the power that went with this sword didn't come back through the gate with me. As if the Immortal who empowered it saw his chance to undo a big mistake."

"We had another one, too," said Bren. "The jade tablet. It let you find things."

"What happened to that one?" said Shveta.

"Gone, I guess," said Bren. "Our friend . . . guide, really . . . Yaozu had it. He went through the Dragon's Gate and never came back, as far as we know."

Bren thought about mentioning his stone as well, but he didn't want to talk about it, so he kept quiet.

"What did you see?" said David. He was looking at Lady Barrett.

"I'm sorry?"

"You said you went to this other place. What did you see?"

She told him the same thing she had told Bren—almost. "There was something I didn't tell you before, Bren. The reason I knew, or thought I knew, I had gone through the Gate, into some other dimension—" She stopped abruptly, as if regretting the path she had started down.

"What?" said Bren. "Please, tell me."

"I saw someone," said Lady Barrett. "Someone I was sure was . . ."

"Dead?"

Lady Barrett nodded. David turned to his son, his eyes wide.

"Bren, did you go through this gate as well?"

Bren felt the saliva in his mouth turn to ash. He knew what his father was asking, and he didn't know what to say. He wasn't even sure it had been real, seeing his mother there, but then he remembered how their hands had touched when she returned the black jade stone to him, and the tremor it had given him. Though that could've just been an aftershock from the earthquake.

He glanced at Lady Barrett. She hadn't mentioned Bren's now-powerless stone, sensing that he might not want to tell his father and Mr. Black about it. And she was right. He didn't. He couldn't.

"I opened the gate, but I didn't actually go through," he lied. "I was too afraid."

His father stared at him in anticipation for a few more agonizing seconds before lowering his eyes and nodding. "I would have been afraid, too."

"You're all fools," said Shveta, standing up and towering over them. "To have that kind of power and just lose it carelessly. It's why magic began to leave our world. Wasted by fools."

"I suppose you wouldn't waste it?" said Lady Barrett. "If you had real power, you would only change the world for the better?"

"Better as I see it," said Shveta. "Now I suggest you all go to bed. We've a long way to go yet."

CHAPTER

14

SURVIVAL LESSONS

Samarkand looked every bit the city where modern magic would have begun. Where Bren had been so awed by China's natural beauty, here it was the architecture that overwhelmed him—perfectly formed marble buildings shimmering with intricate, colorful tile mosaics, gold-domed mosques, mausoleums the size of Rand McNally's Map Emporium. It didn't seem possible that all this was man-made. It had to have been raised out of this bleak landscape by powerful magic.

Black obviously was awed as well. "Do you remember,

Bren, when I let you read my copy of Marco Polo's *Travels*?"

"Of course," said Bren.

"He passed through here, describing it as *a large and splendid city*. In my estimation, a huge understatement from the man who exaggerated everything."

"Where are we going to stay tonight?" David Owen asked.

"An inn nearby," said Shveta. "The two goons will be with me, Ani will stay with you."

Sean laughed. "She's going to keep an eye on us?"

"Yes," Shveta replied flatly.

Bren, his father, Sean, Black, and Ani shared a room with five beds and wooden shutters that let in the cool night air. It was pleasant, and Bren was exhausted, but he couldn't sleep. He kept thinking about what he'd told his father about the Dragon's Gate. Or rather, what he *hadn't* told him. Why had he lied? He told himself it was to protect his father, to keep him from nursing the same aching hope Bren had that his mother wasn't lost to them for good. But had he lied out of selfishness? Because he didn't want to share those few moments he had with her with his father?

He got up and quietly left the inn to walk the streets of Samarkand alone. He didn't know if that was a good idea or not, but he had to try and clear his mind. He didn't even know if he *had* seen his mother. It was probably an illusion.

A delusion, more like it. He had the black jade, yes, but for all he knew he never completely let it go when he dipped his hands into the river.

He'd only walked a few blocks before sensing he was being followed. He got suddenly cold and instinctively reached for the stone, as if it might protect him the way it had against those two cutthroats in Map. He had no sooner touched the stone when he remembered it was powerless to help him anymore, and he broke into a run. He had gone maybe a block when a small figure stepped out of an alley right in front of him.

"Where are you going?" said Ani. She brushed her hair back with one hand and gave Bren a double dose of her catlike eyes.

Bren caught his breath, feeling relieved and then annoyed. "Wait, you *are* keeping an eye on us?"

"Of course, dummy," she said. "Why else wouldn't I stay with my mother?"

"Shveta is your mother?"

Ani shrugged. "She's like a mother to me."

"Except she treats you like one of her servants," said Bren, which wasn't exactly true, but he thought he would try getting under her skin. It worked. Ani half-lowered her eyelids, the way Mr. Grey used to when Bren tried to get him to do something.

"You take orders from a chakka," said Ani.

"I heard Shveta called Lady Barrett that," said Bren. "What does it mean?"

Ani thought about it for a second. "What do you call a man who has been . . . unmanned?"

Bren was confused at first, until Ani made a cutting motion. "Oh! You mean a eunuch?"

"Whatever you call it," said Ani. "It means Shveta thinks your woman wants to be a man." Ani pulled her hair back to mock Lady Barrett's cropped hairstyle.

Bren laughed. "No one would accuse Shveta of that."

"Shveta is a *queen*," Ani replied fiercely. "Don't talk about her with disrespect."

"Okay!" said Bren, and this time Ani opened her eyes so wide Bren was afraid they might be some sort of weapon. But she regained her composure and said simply, "Let's go back."

Bren wanted to argue, but he decided he was ready to get some sleep. His walk, while it hadn't gone as planned, had served its purpose.

On the way back, he kept trying to get more information out of Ani. "Is Shveta really afraid we'll try to escape? Why? Where would we go?"

No answer.

"What if I had been running away and tried to resist you just now? Do you have more weapons up your sleeves?"

Stony silence.

"Do you like cats?"

Ani glanced up at him but quickly looked away and kept up the silent treatment until they arrived back to the inn.

"I could just sneak out again, after you fall asleep," Bren said smugly. "I lived for more than a year on a ship, sleeping less than four hours a night. I can outlast you."

"I never sleep," said Ani. She turned and left, and Bren watched her go with a sort of wonder. Somehow he didn't think she was exaggerating.

▲▲▲

It had taken them less than two weeks to travel from Srinagar to Samarkand, even having to cross the Hindu Kush. Shveta had pushed their horses fifty miles a day, as if they were military grade rather than mounts more suited to merchants and tinkers. Samarkand to the Caspian Sea was twice as far, so before they set off again, she traded their weary horses for new ones, aiming to arrive on the sea's eastern coast by the harvest moon.

A group traveling together for fifteen hundred miles has a long time to get to know one another better. But as Bren had discovered since first leaving Map, being stuck together often had an isolating effect on people. Most of the crew of the *Albatross* had remained complete strangers to him. Those he thought he had gotten to know well, like Mouse and Yaozu and Lady Barrett, ended up confounding his expectations, which hurt even worse in a way.

Bren never expected to grow close to Shveta or her followers, but he had been away from his father for more than a year now. Despite how difficult their relationship had been since Bren's mother died, he had hoped they could forge a new relationship. A better one. But if you have nothing in common with someone, being with them day and night does little to change that.

If anything, Bren and his father spoke even less after their awkward exchange about the Dragon's Gate. Bren didn't know if his father suspected him of lying to him or whether his normally melancholy father had simply sunk deeper into his sadness, but they barely exchanged words for days on end.

Bren was just as reluctant to talk to Mr. Black, his oldest friend in the world (though Black hated it when Bren phrased it that way). Bren had always enjoyed the luxury of having Mr. Black and his father exist, for all practical purposes, in different worlds. His father had always known that Bren spent hours at Black's Books, and that Bren considered Black more like a father. But as long as the three of them were never together, Bren could pretend it wasn't so, that his father wasn't hurt by his being close to Black in a way that he wasn't close to David Owen. Bren even secretly suspected that his father thought Black had been closer to his mother than David had.

With the three of them here together, there was no illusion—just the harsh reality of so many lost years with his father. He didn't want to throw it in his father's face by chatting it up with Black.

Black seemed instinctively to understand. He hardly tried to speak to Bren, either.

Most of what passed for entertainment day in and day out was the conversation, if you could call it that, between Lady Barrett and Shveta. Sean called it a pissing match. While Sean enjoyed it, Bren got the distinct impression that he missed his own sparring matches with Lady Barrett. Sean had thought of himself as Bren's protector, and he had saved Bren, many times. But now Bren's father and friend were here, and Lady Barrett was back. Did Sean feel like he wasn't needed anymore?

What Bren did want to do was get to know Ani better. She fascinated him, in many of the ways Mouse had. Here was a girl, around his age, who seemed to be second in command to a woman aspiring to be queen and to overthrow the entire Mogul Empire. Of course, Mouse hadn't been a girl, strictly speaking. But what were the odds of Ani also being a thousand-year-old demigod trapped in a girl's body? Ani's unusual eyes made her seem *more* uncanny than Mouse, and less like a young girl.

Bren sighed. He was so tired. He rested his hands against the withers of his horse and let his eyes fall shut, the rhythmic trotting rocking him to sleep, until something abruptly woke him.

"Ow!" He opened his eyes to discover that Ani was behind him, poking a knife into his lower back.

"Sleepy boy," she said. "In five seconds I could slit you open and feed your kidneys to the wolves."

"Okay!" he said. "Your point is made!"

She leaned around and showed him her "knife": the top two fingers of her hand. "You thought I really had a weapon, didn't you?"

Bren nodded.

"Funny how fear does that, isn't it?" said Ani. "Your enemy's fear is one of your greatest weapons."

"Just so we're clear, I am not your enemy," said Bren, trying not to sound afraid.

"I know," said Ani, hopping off Bren's moving horse and springing onto the back of her own, which was being led by Aadarsh. "Just thought it might be useful to teach you a few lessons, since you appear to know nothing."

Bren could have sworn that Sean and Lady Barrett were trying not to laugh. Mr. Black arched an eyebrow at him as if to say, *See what we were dealing with before you arrived?*

When they made camp that night, Bren resolved to make the best of it. He had been embarrassed by Ani, but she obviously could take care of herself. Maybe she could teach Bren a thing or two.

"So where did you learn to use weapons like those throwing darts? Did someone teach you? Do children in Cashmere and India typically learn to fight?"

"The most privileged don't have to learn to fight at all," she said. "The defenders of the privileged can proudly display their large, gaudy weapons." She glanced in the direction of Aadesh, who was playing chess with Black, his almost comically large sword by his side. "The rest of us have to be sneaky."

"I am *not* privileged," Bren said stiffly. "My father and I live in a clapboard house in one of Map's poorer parts of town. I ran away from home and lived in the bowels of a ship. And I *did* beat a man twice my size in a fight with loggerheads."

"When I was six years old," said Ani, her voice like a flint, "a man kidnapped me and sold me to a dealer of comfort girls. I escaped and lived on the street for four years before Shveta rescued me. I lived like a rat. I *became* a rat."

Ani quickly turned away. The fierceness she had shown up to now had been fired by pride, but this time it seemed to come from humiliation as she admitted to Bren how she had been forced to grow up.

Bren didn't know how to respond. Here he was complaining about home—a home he'd been yearning for, trying dearly to return to, for months now—and this girl had grown up on the streets. He decided not to say anything. That's probably what she preferred anyway.

Later that night, Ani woke him from sleep for the second time that day. Although this time, it wasn't by threatening him.

"What's wrong?" he said.

"Would you like to learn a few survival tricks?" she asked. "For when you are back on the rough-and-tumble streets of Map?"

Bren's first thought was, *Good heavens, she really doesn't sleep.* But he nodded his head and let Ani pull him away from their camp behind a small hill of scrub grass and gnarled, leafless trees. There she laid out three different weapons: a sharp metal ring; a two-sided dagger; and a short, thick dagger with an unusual handle—a crossbar framed by two long pieces of metal.

"This is the chakram," said Ani, pointing to the metal ring. "I can wear several of these on my arm, like jewelry, or hide them up my sleeves."

Bren tried to pick it up and immediately cut himself. "Ow! How do you hold it?"

"From the inside, dum-dum," said Ani, demonstrating by lifting the chakram with her index finger and then letting it slide down her arm. "Not for beginners."

"So you throw it?" said Bren. "Like those darts you hit me with?"

"We usually tip those with poison," said Ani. "You'd be dead right now."

Bren grabbed the two-sided dagger by the handle in the

middle that joined the two blades, each of which was about six inches long and shaped like a wave. "Why aren't the blades on this straight?" he asked.

"Better to destroy your insides," said Ani, who took the dagger from him and demonstrated how you could thrust forward and then backward at someone sneaking up from behind. Or swipe at attackers from each side. "It's called a haladie."

"Can I have that one?" said Bren.

"No," said Ani. "You'd stab yourself before tomorrow." Finally she picked up the thick dagger with the spade-style handle. "This is the katar. This you can use, because it protects you while you're using it." She showed Bren how to hold the crossbar, which let the other parts of the handle guard your forearm, and then thrust with the blade. "Not as versatile as the others, but at least you won't hurt yourself."

Bren jokingly stepped in front of the chakram and haladie and brandished the katar at Ani. "*Now* who has the advantage?" he said.

Ani looked at him as if she had just heard a chicken speak, and then she slowly undid the belt holding her robe closed. Before Bren knew what hit him, Ani had lashed out with the belt, knocking the katar out of his hand with a loud *clang*.

"What the . . ."

"My most valuable weapon," said Ani. "The urumi.

Essentially a flexible piece of metal, and perhaps the most challenging weapon to master in kalaripayattu, the Indian martial art."

All Bren could say was "Wow." It was like a combination of a whip and a sword.

"I could have slashed your throat open," she said.

"Thank you for not doing that."

She smiled at him. It was the first time he could remember seeing her show any sort of emotion, and it made him happy.

"How about some tea to help us sleep?" she said. Bren eagerly agreed; he was tired of the cold, windy nights. Ani had him wait where he was, and she prepared the tea away from camp, so as not to disturb the others. Whatever it was, it was delicious. An intoxicating mix of spices and just barely sweet. Bren drank greedily.

When he went back to his bed, he fell asleep almost immediately and slipped into a wondrous dream. He was on his back, in a place that felt very familiar. It felt like home. He heard purring and felt a warm body on his chest. He opened his eyes and saw Mr. Grey lying there, staring at him with half-closed eyes. This was what he wanted, so badly. It felt so real it was painful.

And then Mr. Grey spoke.

"Are you in danger, Bren?" he purred.

"I don't know," said Bren. "I may be."

"There's something you didn't tell your friends about the mandala, isn't there?"

Bren didn't answer at first. Lady Barrett and Sean knew the whole story, but he hadn't even told his father or Mr. Black. As Lady Barrett had said, easier to keep a secret if fewer people know it. And he didn't know if he could trust Shveta. But this was Mr. Grey. His old friend.

"A group of monks called the League of Blood wants it back," he began. "They believe in a secret group called the Nine Unknown, who guard nine sacred books of knowledge that would be dangerous if they fell into the wrong hands."

"What's so important about the mandala, then?" said Mr. Grey.

"I don't know," Bren replied honestly. "Ali-Shir said tangkas were used as teaching tools, like books, but he was just guessing."

"Why did the monk who gave it to you want you to take it?"

"I don't know that either," said Bren. "But I wish he hadn't."

A MAP OF
FEVERED DREAMS

Bren woke up feeling uneasy. He was well rested for a change, but he vaguely remembered having strange dreams. He couldn't remember the details, and yet he felt like he needed to. That he had remembered something important, but now had forgotten it again.

As they traveled, he kept looking at Ani. Something about her was strange. Not her eyes—he was used to them by now. More or less. He kept thinking about the night she told him about her childhood, how terrible it must've been. And then it hit him: she used the word *rat* twice. She called *herself* a rat.

Was Ani trying to tell Bren she was Mouse?

The rest of the day Bren could barely contain himself. When they finally made camp, he kept looking for openings to talk to Ani alone. Finally, when it seemed that everyone else had drifted off to sleep, he got up and crept quietly to her small wad of blankets, relieved to learn that she did actually sleep occasionally. He whispered "Mouse!"

She shifted but didn't wake immediately, so Bren put his lips practically on her ear and said again, "Mouse!"

Ani bolted upright and had Bren on his back, a chakram bracelet at his throat, almost before he could get the one word out.

"Are you crazy? Sneaking up on me like that?" she said, wild-eyed. "I could have killed you! You deserved to get killed!"

"Mouse!" he said again, looking for the recognition in her eyes.

She jumped off him immediately and spun around. "Where? Where is a mouse?"

"You!" said Bren, struggling to his feet as well. He was still whispering; Ani was trying to whisper but failing.

"What are you talking about? I ask you again—are you crazy?"

"Keep your voice down!" said Bren, painfully aware now that the others nearby were stirring in their sleep.

When he turned back to Ani, she genuinely seemed to have no idea what he was talking about. She grabbed his arm and dragged him off out of earshot from the camp.

"You mean, you're not . . . I thought, from what you said, the way you've acted toward me . . ." He couldn't finish the thought. How would he ever explain to her what he was talking about?

Ani shook her head in disbelief. She was breathing heavily. "You're a strange boy, Bren. And if that's your first move after all the lessons I've given you, we still have a great deal of work to do."

Bren nodded weakly, but he wasn't really listening. He was heartbroken. Even though the idea was so farfetched, he had somehow hoped . . .

He felt on the verge of bursting into tears, which he guessed was probably the worst thing he could do in front of Ani, so he went quickly back to his bedding and covered his entire head with his blankets. There, in the darkness of his own mind, he wept quietly.

▲▲▲

The next morning, after they'd been on the road for a couple of hours, David Owen pulled his horse alongside Bren's and asked, "Everything okay, Son?"

Bren wondered if he'd heard him crying the night before. He tried to hide his embarrassment with a goofy smile. "Of course! How about you? Bet you never thought you'd be looking forward to being back in Map, at McNally's Map Emporium."

His father smiled back faintly. "If anything's bothering you, I hope you know you can talk to me."

"Yeah, sure I do," said Bren, but he gently pulled his horse a few feet away, and they didn't say much more to each other the rest of the day.

When they were a day out from the Caspian Sea, Shveta said, "We'll hire out a boat to take us to the city of Baku, on the western side. It's where all the traders congregate . . . those heading back north to Novgorod and Rus and Nord, those going farther south into Persia, and those coming from Persia or the Ottoman Empire. We shouldn't have trouble catching on with a Baghdad-bound train."

The "boat" turned out to be little more than a tub with a sail, barely big enough for their party of nine plus the boatman, and Black and David Owen spent most of their time vomiting over the side as they bounced across a choppy, windswept sea.

Both were still violently ill when they reached Baku, and Bren spent his first two nights there tending to them in a small attic room they had rented above a tavern. Emptying the buckets of the two sick men reminded Bren that there were parts of his old life in Map he definitely didn't miss.

"Are they going to be all right?" said Ani, intercepting

Bren as he was returning with two just-washed buckets.

"Sure," said Bren. "Just not used to boats."

"Your father seems worse than that," said Ani. "He's babbling."

"You went up there?" said Bren. "Why?"

He didn't wait for an answer before skipping up the steps of the tavern to see if his father had in fact taken a turn for the worse. Ani came right behind him. Bren opened the door to the attic to find his father half-propped up in his bed, a piece of paper and a pen in hand. Mr. Black was still asleep.

"Dad, what are you doing?" said Bren. "You need rest."

"It *is* a map," said David. "I tell you, it *is*. That's what I've been trying to tell you."

His father didn't seem to be talking to him. Or to anyone in particular. He looked at Ani, who just shrugged. "Told you."

"Give me that and lie down," said Bren, taking the paper and pen from his father. The pen dripped all over him, and he noticed that his father had knocked the inkwell onto the floor. Black ink was pooling next to his bed and slowly filling the cracks of the wooden floorboards.

"Where did you even get all this?" Bren asked, and he looked again at Ani, accusingly this time, but she gave away nothing. "Can you get me something to clean this up?" he asked her, and she left the room.

Bren sat down at the end of his father's bed, trying not to step in ink, and realized he still had the piece of paper in his hand. His father had been drawing something on it . . . a rough circle inside a square, with a smaller circle at the center. It was the mandala from Bren's tangka. Except his father had added a few notations to it—what looked to Bren like latitude markings, horizontal lines with numbers next to them.

He'd just said it was a map. But of what?

"Dad, wake up. Are you asleep?" His father had collapsed back onto his pillow after Bren had taken away his pen and paper, and he barely stirred when Bren shook his shoulder. "Dad, I need to know what this is."

His father mumbled something, his eyes still closed.

"What? I can't hear you," said Bren, leaning closer to his father's mouth while trying to ignore his unbearably bad breath.

"The North Pole," said his father.

Bren sat up. "What are you talking about?" There was no map of the North Pole. No one had ever been there. What it was, what it looked like . . . it was mere speculation. Bren touched his hand to his father's forehead. He must be delirious with fever, except that seasickness didn't usually cause fever.

His father didn't answer, falling back to sleep just as Ani came back with a bucket and scrub brush. Bren was still angry with her. "What were you doing up here? Where did my father get pen and ink? And paper? What are you up to?"

"He asked for it," said Ani. "He kept saying something about a map."

"That doesn't explain what you were doing up here," said Bren.

"I just wanted to see if he and the string bean were all right," said Ani, but Bren didn't believe a word of it. "So what did he draw?" Ani asked.

"Nothing," said Bren firmly, taking the bucket and brush from her. "I can take it from here."

Bren hoped that would be the end of it, but it was wishful thinking. When his father and Mr. Black were recovered and able to join them for a meal, Shveta looked straight at David Owen and said, "I hear you have a map of the North Pole."

Both Bren and his father nearly choked on the fish stew they were eating. His father seemed genuinely baffled.

"The North Pole? Where did you get such a notion? There is no such thing. Er, not exactly anyway."

"It's the 'Er, not exactly' that interests me," said Shveta. "And I'm just repeating what *you* said."

Seeing his father so flummoxed, Bren decided to step in.

"Two nights ago," he said. "You and Mr. Black were still sick. I came to check on you and you had drawn something on a piece of paper. Ani *claims* you had asked for pen and ink." He tried to give Ani the stink eye, but she won the battle of wills handily. "Anyway," he continued, "it was a picture that looked a lot like my mandala. You had made notes around it and kept saying it was a map. When I asked you of what, you said the North Pole."

David Owen was completely astonished, as was Black.

"You're saying that thing sewn into Bren's coat is a map of the North Pole?" said Black.

"I don't know what I'm saying," said David. "I don't remember saying it!"

"I wasn't sure if you meant my mandala was a map, or if you were only talking about your drawing," said Bren.

"Perhaps we can solve this great mystery," said Shveta. "Where is it?"

Bren really wanted to lie. He felt in his gut that showing the drawing to Shveta was dangerous. But denying it could be dangerous too. He simply didn't know enough about her and what she really wanted to devise a good story. The truth would have to do.

"Right here," he said, pulling a folded piece of parchment from his tunic and spreading it on the table between them. Shveta studied it carefully, as did Black and especially David Owen, curious as to what exactly he had done without knowing it.

"It does look like the mandala," said Black, using every inch of his long neck to get a better look. "What are those notes you made, David?"

David pulled the drawing closer, studying it. "They look like latitude lines, don't they?" He paused, as if something were dawning on him. "Years ago, a man came to Rand McNally claiming to have been to the North Pole. He had a map he'd drawn, very detailed, that showed an open polar sea at the top of the world. He said that warm currents from east and west converged there, elevating the water temperature. And that during summertime, when the sun never sets there, the ice completely melted."

"So what?" said Black. "I'm sure kooks come to McNally all the time with fake maps hoping he'll pay them a fortune for them."

"Maybe at one time," said David. "Folks know better now. Nothing gets Rand's approval without verification."

"Which this man didn't have, obviously," said Shveta.

"No," said David, "but part of his map . . . he had shown elevations of three mountains . . ."

He broke off, but everyone looked at the presumed map again, and then Shveta produced the mandala, which appeared to show three mountains against a pale-blue sky.

"Maybe this part is water," said Ani.

"Maybe," said David.

"So what did McNally do?" Bren asked.

"The McNally Prize!" Lady Barrett and Black blurted out at the same time.

"You remember?" said David.

"I do now," said Lady Barrett. "Some extraordinary sum for sailing to the North Pole and verifying the man's claims."

"Why haven't I heard of it?" said Bren.

"Or me?" said Sean. "I've been sailing with the most ambitious explorers I know for years."

"Because McNally withdrew the prize after only two years," David explained. "So many ships and sailors were lost attempting to brave the Arctic that sailors started calling the so-called open polar sea the Sea of the Dead. Bad for business."

"So *now* what?" said Bren, looking to Shveta. But Shveta didn't seem impressed.

"Now nothing," she said. "Your father was probably just dredging up some old memory from his fevered dreams. We already have a plan to make it to Baghdad, where the lot of you can do your best to secure passage home. Unless anyone has other ideas, I suggest we get everyone back on their feet so we can get on with it."

A FORK
IN THE ROAD

The winds that made the Caspian Sea so rough hit Baku square in the face, and Bren wasn't surprised to learn that the name *Baku* came from the Persian for "wind-pounded city." After spending the last year and a half crossing oceans, seas, deserts, high mountains, and the windswept plains of Central Asia, Bren had the face of a man four times his age. Sean had told him he had the skin of an Irish potato.

Bren wasn't exactly vain, but he didn't want to look like a withered old man before his time, and Ani caught him patting mud onto his cheeks, something he had seen Lady Barrett do before. When he noticed Ani, you could see his embarrassment clear through the cakes of mud.

"Are you spying on me?"

"I thought we had established that," said Ani.

Bren furiously wiped his face clean. Mostly.

"They make a special tonic from fish eggs around here," said Ani. "They say it heals the skin."

"What do I care?" said Bren.

"You tell me, mud-face," said Ani.

Bren sighed and threw up his arms. "Fine. Take me to these fish-egg magicians."

She led him down to the densely packed market area, where it seemed everything under the sun was for sale. But all that was overwhelmed by the smell of fish. Specifically, the Caspian sturgeon, a huge, pointy-nosed, startlingly ugly fish being hauled out of boats and piled by the thousands along the shore, where workers stacked them into wooden crates to be hauled to the market. Bren assumed a fish this big must be caught for its meat, but it wasn't—it was caught for the eggs. They were made into something called caviar, which apparently was a delicacy up north. These same eggs were also the magic ingredient in the face tonic Bren and Ani were seeking.

"There's a stall back here," said Ani, leading Bren by the hand down a crooked lane with evil-eyed merchants peering out from under awnings of colorful but worn cloth. "Wait here," she said, and left him in the middle of the lane while she darted off out of sight.

Bren felt his skin prickle with panic as he waited for Ani, feeling all the eyes of the merchants on him. A few called out to him, and though he couldn't understand them he understood them to be making fun of him. Or perhaps threatening him. Finally Ani returned and took him by the hand again.

"This way," she said, leading him to the far end of the lane, past the last of the merchant stalls. There she opened her hand and showed Bren a small folded piece of paper. She unfolded it and poured out a small pyramid of dark-green powder into the palm of her right hand.

"That's made from those oily fish eggs?" Bren asked, surprised.

"Here," said Ani, slightly lifting her right hand while directing Bren to lean in for a closer look. When he did, she suddenly blew a puff of dark-green dust into his face.

He immediately shut his eyes, which burned, and began coughing uncontrollably. "Why . . . *cough, cough* . . . did you . . . *cough, cough* . . . do that?"

"It's what you asked for," said Ani.

Cough, cough, cough. "I mean . . . without warning me."

Ani didn't answer. Or maybe she did, Bren couldn't hear anything at the moment. He suddenly felt like his head was underwater . . . sounds were muffled . . . objects were distorted . . . he couldn't breathe. Ani grew suddenly tall and narrow, then wide and fat, her slight smile changing to a smirk, then a wide grin, then a devilish leer.

Ani, what is happening? What did you do? The words ran through his brain, but he had no idea if they came out of his mouth. He couldn't breathe.

▲▲▲

Archibald Black gathered up his meager possessions and thought about how he and David Owen had come to India burdened with what felt like a thousand pounds of surveying equipment, money, and an outrageously dumb plan. They had disembarked at Bombay Island with four enormous trunks, one of them with a false bottom hiding Black's priceless Gutenberg Bible.

Well, not so priceless after all. Not when it came to Bren. He had been willing to use it to barter his way into the House of Wisdom when he thought doing so might put them on Bren's trail. Several months of misery and failure later, having hauled the huge Bible all the way to Cashmere, Black had, in a way, used it to get to Bren. Indirectly, but still. It was Shveta's now, and frankly, he was glad someone else was having to haul the damned thing to Persia.

As for the rest of what was in those trunks, who knows. Lost? In the possession of the Moguls? Some of it was likely destroyed or buried by the earthquake that had freed him and David from Akbar's army—an earthquake that quite possibly was caused by Bren, the rupture that opened this Dragon's Gate he had told them about.

Had Bren lost his mind? He seemed well enough to Black, if a bit careworn and somewhat distant, but Black knew in his gut that Bren had lied to his father. He had seen his mother—or, at least, believed that he had. Black had thought of Emily Owen every day since her death . . . what, more than three years ago now? He thought often about the day they met, when she walked into his disheveled little bookstore looking for a book for her son. He was just getting old enough to read, and she wanted something special for him. She had asked Black if he had anything appropriate for children, and Black had responded, "If you mean books that teach them there's a rich, vibrant world beyond Map, then yes." She had smiled at him when he said that.

Then she had noticed his chessboard. He explained that he played games by post, and she had wondered if he wouldn't rather complete a game in less than two years. That began their once-a-week chess matches, on Saturdays.

She was the loveliest person Black had ever met, and he wanted to know everything about her. He quickly learned more than he wanted to: she was married to David Owen, the mapmaker over at Rand McNally's. Black had done business with McNally for years, selling him antiquarian maps and books. He had approached McNally with a proposition once—to let Black or Black's customers buy or commission reproductions of historic maps that would be sold through Black's Books. Historic maps and atlases, even reproductions, were becoming prestige items for the wealthy, it so happened. It was a growing market.

McNally thought it was a splendid idea, so he stole it. He didn't need Black's help finding customers.

It was David Owen who approached Black, dropping by the bookstore one evening after work. He would make Black his maps and take a percentage of the sales.

Black was more than six feet tall; David Owen barely five seven. Black had looked down at this unremarkable man, not very well dressed, with the beginnings of a stoop, surprised that he would take such a risk. How would he pull this off? Working at McNally's after hours without being caught? Or worse, trying to sneak one of McNally's valuable maps out of the Emporium?

It turned out this unremarkable man had a remarkable gift. He could take one good look at a map and reproduce it from memory with exacting detail. Black didn't believe him at first, of course, so he tested him and discovered it was true. More than that, David Owen was an exceptionally fine artist.

But it was Emily Owen who kept the business

relationship going even when Black's customers dwindled because of the crash of the Dutch tulip market that left so many destitute. Commissioning maps he didn't need from David Owen was Black's way of helping her family without them knowing it.

It was also his way of making sure she had enough money to keep coming to his store.

Black hadn't meant to grow so fond of Bren, and if Emily hadn't died, maybe it wouldn't have mattered. He wouldn't have had to think of Bren like a son, because he would've had a mother that was seeing to him. But David Owen, without Emily, was lost as a parent. It wasn't his fault, really. It was all he could do to keep their leaky thatched roof over their heads. Educating Bren, helping him grow, making sure he had a chance to do something with his life . . . there was no time for that. Black had to take that on. And he knew David resented him for it.

Black looked at David now through the inn window, saddling his horse. If he resented Black then, what must he think now? If Black had been the real influence on Bren, then it was Black's fault Bren had run away, Black's fault all their lives were in peril, Black's fault they were all still a long way from home.

"David, go get your boy," said Black, leaving the inn. "I'll finish loading up."

"Lady Barrett is with Bren," said Ani, appearing out

of nowhere. "They will meet us at the quay. Shveta has found us a boat."

Sean walked up as Ani was explaining this. "Wasn't Lady Barrett with Shveta?"

"No," said Ani.

Sean and Black exchanged looks, but in the end they followed Ani to the quay. If Bren wasn't there, they could always come back and find him.

The seaside was teeming with people, and it took a while for them to spot Shveta's bodyguards, along with Shveta herself, near a flat-bottomed boat with a tall deck-house near its stern and a single mainmast, flying one large sail. When they reached the gangplank, they were met by a man with no front teeth and two pistols.

"Off you go," said Shveta. "Vlad will take good care of you. I've made sure of that."

"Wait—I thought you were coming too," said Black. "That was the whole reason you left Cashmere."

"Change of plans," said Shveta. "Something's come up."

"Where is Bren?" David Owen almost shouted.

"And don't tell us he's with Lady Barrett, because I know that's a lie," said Sean. "I *did* see her, alone, not long ago."

Shveta shrugged and glanced at Ani, as if to ask, *Should we tell them?* Turning back to David she said, "Bren isn't going with you. He's fine, I assure you, and if you want

I can even promise that he will rejoin you at some point someday. But I've got far more important plans for him."

David Owen lunged for her, but Aadarsh quickly stepped in and stopped him cold with a hand to his throat. David gurgled curses and threats, but he wasn't getting any closer.

"Ani and I will make sure he's safe," said Shveta. "Trust me, he's a valuable young man."

Black felt so angry and at the same time so powerless. He couldn't speak. Sean didn't have that problem. He peppered Shveta with the most ungentlemanly language imaginable, and then asked, "Where *is* Lady Barrett? She's not in on this, is she? She's put Bren at risk before with her crazy schemes."

Shveta laughed. "I have no doubt about that. But Lady Barrett isn't part of *my* schemes. She's too much of a wild card. My companions here have made sure she won't be a problem."

Black was wild-eyed now. "Dear God! You didn't . . ."

"Don't ask questions you don't want the answer to, bub. Now, last call to board."

Black folded his arms. "I'm not going anywhere. None of us are."

Shveta shook her head regretfully. "You are, and you know it. If you force us to do our worst, you guarantee that you and Bren will never be together again. If you make it safely to Baghdad, there's always hope."

Black tried to stand his ground, but his crossed arms slackened, and he looked at David. It was obvious what Bren's father was thinking. He wasn't afraid to die, but he was afraid of losing Bren.

"Could be worse, right?" said Shveta.

Black, David, and Sean turned and shuffled along the crude gangplank, past the smiling captain and onto the boat. Sean put his arm on David's shoulder. "Bren is the most resilient lad I've ever met," he said. "I promise we'll get him back."

David smiled weakly. "That's not a promise you can make," he said.

THE WELL
OF WISDOM

The rocking of the boat woke Bren up. He tried to sit up and immediately felt sick, so he lay back down, but it was too late. Up it came, the contents of his stomach, in a great volcanic eruption of chunky liquid.

He would have to clean that up.

No, wait. He wasn't in Map, working at the vomitorium.

The paiza! He had swallowed it. It was the only way—if he showed it to the admiral they would just take it and not let him come along. He had to trick them. Now the admiral would be furious!

He heard footsteps. It was that awful first mate, van

Decken! Bren panicked . . . he had to find the paiza. He reached out with both hands, looking for it frantically, but all he came up with was handfuls of . . .

"What are you doing?" came a girl's voice. "You can't put that back, you know."

Bren looked up. "Mouse? Is that you?"

"Why do you keep calling me that?"

Ani squatted down next to Bren. He didn't recognize her at first, until she pulled the hair away from those strange green eyes.

"Let me out of here," he said weakly.

"Out of where?" said Ani.

Bren looked around him. No bars. He wasn't in the brig. But the floor was definitely rocking. "Where am I?"

"You're on a barge, on the Volga River," said Ani. "Here, I brought you soup. It will make you feel better."

Her face was right in front of his, and slowly it came back to him . . . the small pile of green powder in her hand, the cloud of dust. He drew back suddenly.

"What did you do to me? Where's my father?"

"I knocked you out, and your father is on another boat, going south."

"What? Why?"

"You really should eat this," said Ani, pushing the bowl closer to him. "It will help relieve the effects of the drug."

Bren pushed the soup back at her, sloshing a third of it

out of the bowl. That's when he heard more footsteps, this time the steady, confident stride of someone in charge. The door to whatever room they were in opened.

"He won't eat the soup," Ani said to Shveta.

"You should eat the soup," said Shveta.

"Did Ani put something in it?" said Bren.

"Yes. Chicken, I think," said Shveta.

Bren stared at the bowl. He was starving, but he couldn't eat now. It would make him look weak.

"I'll feel just fine as long as you don't poison me again."

"Suit yourself," said Ani, who picked up the bowl and began to eat noisily. Bren's stomach growled.

"You want to know what's going on?" said Shveta. "Come with me. I'll fill you in."

She extended one of her heavily bangled arms to him. She was like one of those goddesses they had seen in the tapestries at Leh reaching down from another plane of existence. Bren took her hand, and she lifted him up, pulling him close. He stared into her bottomless brown eyes, which, unlike Ani's, made him want to dive right in and forget his troubles.

"You smell like puke," she said.

"Oh," Bren stammered. "I, uh, got sick."

"My fault," said Ani, polishing off the chicken soup. "I'm still working on the right dosage for my sleeping powder."

Shveta took Bren out of the small room and up through a hatch to a deck that looked all too familiar to Bren: crates and barrels; tools and supplies; sleeping hammocks crammed together to maximize space for whatever cargo they were carrying. It was all on a much smaller scale than the *Albatross*, but it reeked just as bad.

She took him through a second hatch that led to the deck of the barge, which gave Bren a chance to look around. The landscape was an ocean of golden grain, a bright contrast to the murky river. The barge itself was barely moving, and he quickly saw why: it was being towed. On the shore were a dozen men dressed in burlap rags and sackcloth, ropes attached to the front of the barge pulled tight across their bodies.

"They have to pull the boat the length of the river?" Bren asked, astonished.

"They work in shifts," said Shveta. "It's only a couple of thousand miles, give or take."

"But there is a mast and a sail!" said Bren.

"And they work splendidly going downstream," said Shveta. "The Volga current is far too strong to sail upstream. Shouldn't you know that since you claim to be an expert sailor?"

"I never said I was an expert," said Bren.

They continued walking, to the back of the barge and into a deckhouse that had been turned into a makeshift navigation room that was surprisingly well decorated for a cargo barge.

"I had them change it all up for me," Shveta explained. "If I'm going to spend the next month on this tub I need a little something more than vodka and a chamber pot."

"A month?" said Bren, slumping. He didn't even want to think about where *he* was supposed to live during that time.

"A month to sail the Volga," said Shveta. "Then we still need to go north, through Novgorod, all the way to a tiny little frozen village called Murmansk."

"Why?" said Bren. The only consolation he could think of was that maybe he would have time to plan his escape.

She smiled at him, her white teeth sparkling more than the ruby on her forehead. "Sit down, my child. I'll tell you. Are you sure you don't want something to eat?"

Bren wanted to say no. But he was starving. Even prisoners had to eat. "Fine," he said.

Shveta nodded to Ani, who left the room muttering something that sounded like *Make up your mind.* The mandala was on a small table between them.

"I believe your father was right," said Shveta, and Bren opened his mouth to ask again where his father was exactly, but Shveta stopped him. "I'll come to that. But your father is safe, and so is the string bean and the mouthy redhead."

She redirected his attention to the mandala.

"Have you ever heard of the Well of Wisdom?"

Bren shook his head.

"I believe you," said Shveta. "This time."

She did that thing again that unnerved Bren—she folded her arms across each other so they disappeared up her bright-yellow silk sleeves, making it look as if she were preparing to become a blinding force of light and energy. Without meaning to, Bren squinted.

"Remember I told you about natural magic, the kind that comes from understanding the oldest language, the true names for things and their meaning?"

"Yes," said Bren, through clenched teeth. He was determined to let Shveta know that he resented being put through this. "You said the language was lost, just like with the Eight Immortals."

"Through neglect and human selfishness," said Shveta. "Yes. But that wasn't the only reason. Some of the language was hidden."

"By whom?"

"No one knows for sure. One story blames a destroyer-god, an enemy to humankind. Another credits a wise man trying to save humans from themselves by taking away a power they had no control over. A third makes a trickster the hero of the story."

"That's a lot of stories," said Bren. "What makes you

think any of them are true?"

"Two things," said Shveta. "One, a belief that natural magic was real—*is* real. And that the Lost Words of Magic can be recovered."

"But why—" Bren started to ask, when Shveta closed her eyes, lifted her head, and started mumbling something he couldn't understand. Bren looked up as well, and to his horror, the ceiling was writhing with snakes. He shut his eyes, praying it was an illusion, but when he did, the snakes fell, collapsing on the table, the floor, on Bren . . . he jumped up and ran for the door, pulling snakes off his shoulders, but it was locked. Just when he thought he would die of fright, Shveta spoke again and the snakes were gone.

"It's called the Rain of Serpents," she said calmly. "One of the six supposedly mythical Hindu weapons."

"Please don't show me the others," said Bren.

"I don't know them," said Shveta. "That's the problem. Come, sit back down."

Bren obeyed, and Shveta pointed to the center of the mandala.

"This is the other reason," she said. "A Tibetan painting, possibly hundreds of years old, that happens to look just like a European map your father knows. You see, there is another legend, about a group called the Nine Unknown . . ."

Bren flinched. A conversation flashed across his mind . . . a conversation he didn't remember having.

"These nine supposedly guard nine books containing all the knowledge of the world," she continued. "Once upon a time, I thought that one of these books must contain the Lost Words of Magic."

"And now?" said Bren.

"Now, I believe that this book merely reveals where those words are hidden. There may be more than one story about how the words were lost, but all have them ending up in the same place."

"Thrown down the Well of Wisdom," said Bren.

"You got it, bub. And the story I've heard since I was a girl was that the Well was a mouth at the top of the world, which if you live in these parts, means the Himalayas."

Bren suddenly remembered the time Yaozu had called the Tibetan Plateau the "Roof of the World."

"But perhaps that assumption was wrong," said Shveta. "Maybe *this* is the top of the world. The North Pole."

Bren reached out to smooth down the curled edges of the mandala. It looked remarkably good for having been part of his clothing for months.

"So I *did* steal this from the League of Blood?"

"Ah, now we come to the best part of my theory," said Shveta, wagging a finger triumphantly. "I don't think you stole this at all. I think you inherited it."

Bren was already so weak from hunger, sickness, and anger at being kidnapped that he almost fainted. "You think I'm one of the Nine Unknown? Please don't rain snakes down on me, but that's ridiculous."

"Why?"

"Why?" Bren didn't know how to answer. It seemed so self-evident to him that he was nothing special. And the ledger of bad decisions he had been making for the past couple of years certainly contradicted any claim to wisdom he might make.

"Just because the League of Blood is all Himalayan monks doesn't mean the knowledge-keepers have to be," said Shveta. "As far as I know."

"Then why did they try to kill me?" said Bren.

"Good question," Shveta admitted. "I'm sure babies don't come into the world with *Mystical Knowledge-Keeper* written on their forehead. It's probably something the League has to figure out, too. Perhaps chasing you was a test."

Bren lay his head down on the table. He just wanted to go home. Shveta pulled his head back up by the hair.

"I'm quite serious about all this."

"What is it you want?" he pleaded.

"To remake the world," she said.

Bren didn't have a response to that. He only had to look at her to know she was dead serious. "So what am I supposed to do?" he said. "I seem to know less about all this than you do. Here, take the tangka, or mandala, or sacred book, or whatever it is. You don't need me!"

"You're the key to all this," said Shveta. "I know it, and you will know it too, eventually."

"You're going to send me to the North Pole?" said Bren.

Shveta smiled. "Don't look so glum, bub. You're not in this alone. Ani and I will be going with you. Don't you like a good adventure?"

"Not anymore," he said.

CHAPTER

18

GHOST CAT

Bren's trip up the Volga wasn't very adventurous, but it wasn't dull, either. Each of the towns where they stopped to trade was a stew of men and women from both East and West. Along the southern part of the river he met Khazars and Arabs, Greeks and Turks, dealing horses and swords, olives, figs, and honey. When they entered the great plains of Eastern Europe, surrounded by endless miles of golden wheat, Bren met the Volga Bulgars, who traded furs of beaver, fox, and bear for some of the precious caviar, which Bren thought was a really terrible deal for the Bulgars.

And at every stop, his heart raced as he looked for the chance to escape, to return down the Volga and try to catch back up with his father, Mr. Black, Sean, and Lady Barrett. Shveta had finally answered his questions, sort of, about what had happened to them. She had assured him they were safe, and that she had made it clear to them that their best chance of a family reunion was to return to Britannia safely.

But would Bren return to Britannia safely? He believed Shveta wanted him alive, but so what? She was determined to go somewhere no one had ever gone. There was no way she could guarantee Bren's safety. At the same time, he could find no opening to escape. Ani seemed to be there at every turn, not just marking his steps but reading his mind. If he was stuck with them, he might have to swallow his anger and help them, for his own sake.

Surprisingly, Bren traveled in relative comfort, thanks to Shveta. He didn't have to join the poor Volga boatmen who trudged along the shore, towing their barge upriver whenever there wasn't enough wind. He didn't have to do any work at all, in fact. It was nothing like the *Albatross*, except for the one thing—a one-eyed crewman with a salty tongue who reminded him fondly of his old master, Mr. Tybert. This man, who went by the name Scratch, wasn't a navigator (not that a barge needed one). He was what they called the "pole man"—the one who went to the side of the barge with a huge wooden pole to push them free should they get bogged down in mud or garbage or vegetation in a shallower part of the river.

The one time Bren saw him called to duty, it seemed that it was the dozen men on shore yoked to the barge who really freed it. But what did he know about river navigation? He imagined that if he asked Scratch about it, Scratch would probably cuff his ear like Mr. Tybert used to do.

"What are you looking at, boy?" Scratch called to him one afternoon, when Bren was on deck staring across the bird-dotted marshlands they were cruising through. "Are you looking at my eye?"

Bren turned to Scratch. Of course he wasn't! He was clearly staring out into the distance. But now that he was looking at Scratch, of course Bren's gaze went directly to the pole man's missing eye. Unlike Mr. Tybert, who never wore an eye patch, Scratch kept a makeshift rag over the empty socket.

"I wasn't, really," Bren protested, but Scratch came closer. He was shorter than Bren, and about as big around as his pole, but he had a ropy strength about him. Bren's ears began to buzz.

"Well take a good look then!" said Scratch, putting his face right in front of Bren's and lifting his eye rag. Bren reflexively shut his eyes to avoid looking at the rubbery webbing of flesh that he remembered so well from Mr.

Tybert, but just as quickly, he peeked. And what he saw nearly knocked him over—a bright-blue eye staring back at him.

"I don't—" Bren started to say, but Ani appeared on deck.

"What's going on?" she said. "Are you in trouble, Bren?" Ani was standing behind Scratch, so she couldn't see what Bren could. Scratch gently replaced the rag over his eye.

"We'll talk later, boy," he said, and he walked away, seeming to give Ani a wide berth as he went.

▲▲▲

Later that night, Bren followed Scratch from the time he went to the galley for dinner until he reappeared on deck for his evening smoke at the front of the barge. He couldn't wait for the pole man to go to bed—there was no privacy among the sleeping hammocks—so Bren bided his time until Scratch was more or less alone near the rail. Bren ran to him.

"Lady Barrett!" he said, throwing his arms around her. Scratch jumped.

"What the—I ain't no lady, fool boy!" he said, trying not to attract attention.

Bren quickly drew back his arms, thankful the moon wasn't bright enough to show how red his face was. "But . . . but I thought . . ."

"Thought I was a lady?" said Scratch. "God help me, you couldn't pay a woman more of an insult!"

"But then, why are you wearing a disguise?" said Bren.

Scratch seemed puzzled. "Oh, the eye patch? I just like to startle folks. Works, don't it?"

"I guess?" said Bren. "So, you said you wanted to talk to me?"

Scratch clamped an old, wrinkled hand down on Bren's shoulder. "I seen you come aboard with Princess Dazzle and that girl."

"Ani," said Bren.

"Whatever," said Scratch. "Whole thing looked strange to me, so I been keepin' an eye on you."

"And?"

"And the princess don't seem to be bothering you. Quite the contrary. You're more like her little pet."

Bren frowned. "Well, not exactly."

"Now that Ani, she's a different story."

"What do you mean?" said Bren, growing cold in the night air.

"Those eyes!" said Scratch, pointing for some reason at his covered eye instead of the "good" one. "No man or woman has eyes like that!"

"I'm sure there's some explanation," said Bren. "I had a friend once, a surgeon on the ship I was on—"

"I've got an explanation, all right," said Scratch. He

looked around as if to make sure Ani wasn't spying on them. "I worked in India for two years, hired on as one of the men who keeps the crocs at bay in the Ganges when they have religious ceremonies and whatnot. Anyway, I picked up a bit of the culture there . . . the superstitions, if you will."

"And?" said Bren, growing impatient.

"That girl is a bhootbilli!"

"A what?"

Scratch looked around again. It was all getting a bit theatrical. "What the Indians call a ghost cat!"

"I've been traveling with her for more than a month," said Bren. "She definitely has some strange qualities, and she may be dangerous, but I don't think she's a ghost. Or a cat."

Scratch drew back his hand and stood up stiffly—a man whose wisdom had been rebuffed by a mere boy. "Suit yourself. Don't say I didn't warn you."

▲▲▲

When they reached the head of the Volga, they traveled by land to the Slavic Republic of Novgorod, where Bren followed Shveta and Ani, Aadesh, and Aadarsh along cobbled streets past towering spires and onion domes topped with crosses. The market here was the final destination for most of the caviar their barge had been carrying, and men in large fur hats and fur-lined robes eagerly purchased it all.

They were still almost a thousand miles from Murmansk, where Shveta planned to find a ship willing to take them on their insane quest for the North Pole. Bren had no idea how she would convince any captain to do something so foolhardy, but he suspected she would come up with a convincing argument.

If only he could convince Shveta that he wasn't special. That she didn't need him. He had never wanted to be less special in his life.

Their first night in Novgorod, they stayed in a small inn, and Ani and Bren shared a room. When the lights went out, he thought back to all the conversations he used to have with Mouse when they shared their tiny room in the caboose of the *Albatross*. It had been in that room where she told Bren her life story, as she knew it. And it had been in another dark room, aboard the *Fortune*, where she had told Bren she never liked the name Mouse, and told him how much it meant for her to find out who she really was.

Something about the complete darkness made it feel safe to share your secrets.

"Ani, do you understand what Shveta is doing?" said Bren, gently probing the darkness to see if Ani would open up. "Does she understand that sailing that far north is suicide?"

"Shveta can do anything," Ani replied tartly. "It is her destiny to rule."

"And what will your role be when she's in charge?" said Bren.

"Be quiet and go to sleep."

"But why does she need me?" Bren pressed. "I offered to give her the mandala. She knows more about it than I do. I can't help you."

"If Shveta wants you, you're coming," said Ani. Bren was about to speak again, just to annoy her, but she unexpectedly kept going. "What's the big rush to get home, anyway? All you wanted was to get away. Now all you want is to go back. Did it ever occur to you that going home isn't going to solve anything? There life wasn't what you wanted. Out here life hasn't been what you expected. Tough cola nuts! Back home you'll be just where you were, miserable and powerless. Shveta is giving you—giving all of us—a chance to claim power that could make things different for once. The problem isn't with life. Life is what it is. The problem is with you."

"At least I wouldn't be freezing to death back home," said Bren, somewhat petulantly, but he turned over in his cot with a loud squeak, signaling to Ani that he was done talking. What more could he say? After all, she was right.

▲▲▲

When the little boat pulled into port on the south shore of the Caspian Sea, its small crew disembarked, while its three passengers stayed behind. They had no choice—they were bound by ropes near the stern.

"Are they really just going to leave us here?" said David Owen, whose head was still swimming with nausea from being seasick again.

"I don't care anymore," said Black, who was even worse off than David.

"Aye, sit here then," said Sean. "I aim to get off this tub and go find Bren."

They heard footsteps, someone coming back onto the ship. It was their captain, Vlad.

"Not much for sailing, are you?" he said in a thick Russian accent.

"The future queen of India said we were going to Persia," said Sean. "She didn't pay you to leave us tied up here."

"And so I won't," said Vlad. "But you'll be going with someone else. I have secured passage for you with another traveler. Now you can go."

He cut their ropes and then kept the knife raised to make sure no one tried anything. He led them down the gangplank and across the harbor to a small wagon that looked as if it could barely keep its wheels on, much less carry the weight of three men.

"Meet Sven," said Vlad. "Sven is a Swede. He is taking *feesh* oil to Baghdad."

David had assumed all Swedes were giants, but Sven

was a slightly built man with a walrus mustache that covered half his face. A jaunty blue hat covered the other half.

"All aboard!" said Sven, in an almost comically singsong Swedish accent. He helped the two sick passengers into the back, and to Sean he said, "You sit up front with me, Red." And so Sean rode on the stage with their new companion.

Sven whipped their single mule into action, and off they went. Sean could hear the groans of Black and David from the back, as the rutted road did nothing to calm their nausea. For Sean's part, he was trying to plan the perfect time to ditch the Swede so he could begin his pursuit of Bren. Black and David would have to be recovered enough for him to leave them, for starters.

"I know what you're thinking," said Sven.

"You do?" said Sean.

"I do, and I'm going to need you to stop thinking it."

Sean stared at the Swede, wondering what was going on. Sven stared back, before slowly pulling the huge blond mustache off his face. Sean nearly fell off the wagon.

"I thought . . . Shveta said . . ."

"They did try to kill me," said Lady Barrett. "But I dodged them. I doubt the two goons will admit it to the Queen of Sheba. Now, as for your plans to rescue Bren—"

"Don't try to talk me out of it," said Sean.

Lady Barrett smiled. "I know how badly you want

to save him, but I'm the man for the job. Those two back there really need someone to make sure they get back to Britannia. It will probably require hiring out a boat. They'll need you."

Sean tried to protest, but Lady Barrett wouldn't hear him out. All she said was, "Don't make me hurt you, Red."

MURMANSK

Though in the weeks and months to come Bren would long for the relative warmth of Murmansk, he felt at the time that it was the coldest place he'd ever been. There was a wind coming in off the Murman Sea to the north that fought their every step to the tavern. A hundred angry faces turned their way when they opened the tavern door, wondering who had let the outside in.

"Hurry," said Shveta as Aadesh struggled to shut the door against the howling wind. When he finally did, and everyone had turned back to their drink, Shveta scanned the room, her gaze landing on a darkened corner where you could just make out the figure of a man drinking alone. "Come on," she said.

Bren and Ani followed Shveta to the small table and sat on either side of her, facing a short but stocky man, European by the looks of him. Aadesh and Aadarsh stood behind them.

"Do you speak Dutch?" the man asked in Dutch. So he was a Netherlander. When Shveta shook her head, he asked, "English?"

"Yep," she replied.

He looked her over, his eyes taking in her reddish-brown skin. "You're a bit out of your element, aren't you?"

Shveta cocked her head a little. "Just sunburned. Why, I'm as fair-skinned as you, Captain Tromp."

The man laughed, opening his mouth wide and revealing two rows of teeth so filthy they looked like toadstools. His face was stubbled with a greasy beard, and his hair reminded Bren of a mangy spaniel he had secretly fed once outside his father's house. How different from Admiral Bowman, thought Bren, remembering how surprisingly dashing the Dutch admiral had looked, despite years at sea. Almost unnaturally dashing. But then again, maybe that should have been a clue that the admiral was no ordinary man.

"So why, pray tell, do you want to sign on with a rig

sailing into the Arctic?" said Tromp.

"We want you to take us to the North Pole," said Shveta.

Tromp belted out another laugh. His breath reeked. "The North Pole? Oh well, you don't need me for that. The Laplanders have a reindeer taxi that carts people to see ol' Sinterklaas!"

He took another swig of his drink. Shveta wasn't amused.

"You've sailed north many times. You're going that way next spring."

"To find the last damn fool that went too far north," said Tromp, growing serious. "And I'll be rewarded handsomely if I find him."

"As handsomely as if you were the first man to reach the North Pole?" said Shveta. "You'd go down in history."

"More likely, I'd go down with my ship, into an icy grave."

"Where's your courage, man?" said Shveta. "I thought Netherlanders were the greatest sailors, the most fearless explorers on earth?"

Tromp glared at her. Bren couldn't tell if Shveta's tactic was working or not, and she must have felt the same way, for she quickly added, "I can reward you handsomely on the front end, if that's what you want."

"I can't spend Indian money in Amsterdam."

Shveta unfastened the ruby from her forehead and set it on the table. She then reached inside the fur coat she was wearing and pulled a heavily jeweled necklace and set it down, too. She held up both arms and rattled the gold and silver bangles like castanets.

Tromp finished his beer and looked at the table. He touched the ruby and the necklace in turn, saying, "Bring me ten more of these and five more of these and you have a deal. You can keep the bracelets. They don't flatter my hairy arms."

He burst out laughing again as Shveta leaned back, withdrawing the jewelry from the table. She stood up and motioned for Bren and Ani to do the same. "See you soon, bub."

▲▲▲

Bren and company traveled back to the Novgorod Republic, moving around from place to place for the next six months. In the beginning, Bren secretly nursed the hope that his father and Mr. Black, led by Lady Barrett and Sean, would come rescue him. He knew what Shveta had told him, but still. Given what they had put themselves through trying to find Bren the first time, would they really just go back to Map and wait?

But as the days and weeks and then months passed, Bren gave up hope. No one was coming for him. At first he wallowed in self-pity, believing perhaps they had chosen not to come after him. Then it occurred to him that there was a far more logical reason: they couldn't. After all, there was no guarantee that just because they made it to Baghdad, they would make it safely to Britannia. They would still have been a long way from home. And maybe Shveta had lied to him about leaving his family and friends alive.

He would never know for sure unless he escaped, or unless he made it back from the Arctic alive. Whenever the slimmest opportunity to run presented itself, Ani or Shveta or the bodyguard brothers seemed to appear, uncannily. Shveta would never let it happen. So what were the chances he might actually survive her quest?

He had seen Shveta demonstrate her powers. Scratch had insisted that Ani possessed powers, too. Bren hadn't seen her become a ghost cat, or whatever it was the pole man was claiming, though he didn't doubt Ani was special in some way.

But was he special, too, in the way Shveta believed? Could he really be one of these keepers of lost knowledge? If there really was a Well of Wisdom and lost magic that could be recovered, maybe Bren really could change things. At the very least, he might find answers, about Mouse and his mother, and even himself. About what he was meant to do in life, and why.

And so Bren sustained himself on this, and passed the time writing in his journal, playing chess with Aadesh, and practicing weapons with Ani, who finally let him try throwing the chakram rings and darts and using the two-sided dagger. She also showed him how to position his feet properly to use the katar. You punched with it, like it was an extension of your fist. The band-blade she wore as a belt she wouldn't even let him touch, for fear he'd cut off all his fingers.

As for the chess, Bren had been forced into it by Aadesh, who was tired of playing with his brother. Mr. Black had tried to get Bren to play, claiming his scandalous memory would give him a huge advantage, but he never had any interest. Now, though, with little choice, he discovered Mr. Black was right. He and Aadesh would begin a game, and at different points Bren would recognize positions he had seen at Black's Books when his friend was playing one of his postal games or just practicing against himself. Without really understanding the strategy, Bren could still make an effective move, which drove Aadesh crazy. When Bren started to get the game, he became even more formidable, and after a month he finally played Aadesh to a draw, and beat him outright soon after. The look of glee on Aadarsh's face seeing his brother lose was priceless.

Finally, in the spring of 1601, they traveled back to Murmansk. Bren half expected Tromp to renege, or to not be there because he was dead, but there he was, sitting in the same place in the same tavern as if he had never left.

He laughed when he saw Shveta again, and Bren could have sworn he had lost a couple more teeth.

The only change to their bargain was, Tromp wasn't leaving until June. It had been an exceptionally cold winter, which meant the seasonal pack ice in the Arctic would be slower in thawing.

"I don't want to wait," he said. "I hate this place, and leaving later increases the risk we won't finish the job before the packs start to refreeze. But there's no way around it."

Because of this, they spent another two months waiting, this time in Murmansk. It felt as cold to Bren in May as it had in November, even though Shveta had bought all of them luxurious furs. Aadesh and Aadarsh were so large they looked like bears in theirs.

Bren wondered how he could survive the cold, survive another Dutch ship, the Arctic, another mad, mythical quest by a charismatic leader with an undying obsession. And then he found another thread of hope, in a most unlikely place—a water closet.

He normally never left his fur-covered cot in the bedhouse where they were living, but one night his bladder got the best of him. He scampered down the frigid hallway to the closet, did his business, and when he opened the door he nearly knocked over another guest who was standing right outside.

"Sorry," he said.

"I've been trying to run into you for weeks now," the guest said, at which point Bren looked up into a pair of clear blue eyes. "Don't you ever need to relieve yourself at night?"

Bren almost burst into tears, throwing his arms around Lady Barrett and standing there, hugging her, until his feet went numb on the cold wooden floor.

▲▲▲

"I thought . . . I just assumed . . ."

"That no one was coming for you?" said Lady Barrett.

Bren again had to fight back tears.

"Your father and Mr. Black had no choice but to separate from you, I can assure you. As for Sean, he was determined to come back, but once again I had to put my foot down and order him around. He's taking care of them."

Bren allowed himself a slight smile. "I'd feel better if you were still with them too. Sean needs you."

Lady Barrett grabbed Bren's hands in hers. "Darling, whatever do you mean? Right now *you* need me. To get you out of here, and back home, where you belong."

Bren didn't answer right away. Lady Barrett let his hands fall away from hers.

"Bren, what's going on with you?"

"This may be hard for you to understand," he began, then broke off, looking around. "I need to get back to my room. They'll miss me."

"Bren," said Lady Barrett firmly, grabbing his hands again. "What's the matter?"

"It's just, I think I may need to do this," he said.

"Do what?"

"Go with Shveta," he replied. Lady Barrett just looked at him, dumbfounded. He tried to make her understand. "I know what she's after now, and this is bigger than anything Yaozu wanted, bigger than the Eight Immortals. And anyway, I may not have a choice. This may be my destiny, and part of me, a big part, I suppose, wants to know for sure."

"You have a choice," said Lady Barrett. "I'm offering it now."

Bren pulled away from her completely. "I really have to get back to my bed." And that was the last he saw of her before it was time to set sail.

▲▲▲

When Bren stepped aboard the Dutch Bicycle & Tulip Company ship, *Sea Lion*, he felt as if he were dreaming. The sort of dream that feels so real, until you notice strange details or jumps in time. The *Sea Lion* was a company ship, like the *Albatross*, but it had a completely different build, sturdy and double-hulled in places, the better to break through pack ice. The names said it all—the *Albatross* had been a soaring bird; the *Sea Lion* was a plodding beast.

That alone seemed to account for the difference in the

men who captained the two ships. Maarten Tromp was a man built to withstand the hardships of winter. He could stomach any sort of food, was impervious to cold, and had not an ounce of sentiment about him. Around his neck he wore a collar of fur made, he said, from his favorite sled dog. Stranded one winter in the White Sea, he had killed his most loyal companion for food and clothing.

And that was another big difference—dogs. The ship carried at least a dozen huskies for when they might need to sled across the ice with hundreds of pounds of supplies. Bren liked dogs, but this group of wolflike hounds seemed savage, perhaps from being under the lash of Captain Tromp. They were walked on leashes about the deck for fresh air, growling and snapping at the men, and the lower-ranking sailors had to clean up after them. The stench from their kennels below was terrible.

To his surprise, Bren wasn't one of those on dog-poop duty. Unlike Admiral Bowman, Captain Tromp didn't see a need to give his "guests" positions among the crew of forty or so men, even Shveta's burly bodyguards. He berthed them in a separate area at the back of the ship, told them to take the air when they wanted and to stay out of his way, except at suppertime, when they were welcome to take mess with him and the other officers.

"I don't want you, but the crew won't have you," was his explanation for that arrangement.

They had been disarmed before boarding, though. Aadesh and Aadarsh had turned over their giant swords and their daggers; Ani had surrendered her daggers, too. Though Bren took note that the *Sea Lion's* quartermaster hadn't made either Ani or Shveta turn over their "bracelets." Or Ani's belt.

Bren quickly settled into a routine, which included walking one of the dogs—a husky named Caesar. He had sort of made friends with the dog belowdecks, mainly by feeding it occasionally, and the ordinary seamen seemed impressed that Bren wanted to pitch in. But it didn't take him long to make his first mistake.

It was during evening mess with the captain, and Bren's mistake was opening his mouth. Tired of Tromp going on about how Shveta and company had no idea what they were in for, how a pile of jewels wouldn't buy them courage during an Arctic storm, Bren boasted, "I've actually sailed with a Dutch yacht before. A Far Easter."

Tromp stopped (briefly) in the middle of chewing his salted beef, pointed his beer stein at Bren, and said, "Have ya now, jongen?"

Bren swallowed hard, but it didn't bring his words back. "I have," he said cautiously. "Nothing so arduous as a polar journey, of course."

"Oh, now, let's not be modest!" said Tromp, slamming his stein down and gesturing with both hands now.

"Everyone in the world knows Far Easters are the best of the best. A year at sea, each way, maybe more. Touching two, sometimes three oceans. Planting the Orange flag in lands hither and yonder! Tell me, boy. Which ship were you on?"

Bren tried to swallow again, but no luck. "The *Albatross*," he managed to say.

Tromp lowered his arms and a very serious look came over his face. "You were on Reynard Bowman's ship?"

Bren nodded. He noticed that the handful of other officers at the mess table were suddenly very interested.

"A traitor to his country," Tromp said. He was no longer shouting. In fact, his voice was little more than a whisper. "Cape Colony is still in chaos. The butchery there . . ." He looked around at his officers. "I heard they found the governor's head, arms, and legs in different rooms of the house. Same with the other guest. Women, too!" he added, looking at Shveta and Ani. "All Bowman's doing. Was a member of that dark league, what was the name . . ."

"The Order of the Black Tulip," said Bren.

Tromp eyed Bren. "You did know him, then. I suppose you heard folks say he was in league with the Devil?"

"Some thought that, yes."

"Well I knew he was full of crap," said Tromp. "Trying to scare folks, burnish the myth of the great admiral!"

His voice was rising again. "Did he tell you the story about the two-horned narwhal?"

"He did," said Bren. "When I first met him, in fact."

"Bet you thought he was quite the dashing hero, didn't ya? How the beast speared their ship, and the cook to boot, and Bowman saved the day by hacking off both horns single-handedly!"

The other officers laughed. Bren's stomach went sour with humiliation.

"Well, I was on that ship, boy, and nothing like it happened. We took home a narwhal, all right, on a hunt. Bowman wasn't even in the whaling boat. Some hero, huh?" said Tromp, leaning back in his chair and folding his arms across his bulging stomach.

"You're right," Bren admitted. "I thought he was a hero. That's why I wanted to join his ship. But I learned otherwise, on my own, a while ago."

"I hope you pick things up quicker on this ship, boy," said Tromp. "'Cause you don't have a clue what you're in for."

Bren looked at Tromp, trying to hold his eyes to prove he wasn't afraid. He would have no trouble keeping his opinion of his new captain in check; he already despised him. But he also had the sinking feeling that the captain was right.

CHAPTER
20

ICE HAVEN

They had left Murmansk on June 1, sailing east along the Seventieth Parallel until an archipelago called Nova Zembla by the Dutch came into view on their port side. This was the last known location of a crew led by Willem Barentsz, a Netherlander who had gone looking for a Northeast Passage to Asia. Two expeditions had already tried and failed to find any signs of them, which Bren found puzzling, until he saw what Nova Zembla looked like on a map—a long caterpillar of land more than six hundred miles long stretching deep into the Arctic. Most of the interior was mountainous, which meant that if Barentsz and his men had taken shelter in caves, it might be impossible to find them, or what was left of them.

Tromp, though, had a theory. "First two search parties focused their attention on the southern island," he said, pointing to the map where Nova Zembla's two main islands were just barely divided by a narrow strait. "The assumption being, Barentsz would have overwintered in the warmest latitude possible. Logical, yes, but I'm betting he never made it."

Tromp moved his index finger to the northeast. "His ship was retreating from here, having failed again to find a way across. He would have been coming at the island from the north. And if he was forced to overwinter because of storms and ice packs, he would have landed where he could."

"But they could have walked south," said his first mate, Mr. Hein.

"Over mountains? Through storms? When they were likely already exhausted?"

Mr. Hein rubbed his chin. "Man'll do anything to keep warm."

"Yes," Tromp agreed, "and you can keep warm by building shelter and starting a fire. By late fall and midwinter, no part of that island would have been warm."

Bren had to agree with that. The *Sea Lion* had just

started northeast, up the coast of the southern island, and the air was freezing and the wind even worse. And it was the tenth of June. Their entire short voyage had been a slog through slushy waters, and even the never-setting sun barely brought the highest temperatures above freezing.

Another obstacle to rescue also became clear: the fog was dense, replaced occasionally by curtains of sleet and snow.

"Are we going to land and explore on foot?" Bren asked.

Tromp was at the starboard rail of the quarterdeck, taking in the island with a spyglass. "Sounds like a job for a spry young explorer like yourself and your girlfriend."

"Girlfriend?"

"The one with the freakish green eyes."

Bren was horrified. "Ani is *not* my girlfriend."

"Then you won't mind if I throw her overboard for good luck?" said Tromp.

"What?"

"She's spooking the men. The tall one is, too, but she did pay me fair and square."

"You're not serious," said Bren, at which point Tromp closed his spyglass and grabbed Bren by the ear, wrenching it so painfully he was certain he could feel it tearing from his head.

"Everything I say on this ship you should take seriously, jongen. Did Bowman let you backtalk him like that? Whatever bad habits you picked up on that faithless journey, I'll be the one to break you of them. Starting with this: only officers on the quarterdeck."

He pulled Bren by the ear to the ladder leading to the ship's waist and turned him loose at the top step. Bren, unable to keep his balance, stumbled and fell halfway down before catching himself. Tromp laughed and went back to his duties. Bren picked himself up and finished his unplanned journey to the main deck, and as he did so, he caught sight of a crewman eyeing him from the cover of the ratlines. Even more embarrassed now, he hurried belowdecks and went straight to his cabin.

▲▲▲

"Here," said Ani, "this will help." She held out a soft, greenish-brown blob toward Bren, who was standing in front of a dirty mirror in one of the common areas below. He was examining the damage to his ear, which was miraculously still attached, but bleeding. He looked at Ani's offering.

"Help with what? Caulking the ship?"

"Your ear, dum-dum."

"Last time you mixed something up for me, I ended up kidnapped," said Bren. "No thank you."

Ani kicked him behind the knee, causing Bren to crumple

to the floor. With his head at waist level, Ani grabbed his hair and pressed the poultice against his wounded ear. The warm, squishy feeling reminded Bren of the time Duke Swyers had turned a bowl of porridge upside down on his head.

Ah, Duke. I once thought you *were the worst person in the world.*

"Feel better?" said Ani.

Bren pushed her away as he stood up again. "Better? You mean besides the new pain in my knee and yanking my hair out?" But then a cool, soothing sensation came over his ear, the pain receding fast. "Actually, yeah, it does feel pretty good."

"Idiot," said Ani, stomping off.

"Sorry," Bren said to no one in particular.

Even as his ear healed, the captain's attack opened his eyes to just how cruel Tromp was to his men. At least, some of his men. The disposable ones, or the ones who couldn't fight back. Tromp struck them, gave them the worst jobs and the worst watches, humiliated them in front of their crewmates, and frequently had the purser dock their future pay for vague "insubordination."

Bren could only imagine how badly Tromp would treat him if he could. If Shveta weren't paying for Bren's protection.

Shveta herself, meanwhile, seemed to go into suspended

animation. She appeared for supper but spoke little, then retired to the cabin she shared with Ani for the rest of the evening. She could occasionally be seen taking the air at midday (she was impossible to miss with her radiant clothing), but she spoke to no one and the men avoided her. Even when Bren walked Caesar by her, the husky whimpered and shrunk away.

The farther north they went along the coast of Nova Zembla, the more frozen the slushy water, and it took the *Sea Lion* more than a week to reach the top of the archipelago—the "rump" of the caterpillar. Everyone was on the lookout for black flags, the official Dutch distress signal. Bren, for his part, began to regret turning away Lady Barrett. He didn't regret his decision to go north, not yet anyway, but he wished she had offered to come with him. He could have used an ally.

Finally a man in the crow's nest spotted something, though it wasn't a flag.

"A house, Cap'n!" he called out. "What's left of one!"

In fact, the sun was so bright and the tip of the island so bare, Bren could see the structure with his naked eye. It looked like a raised wooden cabin that had either never been finished or was already coming apart. Once they landed it was clear where Barentsz and his men had gotten their wood.

"They took apart their ship," said a man named

Nindemann, the *Sea Lion*'s chief engineer. "You can see how they warped the hull boards to make walls. That's the keel there, cut in two, to make the foundation."

"So shelter wasn't an issue," said Tromp. "Not at first, anyway." He and the engineer were examining what was left of the structure. "They got the cabin built, looks like. I'd wager that weather has taken it apart in the three years since."

"Or bears," said Nindemann.

The wind was so loud Bren could hardly hear, but he heard the word *bears*. "Polar bears?" he asked, trying not to sound afraid. Black had once had a book at his store called *Terrors of the North*. It described in lurid detail the dangers of animals such as polar bears, narwhals, killer whales, sharks, and a few ghoulish things Bren was pretty sure were mythological, like something called the Highland Nightmare, a creature with the body of a horse and the head and torso of a Scotsman, said to haunt the Caledonian forests. "Why would polar bears take apart a cabin?"

Tromp scowled at him. "Are you daft? Same reason a man opens a tin of sardines: to eat what's inside."

"You think Barentsz and his crew were eaten by bears?" Bren asked Nindemann, not wanted to invite more abuse from the captain.

"He had camped on Nova Zembla before, on an earlier expedition," the engineer explained. "Talked about bears as if they ran amok here. Two of his men on that occasion were killed by bears. Barentsz hated the things. Was terrified of 'em."

Bren shivered, telling himself it was just the cold. He couldn't get the stories from that book out of his head, about how polar bears could smell seals through the ice, and how they'd been known to track prey for dozens of miles if they were hungry. They could swim, climb, and run as fast as a lion but were twice as big.

"Don't worry, jongen," said Tromp, patting Bren on the back, which slowly turned into a squeezing of his neck by the captain's massive, rough hand. "You've got a sight more to fear from me than some old bear."

He laughed as he walked off, preparing to disembark with a landing party, and Nindemann gave Bren a look that said, *Be careful.* A warning Bren hardly needed. As the landing party gathered to leave, the man that had seen Bren's embarrassing fall down the ladder sidled over to Bren and said, "Don't worry, jongen. I'm looking out for you." And Lady Barrett winked at him.

▲▲▲

When the party returned to the ship, Bren tried to get Lady Barrett alone as soon as he could, which proved less difficult than he would have imagined. The crew was in a frenzy, going through all the abandoned supplies the landing party had dumped onto the deck: copper pots and iron pans; a few rifles; a box of books; and sacks of bones, presumably human. In the hubbub, Bren and Lady Barrett slipped off to the far side of the ship.

"You didn't think I'd let you take off with these lunatics on your own, did you, Bren?"

"I'm sorry," he said. "I'm glad you're here, but I'm sorry you felt obligated to follow me into this foolishness, if that's what it is."

She gently elbowed him. "Don't look so glum, bub. Who do you think you're talking to? I'm always up for an epic adventure and a chance to claim godlike power."

Bren laughed. "Why didn't you tell me before?"

"The fewer people to know a secret, the better, remember?" said Lady Barrett. "I didn't want you looking for me. Might've aroused suspicion. But this compulsion you had to stay with Shveta . . . you need to tell me more. What is she after?"

"She wants to remake the world," said Bren. "And I'm not sure that's a bad thing."

They turned their attention back to activity in the middle of the ship, where the ship's surgeon was assembling all the bones they had found.

"What's he doing?" Bren asked.

"The Dutch Bicycle and Tulip Company makes anatomical measurements of all their officers, using the results to estimate the shape and length of their major bones and skull," Lady Barrett explained. "Helps them identify remains."

"Oh," said Bren, who watched with fascination while the surgeon put what was left of these men back together, constantly referring back to a thick leather book of records. When he had finished, there were thirteen skeletons, more or less, and seeing them lined up across the deck like that cast a pall over the other men.

After carefully studying and measuring them all, the surgeon concluded that none of the men was Barentsz. Everyone went back to their duties, and Bren went belowdecks, where he accidentally stumbled within earshot of a conversation between the first mate, Mr. Hein, and Tromp. They were at one end of the gangway leading to the caboose; he was at the other, just out of sight.

"So now what?" said Mr. Hein.

"We go through the books," said Tromp in a low voice. "If those men were part of Barentsz's crew, there might be a journal or some other clue where to find him."

"What about . . . you know," said Mr. Hein.

Tromp didn't answer right away, and Bren felt a creeping sense of dread.

"Plan still holds," said Tromp. "We'll kill the Indian woman and her bodyguards. She won't be a problem, for obvious reasons, but I'd suggest getting the two goons drunk."

"And the children?" said Mr. Hein.

"We'll maroon them at our next stop. They won't last the winter. Then we head home with or without Barentsz."

Bren heard footsteps coming through the gangway, and he fought every impulse to run. All he could do was remain perfectly still, and hopefully invisible, until the men went by. It was only Mr. Hein, and he walked right past where Bren was eavesdropping without noticing. Bren then ran as fast as he could to find Lady Barrett.

MONSTER ISLAND

B ren threw open the door to Shveta's cabin without knocking. Still trying to catch his breath, he panted, "We're in dang—"

Shveta was sitting cross-legged on the floor, her arms resting on each knee and the middle finger and thumb on each hand curled into a circle. She was facing her cabin's one portal, away from Bren, but as soon as the door had flung open she spun her head over her shoulder, and her furious gaze froze Bren in his tracks. For a brief moment, the whites of her eyes were a brilliant green.

"I tried to stop him," said Lady Barrett, who had obviously been chasing him. "Never enter a lady's chambers without knocking, I always say."

"Ani said I could find her in her cabin," said Bren.

"Don't blame me," said Ani, who was right behind them.

Bren looked at Shveta again. Her eyes were normal, but she was still angry, and she was staring at Lady Barrett. It was obvious she could tell it was her, despite her seaman's trousers and shirt and fake beard.

"Where did you come from?" said Shveta, her voice like an icicle.

"Originally?" said Lady Barrett, half smirking.

Shveta turned to Bren. "Finish your thought."

"We're in danger," he said. "I overheard the captain. They plan to kill you and your men and maroon Ani and me, then head back to Amsterdam. He never had any intention of taking you to the North Pole."

"And when is he thinking he'll carry out this ill-advised maneuver?"

"Soon," said Bren. "They plan to sail north a bit longer, if the journals they found tell them anything. If not, maybe sooner."

Shveta rose from the floor without using her arms, her folded legs gracefully returning to upright form as if her body were on a spring.

"I may kill Aadesh and Aadarsh myself," she said, glancing at Lady Barrett. To Bren she said, "You draw maps, right, bub?"

▲▲▲

"We should go ahead and kill him," said Aadesh. "We know he's planning to kill us."

"Planning to *try,*" said Aadarsh. "I'll cut his fat little body in half."

"With what?" said Lady Barrett. "He took your weapons. You're severely outnumbered. And I'm not sure you're much of a killer, at that."

Aadarsh growled.

"I don't think the whole ship's in on it," said Bren. "It sounded like something between Captain Tromp and Mr. Hein."

"Tromp knows the Arctic," Shveta reminded them.

"So does his first mate," said Aadesh.

"And what if *he* doesn't want to cooperate, either?" said Shveta.

"On to the next one," said Aadarsh, slamming his hand onto the table.

Shveta slapped Aadarsh upside the head. "Use your brain! We can't kill everyone. Unless you dum-dums know how to sail through ice."

"In my brother's defense," said Aadesh, "we wouldn't have to kill that many before the rest were persuaded." He subtly leaned out of arm's reach from Shveta as he finished talking.

"No!" said Bren, who had been sitting quietly with Ani but couldn't take it anymore. "This will not become a bloodbath!"

The look Shveta gave him halted him midspeech, but somehow he found the nerve to go on. "Mutiny is a terrible thing. I learned that firsthand on the *Albatross*. It may solve one problem, but it creates many more. The best course is to work with the evil you know."

He sat back, expecting Shveta to lash out at him, but she didn't. No one said anything for a minute, until Lady Barrett spoke up.

"Bren's right. There are enough of us to . . . *persuade* Captain Tromp to stick to the plan he was paid for."

Shveta closed her eyes and took a deep breath. "You have seen the daily navigational charts, though, right, Bren?"

"Yes. I can duplicate them," said Bren. "If you can get me parchment and ink."

"Ani can," said Shveta. "Go ahead and map our way forward. We'll see where Tromp takes us from here. If we have to remove him, we'll have your forged charts to keep the crew going our way."

"That will never work," said Lady Barrett.

"Perhaps it won't have to," said Shveta. "I can be very persuasive."

The six of them left Shveta's room and went about their business as usual. For Shveta, that actually meant staying put and doing whatever it was she did in private. For Aadesh and Aadarsh, it meant playing chess in the officers' saloon. Lady Barrett went back to her watch in her guise as an ordinary seaman, and Bren and Ani went to the kennels to fetch their dogs. Just as Bren had taken ownership of Caesar, Ani had struck up a friendship with another husky, named Rotter, and had begun joining Bren on walks around the deck. Most of the men and officers were amused by the sight of the two children walking their dogs, but Nindemann was not one of them. One day he had said to Bren, "You shouldn't grow too attached to a dog in the Arctic."

Bren had immediately remembered Tromp's fur collar and his horrible story about having to kill and eat his favorite husky. Assuming it was even true.

That night at supper, Bren could hardly eat. Here they were—Shveta, Ani and Bren, Aadesh and Aadarsh, sitting with Captain Tromp and his first mate, knowing they planned to kill them. It turned his stomach, but apparently not the twins', who ate heartily as usual. So did Nindemann, the engineer, and Bren took that as a good sign. He liked Nindemann. He didn't want to believe he was in on this. Tromp and Mr. Hein sort of stabbed at their food, distracted. Nindemann obviously had nothing on his mind except a good meal after a day's work.

"Did you learn anything from the journals you found?" Shveta asked innocently.

"Indeed," said Tromp. "Those bones we found were Barentsz's men, and one of the journals belonged to Barentsz himself. Apparently they found land, above the Eightieth Parallel."

"The Eightieth Parallel?" said Nindemann. "Have you ever seen a map showing land that far north?"

Tromp shook his head. "It gets better. They claim it was inhabited."

Nindemann stopped chewing. "Who could live there?"

"According to them, monsters."

If Bren hadn't already lost his appetite, he would have now. "Monsters?"

Tromp smiled at him. The cruelest smile Bren had ever seen. "What are you afraid of, jongen? You're already traveling with these two freaks."

Shveta didn't react. Ani just narrowed her green eyes at the captain.

"Anyway," said Tromp, "they found this new land, a group of islands. It's as far as they could go, so Barentsz and half the crew decided to overwinter; the other half took the ship back toward Nova Zembla. They knew if something happened no one would know they made it that far north. 'Course, we know what happened after that, at least to the men on Nova Zembla."

"And Barentsz?" said Nindemann.

"I think we know where to find him," said Tromp, eyeing Shveta and Ani as he said it.

"Can I read his journal?" said Bren. The question drew a scowl from Tromp, so Bren added, "I'm a journalist myself."

"Are you, jongen? A regular scribe? Good for you. And no. That is company property."

That night, before Bren snuffed the candle in their tiny room, Ani stopped him. "Don't you want to read before bed?" She was holding up a weather-beaten leather journal.

"Where did you get that?" said Bren, eagerly taking it and opening to the first pages.

"Don't ask so many questions," said Ani. "But tonight is the only night we have with it. So scoot over."

Bren made room for her on his cot, and by their one light they read the harrowing account of Barentsz and his crew pushing farther into the Arctic than any European had before.

Their plan had been to cross the northern coast of Russia and Siberia, in search of a major river that would take them into China. But the seas had proven more frozen than expected during summer, and the weather and storms far more unpredictable. Instead of returning home directly, they sailed north, based on little, it seemed, other than the unproven theory that the Arctic was actually warmer the farther north you went in summer because of the unending daylight and the convergence of two warm ocean currents. It was the same theory that had once led Rand McNally to offer a reward to anyone who could map the way to the supposed island paradise at the top of the world.

Tromp had told them what happened next—the discovery of an unknown land; the decision to send half the crew back home. This part of the journal, once the crew was forced to overwinter, was crushingly sad. Barentsz described in poetic detail the loneliness, how the permanent darkness infected his soul and mind, the inescapable cold, his debilitating fear of bears, and the eerie sounds of nature: ice moving and cracking, howling winds, and icebergs flipping or crashing into the sea.

Then he talked about the monsters.

It was never clear to Bren what the doomed navigator was describing. People that lived like animals? Animals that behaved like people? Some horrifying hybrid of man and beast? Or perhaps it was all just hallucination, brought on by privation and fear.

The last part of the journal had been written by one of the crewmen sent home, after these men had been forced to disembark at Nova Zembla. They had been preyed upon by a bear. Four men had been lost already. So the rest went south and into the mountains, hoping for a miracle. When none had come, the man writing the journal had decided, according to his last entry, dated January 1598, to return to the makeshift house to die, so that Barentsz's journal could be found.

When they finished reading, Ani snuck out of their room to return the journal, and Bren lay back in his cot. The pages haunted him all night, and for nights after. They were enduring the same bitter cold, hearing the same ill winds, and the same ice moaning and cracking. There were constant reminders of how close and violent death could be. It was hard for Bren not to think of the Barentsz journal as some forbidding omen, almost as if he had traveled in time to read the journal he himself had written of their own doomed voyage.

CHAPTER
22

ICEBREAKERS

Barentsz's journal described the unknown lands as approximately two hundred miles due north of Nova Zembla. Even with its reinforced hull, the *Sea Lion* was barely able to make a knot of speed through the slushy sea, which meant it might be July before they found what Bren had started calling Monster Island.

When they crossed the Eightieth Parallel, the men let out a great *whoop*. Before the Barentsz journal proved otherwise, it was believed that no one had penetrated this far into the Arctic. Now this crew, while not first, had the chance to return home as the only living explorers to go here. But their elation was quickly tempered by caution. None of them knew what to expect, except hardship. Tromp had not told the crew at large all of what Barentsz wrote.

They spotted land soon enough—a cluster of islands small and large, dozens of them, that reminded Bren of the Dragon Islands in the East Netherlands. Except these islands seemed wholly deserted, barren of any settlement, if not life. The southernmost lands were snow-capped but covered by moss, lichen, and nesting birds, and they passed congregations of seals and walruses covering entire shorelines. With no clear idea how to navigate the islands, Tromp and his navigator plotted their course by the ice, choosing places where the floes were more broken, allowing for movement, if you could call it that. The ship crawled north with less speed than anyone on board could've walked.

Bren, the boy who had never wanted to draw maps, eagerly stood shivering by the navigator as he sat atop the deckhouse at the rear of the ship, trying to map their path with frozen hands. This was, after all, what Bren had once dreamt of—experiencing the thrill of discovering new lands and sending men like his father back to his drawing table to revise the collective image of the known world.

"How the devil are we to find where Barentsz might've landed?" Tromp wondered aloud. "There could be a thousand islands here."

The navigator eagerly offered, "We circle the islands, try every channel, until we see a black flag or anything resembling a camp."

Bren knew he just wanted the chance to map their new discovery whole, but Tromp shook his head.

"We don't have the time or the resources to sail in circles," he said.

In the end, it wouldn't matter. They were forced to anchor the ship at the cape of a large island around the Eighty-First Parallel. The ice would give no more.

"We'll rest. Then send the icebreakers out," ordered Tromp.

When Bren was growing up in Map, his father used to remind him that there were worse jobs than being a mapmaker. Stonemasons were a favorite example of David Owen's, those broad-backed men who broke and shaped rock. If you visited their guildhall, you were sure to see men with mangled feet and hands, warped spines, crushed arms and legs. They took immense pride in their work, but it crippled their bodies.

The icebreakers made Bren remember those proud but damaged tradesmen. There was no wind strong enough to propel a sailing ship through solid ice. So ships like the *Sea Lion* designated parts of the crew to go out on the ice with picks and sledgehammers and axes and chisel the ship free.

They were in the latitudes where the ice was permanent, fifteen feet thick in places. Their task was nothing short of Herculean.

Common perils included falling through the ice, accidentally striking another man's hands or feet, or worst of all, getting crushed by the ship lurching forward into a gap they had just made.

The engineer, Nindemann, led the icebreakers and worked on the gang himself. From the prow of the ship, Bren watched him. Despite the cold he had taken off his furs and rolled up his sleeves in the bright sunshine. His arms had the same ropy muscles as Bren's old nemesis, Otto Bruun, and he had the same dark hair and dark, determined look in his eyes at all times. Yet he was kind to Bren, and he wondered if Otto had once been like this . . . friendly, hopeful, until driven mad by the cruelty of a ship's captain or simply the cruelty of a life spent at sea. Was there some way of predicting who would break? Would Nindemann change?

They made only halting progress through the thicker ice, while scouts used the midnight sun to search day and night from the crow's nest for signs of Barentsz's camp or black flags. After several days, they had spotted none, and so Tromp made the fateful decision to anchor the *Sea Lion* and organize a search party that would go ashore, starting with one of the larger islands where they had seen plenty of animals that could have sustained a stranded party.

Tromp left Mr. Hein, his first mate, in charge of the ship. He chose Nindemann and eight others to go with him. And then he surprised everyone by calling on Bren and Ani to go along as well.

"We're taking the dogs, and the jongens have made pets of two of 'em," said Tromp. "Will keep 'em calm."

Bren and Ani knew the real reason—this was where Tromp planned to finally maroon them. Nindemann also suggested taking Aadesh and Aadarsh, but Tromp dismissed that, too. His excuse was that the men would be useless exposed to weather like this, having lived their lives in much warmer climates, but again, Bren knew the real reason: the brothers' presence would make it more difficult for Tromp to leave Ani behind. Bren's spirits lifted, though, when he noticed that Lady Barrett had somehow gotten herself on the landing party.

They hitched six of the dogs, including Caesar and Rotter, to a pair of sleds holding supplies and weapons, but the search party walked. When they got farther from the ship, where the snow and ice began to pile up, they all shod their feet with what looked like lawn tennis racquets to Bren. But these snowshoes did keep his feet from sinking into the wet snow and slush, keeping his already freezing feet from hurting any worse.

They found nothing the first day, camped, and tried

again. They kept following false leads, or mirages. It was a funny thing about Arctic light—it was so bright and clear in summer, and brought everything into such sharp relief, and yet so often it showed you nothing but distortion or trickery. After three days, Bren and Ani were exhausted, afraid to sleep because of Tromp. Finally, as they neared the shore again, they found something . . . feces filled with fish bones, along with what looked to be the remains of a fire.

"Could this be from three years ago?" Nindemann asked.

Tromp was kneeling by the burnt wood and ash, sifting it with his hand. "Barentsz mentioned an encounter in his journal," said Tromp. "With people, of a sort."

"People?" said Nindemann. "Living here? Another group of explorers?"

Before Tromp could answer, a storm kicked up suddenly, the wind tearing across their faces, sleet and snow so fierce they could scarcely see one another.

The dogs started barking, pulling at their restraints. Bren knelt next to Caesar, saying, "It's okay, boy. It's just a storm. It'll pass."

From his knees, Bren could just see to the shoreline, as if he were peeking under a twisting, windblown curtain. The storm was pushing the ice floes toward the island, where they would collide and ricochet away again. The dogs seemed to be barking not at the storm, but at the shore, and as Bren stared out, he saw what could have been a group of men emerge from the frozen sea onto land.

He tried to call out, but the wind beat away his warnings. The snow had grown worse, too, and his brief glimpse of the shoreline vanished. It was all any of them could do to keep from being overwhelmed. Even the dogs had stopped barking, to keep the daggers of ice out of their mouths.

When the storm relented after several minutes, Bren cautiously opened his eyes, and when he did, he saw one of the men jerk backward, as if grabbed from behind. A second man was attacked as well, and this time, Tromp noticed.

"Bears!" he shouted over the wind, and his men immediately went to the sleds for their weapons.

But they weren't bears. Bren wasn't sure what they were. They weren't animals, nor were they fully human. Some had long tusks for canines, others had fins for hands. There was a man with one forward-facing eye and one bulbous eye around the side of his head, where his ear should have been. Another rose up from the ice on a thick, leathery torso that terminated in a tail. Something near the back nursed at least six children on rows of teats along her stomach. All were dressed in skins of walrus, seal, reindeer, polar bear, and muskox, wearing necklaces of stone and white feathers.

Even through the sleet Bren could see that the two men who had been ambushed were already dead. One lay pinned to the ice with a massive spear. The other's head was barely attached, blood pulsing from his neck.

"There's only a dozen of them," said Tromp, though he said it without a hint of confidence. He now had half that number.

This ghastly clan's weapons were even stranger than the ones Ani had shown Bren. One gripped a long pole that branched into half a dozen spikes. Two appeared to have fashioned whips from barbed arms of jellyfish. Others had long bones, filed into blades and attached to the undersides of their arms. Most brandished daggers, scythes, swords, and spears made of bone and ivory, all of which were pink with old blood. There was one with tusks as large as a walrus's, and a body to match, massive and shapeless, oozing onto the ice.

There was no time to discuss their strategy. The walrus-sized one opened his blood-stained mouth and let out a cry that shook Bren to his core. It was the same terrible sound that had come from a berserk Otto before he had attacked them in the hold of the *Albatross*.

The one with the long spiked pole raised it over his head, and by reflex Bren and the others crouched, expecting him to hurl it like a spear. Instead, he spun the weapon around and brought it down, spikes first, into the ice with a thunderous crack, then used the pole to vault himself into the air, covering the distance between the two forces in one motion. He landed before a stunned crew member, who stood there with a pistol in hand, and sliced his neck open with the back of his fin-shaped hand before the hapless victim could fire a shot.

Tromp and the others briefly stood frozen, watching their mate fall to the ground into a puddle of bright-red blood. Bren just stared at it, this sudden, shocking burst of color in the vast whiteness, growing and spreading like a living thing that had just escaped its shell.

What felt like minutes, though, was but a fleeting second. The others attacked; Bren was yanked backward by Lady Barrett, who flung herself into the fray.

Shots were fired. Metal weapons clashed with bone and ivory, filling the empty wastes with an eerie, blunt symphony of battle. The huskies charged, and animal and human guttural cries mixed with the wind and were carried away. The ice was soon slick with blood and fat from bodies that had been cut open.

Bren, to his shame, never got up. He had no weapon but a short dagger, and his useless black jade stone was stashed away among his things onboard the ship. There was nothing to protect him, except his own cowardly desire to run from the battle.

He turned to find Ani, who was on her hands and

knees against the pounding winds. He went to help her, but just as he got closer she took off running full speed—toward the battle.

"Ani, no!" Bren cried, but again the wind swept away his voice. She was running directly at the man with the walrus tusks, and when she was perhaps twenty feet away she leaped into the air, stretching her arms out before her like a swimmer diving off a cliff.

The girl Bren knew as Ani plunged headfirst toward the ice, but what landed and sprung up again was a huge grey cat, the size of a panther, lunging at the leader of the beastly clan.

The cat knocked the tusked man to the ground and pinned him there, tearing at his throat with her teeth until he managed to push her away with his staff. She landed on her feet and quickly lunged at another, trying to even the odds.

Tromp and the others seized the advantage. Nindemann was a force, fighting two and three opponents at once with an ice ax in one hand and a pick in the other. The rifles and pistols took too long to reload, so those weapons were quickly tossed aside, forcing the crew to fight close in, which resulted in ghastly wounds. The creatures who had lined the undersides of their arms with sharpened bones sliced open men left and right like windmills. Bren watched as the joint end of a massive femur bone came crashing down on one man's head, caving in his skull. Others fought more like the animals they resembled, biting and clawing.

Lady Barrett had managed to secret her sword off the ship, and she was thrusting and slicing and parrying, looking as if it were old hat to fight three or four men at a time. But during one flourish as she raised her sword arm, Bren saw that she, too, had been badly wounded, a long lateral gash across her side and back.

It was sheer butchery, but Ani, or the cat, was turning the tide. It took more and more of the clan to battle her, leaving them vulnerable to attack from behind. But then, to Bren's horror, he saw the nursing woman, who had retreated from the battle, one by one pull her suckling children from her belly and throw them at the cat. Whatever sort of children they were, they clung to Ani, attacking her legs and her neck, trying to disable her.

Finally they pulled her down to the ice, and Bren thought she was finished. The tusked monster, despite bleeding profusely from the wounds Ani had left in his neck, slowly crawled toward her, using his tusks like walking sticks. He was going to finish her.

Bren frantically looked around. Where Ani had transformed, there was a pile of fur on the ground. He fished around until he found them—her chakram bracelets and the bladed whip.

He picked up the chakram and raised an arm to throw them, but his confidence dissolved. What if he hit one of his own men, or Ani? And so he reached for the urumi, the one Ani had not even let him hold. He found the handle and stood up, praying his aim would be true, and he drew his arm up and back, the whip rising up and rearing back like a striking snake. He threw his arm forward, and the whip lashed out into the blur of snow and ice, landing squarely across the back of the tusked leader.

He howled in pain like nothing Bren had ever heard, and a bright-red vein of blood opened from his neck to his waist. Bren was so stunned at his lucky aim that he forgot to draw the whip back, and suddenly his victim turned and grabbed the end of it, his thick, walruslike skin somehow bearing the pain, and pulled Bren toward him.

Bren could have simply dropped the urumi, but fear froze his brain. Before he knew it, he was face-to-face with the half-human, warmed by his putrid breath, about to be devoured.

His dagger. He felt for it . . . if he could place it just right . . . there! He firmly closed his hand around the handle and swung his arm up, stabbing the blade up to the hilt into the roll of fat around the walrus-man's neck.

He howled again and reached up, grabbing Bren by the hair and tossing him away. Bren hit the ice so hard his lungs emptied. In the frozen air he could see every ounce of breath he had leaving his body like a ghost. Then, to his despair, he saw that the leader, after briefly collapsing to one knee, was up again and advancing on Ani, Bren's dagger still sticking out of his neck.

And then he stopped again. They all did, when they heard the overpowering roar of the bear.

The half-humans knew it well—they lived among polar bears. But what they didn't expect, what none of them expected, was what they saw next. The bear was stalking toward them, and walking by its side was a person, dressed head to toe in thick black fur.

It was Shveta, and when she raised her hand the bear charged.

From his back, dizzy with pain, all Bren could see at first was a confusion of legs and white fur, and then the mauled figure of one of the clan skidded to the ground right next to him. Bren pushed himself half upright and saw that the grey cat, despite her wounds, had shaken off the savage children and was ferociously dragging men down in tandem with the bear. The nursing creature gathered her children back to her and retreated. A few others did as well, leaving their wounded to die. The last to give up was the tusked leader, who rose up one last time and attacked the bear from behind, plunging both his tusks into the bear's back. He hung there, burying his face into the bear's blood-stained back, trying to use his weight to force the bear down, but just when it seemed he might succeed, the cat sunk her front claws into his shoulders, pulling him away, and then finished tearing out his throat.

The victors looked anything but victorious. Nindemann was on one knee, propping himself with his ice ax. Tromp was on both knees, eyeing the white bear and the woman now standing over it, running her hands over its wounds. Only two of the remaining crew were still alive, and Bren was relieved to see that Lady Barrett was still among the living. But for how long? Everyone's wounds looked terrible. The carnage was unlike anything he had ever seen, even at Cape Colony.

The cat approached Shveta cautiously, and the wounded bear took in her scent. The two remaining dogs, including Caesar, bristled and growled, but the cat and bear followed Shveta as she left the scene of battle, walking across the white landscape in the direction of the ship.

Bren expected Tromp and his wounded men to do the same, but instead the captain hoisted himself up and pointed in the direction of the retreating enemy. "Strip the dead, rend their clothes, bandage your wounds as best you can," he ordered. "We follow them now. It's our best chance to find what happened to Barentsz."

SKULLS, BONES, AND LIVER

They discovered that the clan had arrived on a pair of leather canoes, but had retreated in just one. To follow them, Tromp and Nindemann had to paddle the abandoned canoe through shifting floes, which proved treacherous. Fortunately it was a short trip to the next island, where they did find the remains of Barentsz, at last.

The surviving clan members had already gathered up their most vital possessions from their camp and retreated again. When they were out of sight, even by spyglass,

Tromp led them to the campsite, where they found several skulls (some human, some animal) and piles of bones that may have been intended for weapons. The only real proof that Barentsz was among them was another leather journal, one the doomed navigator must have started after sending the other half of his crew back to Nova Zembla with his old one.

"So which skull is his?" said Nindemann. "What do we carry back?"

Tromp walked among the bones, scattering them with his foot. "Leave all these," he said. "Pick one of the skulls. Doesn't matter which. King Max, the Company, and Barentsz's family will just be happy to have something to bury."

They hiked back to the canoe, paddled across, and then loaded their own dead onto the two sleds and began pulling them back to the *Sea Lion*. All Bren could think about as the midnight sun rolled along the horizon without setting was, When would Tromp make his move? Would Lady Barrett, as badly wounded as she was, be able to thwart him? Bren now knew Barentsz's nightmares had been all too real. The thought of being stranded in such a remote, lonely place made him ill with fear.

But if the captain had a plan, it must have been buried under his fear and anger over what he had witnessed in Ani and Shveta. As they all reboarded the ship, Tromp barked an order: "Find the queen, her freak orphan, the two goons, and throw 'em in the brig."

To his surprise, the answer he got was: "Captain, they're already there. In the hold, anyway. With a white bear. They went down there on their own, through the cargo hatch. No one dared come near 'em."

Bren ran as fast as he could to the hold before Tromp could gather himself. Sure enough, there was the bear, on its side, with Shveta and Ani—human Ani—kneeling next to it, stroking its fur.

"Tromp will be down here any minute," said Bren. "He was ranting the whole time about what happened. You're going to have to explain it to him. And then of course there's the small matter of him planning to kill you, Aadesh, and Aadarsh, and leaving Ani and me here to die."

Shveta didn't seem concerned. "And you don't need an explanation of what happened, Bren?"

He hesitated. "I had a friend . . . she could do some extraordinary things."

"Mouse?" said Ani.

Bren nodded. The thunder of footsteps shook the hold as Tromp, Nindemann, and four others came looking for Shveta. Tromp was so angry he forgot to switch from Dutch to English.

"You translate, boy," he ordered Bren, when he realized what he'd done.

"Pretty much just what I said before," said Bren. "He wants answers."

Shveta stood up and walked slowly toward Tromp, who stood his ground but clearly seemed afraid. She was taller than he was, too, and let that fact sink in as she stood face-to-face with him, her chin angled down slightly to meet his beady eyes.

"You want answers?" she said. "Pay me for them." She pointed to her forehead, where she had replaced the ruby bindi with a vermilion dot, some sort of chalk Ani had made for her.

Tromp smirked. "I'll pay you if what you tell me means anything. Not before. And that bear can't stay here."

"He's dying," said Shveta, returning to its side. "The tusks punctured his lungs."

Tromp had no sympathy. "Until then, we chain him here. And you and the freak are confined to the brig. If either of your two large friends tries to do anything about it, I'll execute them on the spot."

No one moved. No one wanted to be near the bear if it suddenly revived. Tromp, furious, grabbed two men at a time by the neck and pushed them forward until he had four "volunteers."

"And for being such cowards, you better hope the bear mauls you compared to what you've got coming from me."

The men chaining the bear survived, except for one,

and it wasn't the bear that killed him. Tromp lashed all four publicly until they bled, and one, already weak with dysentery, died on the spot. Because he had been punished for cowardice, Tromp had him dumped overboard without a proper burial.

The men killed in battle he did bury with ceremony, but apparently that act exhausted his humanity; he sent everyone to work or to bed without supper. An exhausted Bren collapsed into his cot, looking at Ani's empty cot before snuffing the candle. In the darkness, some hours later, he heard the bear awake. A great moan came from the bowels of the ship, followed by the terrible rattling of chains.

▲▲▲

Bren slept maybe an hour, leaving his room before the fifth bell to find Lady Barrett. He went to where the ordinary seamen slept, looking for "Speler," fearing they would say he had died during the night or was in the surgeon's ward. But he was told Speler was above, on his regular watch.

Bren almost ran to her when he saw her on deck, but Lady Barrett put a hand out, reminding him they were in plain view. When he got within earshot, she said, "I'm fine. I'll live, for now." She took a deep breath, which seemed to cost her dearly. "I guess I underestimated Queen Shveta," she said. "If you knew half of what we all know now, I can't blame you for wanting to see what she's after.

But we still need a plan, and soon."

Bren ran to the hold, where he found Shveta and Ani sitting in their meditative poses in the small iron cage. Aadesh and Aadarsh were both leaning against the cage, asleep, having apparently kept guard all night. The bear lay still, making no sound.

"He's dead," said Shveta without opening her eyes.

"It's me," said Bren.

"I figured," said Shveta, opening her eyes but remaining in her pose.

"Are you two all right?"

"I'm fine," said Shveta. "Ani is weak. Transformation is taxing."

They were interrupted by the pounding of boots coming down the ladder and across the hold. Aadesh and Aadarsh awoke and stood, but Tromp walked past them to the bear, nudging its head with his foot.

"Did you bring my jewels?" said Shveta.

"You first," said Tromp. "That's the deal I gave you last night."

"We need to eat," she said.

"Mess isn't for another hour."

"No, we need to eat the bear," said Shveta. "The organs."

Tromp barked a laugh. "What sort of witchery are you getting at?"

"I thought you wanted to know how to acquire my power," said Shveta. "This is how. Besides, I'm hungry."

Tromp turned to Nindemann, as well as the others with him. Bren knew exactly what he was thinking. He was planning to kill Shveta. It didn't matter if she was conning him. He had the upper hand.

Except he didn't, and Bren knew it. He just didn't know what Shveta had in mind.

The ship's cook came down to the hold, and with the help of six other men, he turned the bear on its back and slit open its belly. He removed the heart, the liver, the kidneys, the stomach, and the pancreas. Tromp wanted to eat the brain, too, but Shveta assured him it wasn't the bear's intellect he was after.

"Boil the organs, and let us know when soup's on," said Shveta. "We're just fine right here."

"Cook them?" said Tromp. "You should eat them raw!"

"Only if you want to make yourself sick," said Shveta.

▲▲▲

They gathered two hours later in the officers' saloon, where the cook had prepared three large platters of organ meat. Tromp, Nindemann, Bren, Shveta and Ani, Aadesh and Aadarsh, the first mate, and the navigator all sat around the stained wooden table.

"There must have been men who've eaten polar bear meat before," said Tromp. "Don't recall hearing of any

Arctic explorers with supernatural powers."

"Maybe they didn't eat the organs," said Shveta. "They are an acquired taste."

Tromp picked up his fork and knife, then pushed his plate across the table to Shveta. "You go ahead. I want to see how you like it."

Shveta smiled. "You don't really think I'm dumb enough to believe I could poison you so obviously."

"I do," said Tromp. "The obvious part is the trick of it. Now go ahead, eat up."

Shveta glanced at Ani and Bren, then carefully cut a piece of pancreas and placed it in her mouth. She chewed slowly, seeming to savor the bite. Tromp made all of them try some, except his officers, and when it was Bren's turn, he got to try the liver. Despite growing up in Map, with the worst cooking in the world, he decided he had never tasted anything so foul. The liver tasted like metal, with the aftertaste of medicine. The texture was horrible, too, somehow slimy and chalky at the same time.

Tromp sat there, his knife and fork propped in each hand, watching them eat. This went on for twenty minutes before Nindemann said, "I don't think the food is poisoned, Captain."

Tromp snorted. "I guess not. Perhaps you are on the level, Queen Shveta." He laughed as he overemphasized the word *queen*, and Bren could see the murderous look in Shveta's eyes. But the look softened a bit when Tromp began to eat. He dug into his organ meat with gusto, polishing off an entire kidney by himself, wolfing down half a pancreas, and then cutting long strips of liver, which hung from his lips like wriggling worms before he slurped them down. Bren wondered if Shveta's plan was to disable Tromp by way of a powerful stomachache.

"Here, finish the liver, Mr. Hein. It's delicious," said Tromp as he leaned back from the table, rubbed his belly, and let out a disgusting, loud belch. Then he stood up, raised his arms and curled his fingers like claws, and let out a great animal roar, which quickly morphed into laughter.

"I better wake up with white fur on my chest, Your Highness," he said, then barged out of the saloon like a drunk.

After Mr. Hein had polished off the remaining liver, he and the other officers followed, except for Nindemann, who sat there, looking at Shveta, Ani, and Bren in turn before finally standing and walking out of the saloon without saying anything.

"What's the plan?" Bren asked.

"You're about to get very sick," said Shveta.

"You . . . you poisoned me?"

"I poisoned all of us," said Shveta. "Polar bear liver is toxic. But we'll be the only ones to survive it."

Ani pulled out another vial of crushed powder. This

one was green. She stirred it up in their water cups and ordered Bren to drink.

"This will keep us from getting sick?"

"Oh no," said Ani. "We're going to start puking like volcanoes before the night is over."

"How did you know all this?" said Bren.

"My father was a physician," said Shveta. "One of his patients ran the zoological park in Jammu. When animals died he would let my father poke around. He was also an amateur apothecary . . . it was useful to him to be able to grind his own medicines. I still have his notebooks, and Ani is fond of reading."

Sometime around three bells, Bren rushed to the head—a chute at the back of the ship that emptied into the ocean—and threw up so violently that he was sure his own liver and at least a couple of other organs had been ejected from his body. The only consolation was that he didn't have to clean it up.

He was so weak he barely made it back to his cabin. When it came time for the seven a.m. watch—the one Tromp always commanded—the captain was nowhere to be seen. Bren had no idea if Tromp had given the order to turn back or not, but either way they had a difficult task ahead of them. They had to break through the pack ice and find a way out.

The icebreakers went to work, this time with

Nindemann watching them from the bow of the ship. He had jerry-rigged a device to hold the ship in place to prevent the ghastly consequences of the ship slipping forward into open cracks. Bren, braving the cold, sneaked onto the forecastle and stood by his side, watching with him.

"Is Captain Tromp sick?" Bren finally asked.

Without looking at him, Nindemann replied, "Would that surprise you?"

Bren didn't know how to take this response. "I just . . . I mean, I was throwing up all night. I guess my stomach isn't used to organ meat."

"No one's stomach is used to poison," said Nindemann, and this time he turned and looked Bren squarely in the eye. Bren felt himself getting sick again. "You found out he was going to abandon you and kill the others, didn't you?"

Bren nodded. Nindemann turned back toward the icebreakers.

"You may have saved me the trouble," he said.

"I'm sorry?" said Bren.

"The trouble of killing Tromp myself," said Nindemann. "I'm not a murderer; I am an explorer. And ever since you showed me this map of the Pole, getting there is all I can think about. I wasn't about to let Tromp stop us."

"Oh," said Bren.

Nindemann took off his furs and leaned against the gunwale with both arms, now wearing just his grey company shirt, which was heavily soiled and threadbare in places, especially the sleeves, where the engineer's massive shoulders had nearly rubbed through the fabric. "Look at my right arm," he said.

And that's when Bren noticed it, scarcely visible through the translucent threads—a black *V*, bracketed by a smaller *Z* and *T*, and cupping a small black tulip.

TRAPPED

"You're in the Order of the Black Tulip?" cried Bren, before realizing how loudly he'd spoken. Nindemann cringed; they both looked around, but no other crewman was close enough to hear them.

"I am," said Nindemann. "And your friend, Reynard Bowman, wasn't. Not when you sailed with him."

"He wasn't my friend," said Bren. "But I thought there was no Order anymore."

"He tell you that?"

Bren nodded, embarrassed even now to learn one more

thing about the admiral he had been foolish enough to believe.

"I guess maybe that was only a half lie," said Nindemann. "There was more than one Order once, both claiming to be real. I like to think I believe in the true mission, to believe anything is possible."

"How many are in the Order now?" said Bren. "Are there more on this ship?"

Nindemann barked a few orders down to his icebreakers before answering. "That's a secret, jongen. Because of the split, most men don't even get the tattoo anymore. Or they hide it, like I do."

"So what is it you believe is up there?" said Bren. "The North Pole, I mean."

"I'm not sure," said Nindemann. "I've heard rumors, stories. I remember the man's claim to have found a warmwater paradise. I just know that no man has ever made it that far, and many think it can't be done. I say we find out." He shrugged his furs back on. "I'm sure the Indian woman is looking for something besides warm weather. Nor does she seem like the adventurous type. What does *she* think we're going to find?"

"You wouldn't believe it if I told you," said Bren, trying to imagine explaining the Well of Wisdom and Lost Words of Magic to the engineer. And the fact that Bren himself was nursing the hope that she was right.

"Wouldn't I?" said Nindemann, but when Bren was unable to find an answer, he half smiled. "It doesn't matter. Like I said, I want to find out, whatever it is. Whatever the cost."

"I feel the same way," Bren mumbled, but when the engineer gave him a puzzled look, Bren said, "I've made a fake navigation chart. It was Shveta's idea when she learned of Tromp's plan. The idea was to eliminate him and have the navigator go by what he thought were Tromp's orders."

"Mr. Hein will still be a problem," said Nindemann. "But I can deal with him. Slip the chart under my cabin door tonight."

Bren went to find Shveta and Ani to tell them they had an ally. He was halfway belowdecks when he realized he was practically running. He was excited. The sensation stunned him, unexpected as it was. Here he was, on this horrible ship in the most unforgiving climate he'd ever experienced. He had been brought to the brink of departure against his will, taken from his father and Mr. Black just when it seemed he would finally get to go home.

So what was this? He had willingly boarded the *Sea Lion,* but this was something different. Belief.

Somewhere along the way, he had come to believe that the part of him that yearned for adventure, to be an explorer, was childish. Shveta and Ani had sparked something. And here was Nindemann, the engineer, the problem solver, the practical man, admitting that he believed anything was possible. He was upholding an ideal that Bren still badly wanted to cherish.

Tromp didn't die, not right away, but he was so sick he couldn't leave his bed. Mr. Hein, despite having a smaller portion of the liver, had become violently ill, too. Nindemann, in charge with Tromp and Hein debilitated, would set their course for the Pole, if they could ever get free of the ice.

The icebreakers did their work tirelessly for seven days and nights, slowly but surely carving space for the *Sea Lion* to push through the floes. But each time the ship filled the space where ice had been, the packs shifted and regrouped, pressing in on them from all sides. If it had been a trap, it would have been a brilliant one. There was no turning back, but the way forward might be a prison.

It took them three weeks to sail clear of the islands of the barbarians. It was now August. Bren, having spent months on the *Albatross*, knew that life on a ship was a hard one. But at least sailing from Britannia to Asia there had been periods of relief—tropical waters, relatively easy days of clear sailing, and an end in sight. They knew where they were headed, and could look forward to the comfort of reaching ports like Cape Colony and Bantam. But on the *Sea Lion* there was no relief, ever. The unbearable cold became colder, the brutal work and conditions even more brutal.

He also remembered how frightened he had been at

first by the strange noises on the *Albatross*. No sailor's account can really prepare you for living in the bowels of a ship, trying to sleep while the planks and boards moan and the rats scrape and scurry with such abandon that it feels like they're inside your skull.

The *Sea Lion* was no different, but in addition to all the sounds of the ship there were the sounds of the ice. The grinding when floes rubbed across one another. Cracking that sounded like rifle shots. And when an iceberg calved, sending a mountainous chunk plunging into the sea with concussive force, it sounded to Bren like the world was ending.

Nindemann was used to the noises; what he was worried about was the ship itself. So congested was the pack ice that the *Sea Lion* was often pinched at its sides, warping the hull and the decks. The boards would become so separated that the black tar used to waterproof the ship would ooze forth, and the caulkers and joiners worked nonstop to reseal the ship once it had become unpinched and sighed back into shape.

But they could not work fast enough to keep the water out. The slush seeped in, filling the bilge and sloshing into the hold. It was critical for them to keep their food stores and other supplies dry; they had no alternatives, other than what they could hunt, and it might be months before they returned to inhabited lands.

Nindemann had built a sump pump able to handle the weight of icy water, but it was a constant struggle and required constant manpower. Men were forced to stand waist-deep in sub-freezing water, bailing and pumping. And Nindemann was right there with them, as were Aadesh and Aadarsh, who won the respect of the crew for their efforts. All three could work the pump for hours at a time, never seeming to tire. But Bren knew better, because at morning and evening meals he could see how hollow their eyes were, how they were so weary it was a struggle for them to lift their spoons or cups.

The crew was now so afraid of Shveta and Ani that they didn't even want to see them, which was fine by them. They spent hours at a time in their cabin, meditating, and it finally dawned on Bren that they were practicing magic. Natural magic, what little of it they knew. Before they had poisoned Tromp, Bren had asked Shveta why she didn't just rain snakes down on him.

"That was just an illusion, a shadow of the full spell," she had explained. "I need the Lost Words to master my full powers, the kind that can take down an empire."

An illusion, a shadow . . . Mouse had said similar things on the mountain in China, when she was trying to explain the power of their stones and the artifacts. When she was trying in vain to convince him not to open the Dragon's Gate. Given what had happened since—his stone and Lady

Barrett's sword now useless—had Mouse been wrong? Or had Bren's mother, in changing his mind, prevented real catastrophe?

Bren had too much time to think about such things, because there was so little he could do to help the crew. Finally, seeing Nindemann and the rest down in the bottom of the ship, freezing and yet sweating from exertion, delirious from lack of sleep, was too much. Bren pleaded with the cook on their behalf—rations were tight, but he convinced the cook to let him concoct a sort of paste from lard, beef trimmings, and soup stock to help the men keep up their energy. It was a trick Bren had learned from Beatrice, of all people, back at the Gooey Duck in Map, when the pub had been forced to scrape meals together out of next to nothing.

"What is this gruel?" said Nindemann, when he smelled what Bren had brought him.

"Food," said Bren. "Maybe sustenance is a better word. I know it's not bear chops and peas, but it's all we could manage in order to give you and your men extra portions without making a dent in the rations."

"This was your doing?" said Nindemann.

"I wanted to help," said Bren. "I'm sorry if it's gross."

Nindemann smiled, even though just lifting up the corners of his mouth seemed like a struggle. "You're a good jongen, Bren."

Bren smiled, dipped one finger into the paste, and touched

a small amount to his tongue. He grimaced. "You may change your mind after you try this."

Nindemann grabbed his shoulder with affection and then scooped up a mouthful of the foul stuff with his first two fingers. The look on his face suggested he had just had the best meal of his life.

"The men will appreciate this," he said. "Thank you. And thank Cook."

"I will," said Bren, who turned to go back above. But he noticed something he had overlooked on his previous trips to the hold—a large sheet of canvas, the size of a mainsail, draped over a cylinder-shaped object that stretched a third of the length of the ship. It was common for supplies to be covered by tarp, but the shape of whatever lay beneath looked like neither crates nor barrels.

Nindemann, noticing Bren's curiosity, took his men the food and came back. "Wondering about that, I see?"

Bren had just been about to lift a corner of the canvas when the engineer caught him off guard. The water had been pumped out, for now, and more repairs were being made to the joints. Nindemann could rest. He grabbed the canvas and pulled it back, revealing what looked like the great bulbous nose of a wooden whale. He pulled the canvas back farther to show Bren not fins, but oars, a row of six on each side that appeared to grow straight from the middle of the round body.

"It's an onderzeeer," said Nindemann.

"It goes under the water?" said Bren, who'd never heard anything crazier. "How do you keep from drowning?" Even as he asked, he was running the palm of his hand along the surprisingly smooth sides of the curved hull. The seams were so solid they seemed more like decoration. He examined one of the oarlocks more closely. Surely there was no way to keep water from leaking in there.

"There's a rubber collar there," said Nindemann. "Flexible, but it stays with the oar as it moves. The collar itself is fixed to the inside of the hull with pitch."

"What about the hull?" Bren asked, again marveling at how seamlessly the boards came together.

"Pitch on the inside, just like a ship," said Nindemann. "But I sealed the exterior with beeswax, then varnished the entire hull with sap from the lacquer tree."

"You designed this yourself?"

Nindemann allowed himself a smile.

"Have you tried it?" said Bren.

"Only in the Amstel River, to impress King Max enough to bankroll this prototype. Lacquer sap is like liquid gold."

Bren studied the size of the vessel. He tried to imagine what it would be like to be inside, no natural light or air, under the sea. And here in the Arctic, under masses of ice as well. Plus there didn't seem to be any way to see out of it, or navigate.

Nindemann seemed to read his mind. "I hope we don't have to use it. The men won't admit it, but they're terrified of being in the water. King Max sees the onderzeeer more as a weapon, to sneak up on enemy ships. I see it as the ideal scientific vessel for polar expeditions, freeing you from the mercy of the water's surface."

"Except, unlike a river, how do you get it down there, and then back up, with all the ice?" said Bren.

Nindemann frowned. "I haven't figured everything out yet."

He didn't admit it to Nindemann, but Bren could see why the men were afraid. He didn't want to be under the sea, either. He had been in the ocean once, when the *Albatross* foundered, and he never wanted to be overboard again. Or underboard, for that matter.

Another problem cropped up as well. The navigator, Mr. Duval, who had sailed with Tromp for several years, took it upon himself to tend to his woefully ill captain and first mate when the surgeon allowed it. At supper one evening he confronted Nindemann with something Tromp had been mumbling in his half sleep, about how he was dying, and when would he see Amsterdam?

"Why does he think he's going to see Amsterdam soon?"

"He's sick," said Nindemann. "Delirious."

"I've never seen Maarten Tromp sick a day in his life,"

said Duval. "Once saw him eat a dead man's hand on a dare."

"You sure the man was dead?" said Nindemann, at which point Duval became indignant and pointed his fork at the engineer.

"You did something!" he said, his eyes now scanning the whole table. "All of you!"

Aadesh, who was sitting next to Duval, gently but firmly grabbed the navigator's wrist and wrenched the fork out of his hand.

"You don't respect that bastard any more than I do," said Nindemann.

"I respect the position, and so should you," said Duval. He tried to pull his arm free of Aadesh, but he may as well have been trying to tear free of a crocodile.

"Tromp was planning to murder our guests," said Nindemann. "He was planning to murder these children."

Duval again recoiled, not wanting to believe it. But Bren could tell by the look in his eyes that he knew it was true, or at least believable. Aadesh released him.

"So what, you poisoned him? This is mutiny?"

"It's something much bigger than that," said Nindemann. He looked to Shveta, who left the saloon and came back with both the mandala and the crude map David Owen had drawn. "Where we are now," Nindemann continued, "is roughly five hundred miles from the North Pole.

The magnetic pole. But if we're right, we could be free of ice and sailing into a warm ocean in half that distance."

Duval was just shaking his head. "And if you're wrong?"

"Then it takes us a sight longer to get there," said Nindemann, trying to sound lighthearted. "But we'll still be the first explorers to reach the North Pole. Even now we're mapping lands never known. We'll return home heroes."

Duval didn't say what he must have been thinking: *if we return home.* But he nodded and agreed to do his best to pilot them. Meanwhile, the ship, while taking on less water now, was weakened and would be unable to withstand much more of a beating like the one they had just come through.

And the days of August were slipping away. Even if there was a warm polar sea waiting for them, if the summer didn't produce a late-season burst of warmth, they might very likely be stuck wintering on the ice; no way forward, no way back.

SHIP,
ABANDONED

Bren remembered lying in his cot, in the cabin he shared with Ani, watching the hull of the ship as it slowly bulged and exhaled, like a dying animal. The whole ship was like an expiring body, gasping and groaning as the ice relentlessly crushed it.

It was the last week of August when Nindemann and Duval realized they could go no farther, not on the *Sea Lion*. It was beyond repair; beyond saving. The decision was made to abandon ship and take what resources they could for shelter and firewood, food and medicine. Duval insisted they go on foot, with their sleds, which the remaining twenty-six crew members would have to pull themselves. They had but two dogs left after their battle with the barbarians.

Nindemann had other ideas. He took the entire crew down to the hold, to show them the onderzeeer.

They all stood there, ankle deep in freezing water, looking at the thing as if it might come alive. None of the men wanted to get in, save two. Nindemann and the ordinary seaman being played by Lady Barrett. No one except Bren, Shveta, Ani, the brothers, and now Nindemann were in on her secret yet.

"What's the fewest number of men needed to row this tub?" said Shveta.

Nindemann rubbed his chin. "Two, I suppose. Though your progress would surely not be swift."

Shveta snapped her fingers at Aadesh and Aadarsh. "Let's go. You too," she said to Ani and Bren and Lady Barrett. "Show us how to get in."

There was an awkward silence and some murmuring as the men weighed the benefits of letting these strangers be the ones to test the submarine versus the shame of being upstaged by women and children. In the end they decided shame was temporary, drowning was permanent.

Nindemann, though, shook his head. "Duval's right. We're better off walking. The onderzeeer's too risky. I've never tested it in a frozen sea. Bren himself saw right off the problem of getting it below the surface and back up again."

Bren felt bad for the engineer. He had been so proud of his invention. But he was probably right, and in the end they decided to walk. Though after they began dismantling the ship for firewood, they did leave the onderzeeer atop the ice, on a row of timber, just in case. It seemed a waste to destroy it.

Once they set off, Captain Tromp and Mr. Hein had to be carried on one of the sleds. The first mate had slipped into a sort of permanent sleep, though the surgeon refused to pronounce him dead. Tromp had lost the use of his legs and had spoken nothing but gibberish for weeks.

Bren and Lady Barrett had walked twenty-five miles a day across China with Yaozu, but the Arctic was something else entirely. The storms and snow-blindness made it nearly impossible to forge ahead for hours at a time. Bren felt as if he had walked for days just to advance a few hundred yards. They would never make it.

When they had burned the last of the wood they had carried from the ship, Nindemann led a hunting party and came back with an enormous walrus. Cook prepared steaks, and they burned blubber for a fire, adding in scraps from supplies they could sacrifice, until they could carry what was left on one sled. Then they burned the other sled. Mr.

Hein was the first to die; two men who began the journey already malnourished died of exposure shortly after. Their remains were used to feed the two dogs, so the remaining men could have more rations. Bren didn't want to think about what would happen to Caesar if he didn't survive.

They all were suffering from frostbite. Bren's toes hurt so much he wanted to cry. Why couldn't the cold just numb them? Instead it was like he was walking barefoot across a field of sharp stones. He saw the ghastly results of frostbite firsthand when the surgeon peeled the shoes off Captain Tromp, who had been suffering from extreme fever, and one of his swollen, blackened toes came off in the surgeon's hand.

"Is he going to lose the whole foot?" Bren asked, feeling panicky about his own condition. The surgeon shook his head.

"He won't live that long. I can't treat his fever."

He was right. They woke up the next morning to find the indomitable Maarten Tromp cold and stiff, a pained scowl frozen onto his face.

"Don't feed him to the dogs," Shveta told Nindemann. "He ate almost the whole liver by himself."

"I say we burn him," said Duval. "And good riddance."

And so they did. The remaining crew cheered the only warmth ever given off by their despotic captain.

Before they turned in that night, Nindemann came to

Bren, Lady Barrett, Ani, and Shveta with a new plan. "I don't like the progress we're making," he said. "We don't know for sure how far the polar sea extends, which makes it almost impossible to ration for all of us. We don't know if we're on a five-hundred-mile trek or a fifty-mile trek."

"What do you want to do?" said Shveta. Her face was barely visible through her fur hood. All Bren could see were her deep black eyes and the scarlet jewel which had regained its rightful place on her forehead. Of all of them, she seemed the most impervious to the cold. Bren had no idea if she had frostbite—he wasn't sure he had ever seen her feet.

"The onderzeeer," said Nindemann. "We walk back . . . it won't take us as long without sleds . . . and launch it. I can solve the problem of getting under the ice and back out. I think."

"You think?" said Shveta. "Or you're sure?"

"I can't be sure of anything," he admitted. "But I like our chances better than continuing on foot."

Shveta shrugged. "I wanted to take the thing to begin with, if you remember. You were the scaredy cat."

Nindemann laughed. "That I was. I just wish I had nine lives."

He actually drew a smile from Shveta. At least, that's what Bren thought. He couldn't see her mouth, but her eyes lit up.

Nindemann met with Duval and came to an agreement on rations they would take and also where and when they would try to meet up again. Neither seemed to have much conviction that would happen.

After a brief sleep, they were off, Nindemann, Aadesh, and Aadarsh carrying all their supplies. As a smaller group, without the sleds, they made better time going back, but they still had to make camp twice, cocooning themselves in furs. The entire trek, Shveta, Bren, and Ani had been sleeping in the polar bear hide that Shveta had saved. But on this return trip, Bren had the strangest dreams.

He awoke in the middle of the night—real night, pitch-black—but he could see. Even more, he could smell. His nose picked up scents that seemed to come from everywhere, and from great distances: salt; blooms of algae; the warm flesh of a newborn seal; smoke from a faraway fire; and when the wind blew violently, a thousand other sudden sensations. But it was another smell that drew him—it smelled like . . . him. He began walking toward it, and Bren realized he was walking on all fours. He briefly stood, but it wasn't natural, so he let himself fall back on his hands, which is when he saw that he didn't have hands, he had paws. Massive paws covered in pinkish-white fur.

After his initial surprise, he relished how easy it was to cross the frozen ground. There was no pain, no numbness. His body was warm, too. But he was hungry. He followed the scent of flesh, covering what felt like dozens of miles, but he could find nothing. His stomach growled. Or was that him? He wondered if this was how Ani felt when she became a cat. Was it how Mouse had felt when she soul-traveled into an animal?

A moon had risen and bathed the entire Arctic landscape in pale blue. Bren came to a pool of water and looked at his bear reflection, the solid black eyes. He could see Mouse there, her opaque, fathomless eyes. The monk at the Leopard's Nest had looked at him with those same eyes, trying to make Bren understand as he drew signal flags in the sand.

The next night was just the same, except for one thing: Bren came upon another bear, lying on its stomach, next to a hole in the ice. He was far away and the other bear didn't notice him, but Bren knew he shouldn't approach. He slowly turned and walked away.

Bren woke up suddenly and rousted the others. "We need to get going. I think we're being stalked."

They reached the spot where they had abandoned ship by midday, and the onderzeeer was still there, untouched except for a coating of snow and frost. They had propped it on a row of timbers, from which they could launch it into the water, but the first obstacle was making a hole in the ice big enough. Here, they caught a break. The bulk of the *Sea Lion*'s skeleton was still there. They had only salvaged as much of the hull as they could carry. They had only to burn the rest of the ship, which would also melt away some of the surrounding ice.

Bren basked in the warmth of the raging fire once it was going strong. They all did. It was almost painful to be so warm after their constant exposure to the Arctic weather, their misery scarcely relieved by the weak summer daylight or their puny campfires. Bren felt alive again. More important, he felt like they all might actually survive.

"Any sign of bears?" Nindemann asked, when Lady Barrett came back to the group. They had been taking turns scouting the area for the predator or predators Bren had warned them about. But she just shook her head and buried her hands and face in the radiant heat. They enjoyed their finest meal in ages, too. Walrus steaks and the one bottle of wine Duval had parted with, probably because he thought he was sending them to their deaths.

This time, they didn't risk sleep before setting off. It was time for their voyage into the great unknown, inside a great unknown.

"There's a hatch above and one below," Nindemann explained. "Everyone but me and the two brothers will go in now, and then the three of us will push her into the water and climb in before we seal and descend. Everyone ready?"

They all nodded, Bren wondering if he were the only

one who really wasn't. Nindemann climbed to the top, opened the hatch, and then Aadesh and Aadarsh helped boost the others up. The engineer unfolded a rope ladder for everyone to climb down, and when they were all inside, he closed the hatch behind them.

Bren expected it to be pitch black until they could light some lamps. But to his surprise, the inside of the submarine was aglow with soft, bluish light. He looked up and saw that the engineer had installed three portals in a row along the top, like a whale with three blowholes. Suddenly Nindemann's craggy, bearded face appeared through one, staring right at Bren.

"Couldn't stand the thought of not being able to see anything," he shouted. "Plus, we're going where no sailors have gone, with a chance to see ocean life up close. Couldn't resist."

Bren smiled. Nindemann had a little bit of Mr. Leiden in him, too, the long-lost surgeon from the *Albatross* who had taught Bren so many things about botany and zoology and medicine.

Shveta, meanwhile, was looking for a comfortable chair.

"We should all sit," said Lady Barrett. "It will be quite jarring when they put us into the water."

For the moment they all took seats next to the oars and held on tight. They felt the vessel lift up from the stern, and then with unexpected speed they were rushing forward until the surface of the water brought them to a jarring halt. The oar Bren was holding on to for dear life rammed into his ribs.

"Everyone okay?" said Lady Barrett, when the worst was over.

She was answered mainly with groans, but it appeared everyone was fine. It was obvious they were in the water; Bren could feel them bobbing, and despite how well-sealed the vessel was, he could hear the two brothers on the ice murmuring their amazement at the fact that the contraption didn't sink immediately.

A few minutes later, they heard some splashing and then the chuff of boots atop the vessel, and the hatch opened again.

"May we come in?" said Nindemann. He and the brothers climbed down, and this time Nindemann locked the hatch, a slight *hiss* letting him know it was sealed shut. "How about a tour?" he asked.

Despite being small, the inside of the submarine was fairly cozy—more so than any of the ships Bren had sailed on. Ahead of the rowing stations was the navigation area, with a compass set into a gimbal, plus a tube lined with mirrors that extended out of the vessel so the pilot could see where they were going. Nindemann had made the rest of this area into a living room of sorts, and Shveta plopped herself cross-legged on a floor cushion.

Behind the rowers was the magic that made the submarine livable. There was a brazier where Nindemann would burn saltpeter for fresh oxygen. As a bonus, the fire would provide warmth. There was an open container of soda lime to absorb the moisture from the air they exhaled. And rising from the floor was a massive screw, topped by a crank. Nindemann explained how it was connected to bladders on either side of the vessel's stern that either took in or expelled water. Turning the screw controlled their ability to descend or resurface.

"Speaking of which," said Nindemann, who grabbed the crank and, even with his prodigious strength, struggled to move the massive handle. But move it he did, and with each clockwise rotation, the screw turned and the submarine slowly began to sink.

Bren could tell by the looks on the others' faces that he wasn't the only one unsettled by the downward motion of the vessel. A ship wasn't supposed to sink! Ice packs juddered the hull and created the unnerving sensation for those inside of being crushed.

But as Nindemann continued to turn the screw, the grinding subsided and they felt . . . nothing. Just the sensation of being suspended in water.

"Now's as good a time as any to test our ability to propel ourselves," said Nindemann, taking a seat at one of the oars. "I'm a bit worried about loose ice."

"Now you tell us," said Shveta, who closed her eyes and assumed her meditation pose. She obviously wasn't planning to help row.

Aadesh and Aadarsh took seats opposite each other, Lady Barrett sat opposite Nindemann, and Bren and Ani took two more. That left three pairs of oars unmanned, but Nindemann said they would help with balance.

"If our earlier calculations were correct," said Nindemann, "we should have ample supplies of air and water and food until we reach the polar ocean."

"And if they weren't correct?" said Lady Barrett.

"We chisel our way back to the surface and see where we are," Nindemann replied. When he noticed that Lady Barrett was about to ask more questions, he stopped her. "Let's see how this goes before we assume the worst, shall we?"

UNDER THE ICE

Bren, of course, had helped row the longboat from the *Albatross* from the Vanishing Island to the East Netherlands, a voyage of a thousand miles across open ocean. Even with the dozen surviving crewmen from that ship doing the lion's share of work at the oars, he had nearly died of exhaustion.

But this was even more difficult than that. Yes, there were fewer rowers. But they were underwater, which meant resistance throughout the entire stroke. No coming up for air, so to speak. And Nindemann was right about the loose ice and slush beneath the pack ice. Bren felt he could never get a clean stroke without hitting something, or feeling like he was dragging his oar through quicksand.

He let out a sigh of frustration and looked up. He was sitting directly under one of the portals, and it was as if he were looking into the purest blue sky he had ever seen. The ice was like crystal clouds, pulled along gently on a current of wind.

Bren's brief reverie was interrupted when Lady Barrett yelled at Shveta, "Unless you're using magic mind power to propel the ship, maybe you could make yourself useful."

"Meditation keeps me from killing you," said Shveta. "Is that useful enough for you?"

This went on for three days, judging by the number of times Nindemann turned his hourglass. There was no getting away from one another. They ate rations where they sat and slept like dogs in two narrow spaces at the front and back of the sub. Bren tried to push away the pain of rowing by lifting his gaze toward the portals, dreaming not just of being under a perfect sky, but in it, floating above the world. Until the day a dark cloud intruded . . . a shadow of something darkening each portal in turn.

"Was that ice?" said Bren, hoping that Nindemann or someone else had noticed it.

"Probably a seal," said Nindemann. "Thousands of them in these waters."

Something bumped the submarine. Gently at first, but then again, hard enough that Ani fell off her seat and Bren slid hard against the hull.

"Would a seal do that?" asked Lady Barrett.

"Possibly," said Nindemann. "Might be curious about us, or think we're a fellow marine mammal or a big fish."

Bump.

This time it was hard enough that Shveta fell over, still cross-legged, and had to brace herself with one hand.

"Row faster," said Aadarsh.

"*You* row faster," said Aadesh.

"Stop rowing altogether," said Nindemann. "The swinging oars are probably making whatever it is more agitated."

They all stopped rowing, which was a relief to Bren, who rubbed his aching muscles as they waited to see what happened.

THUMP!

This time the submarine was knocked sideways through the water like a booted ball, rotating on its axis until they were upside down. The seven passengers fell together in a heap.

"Did you think to arm this thing?" said Lady Barrett, trying to push Aadesh off her.

"It's an exploration vessel," said Nindemann, "not a war machine."

"Feels more like a fish toy," said Shveta.

They had slowly rotated another quarter turn, so the portals were on the side now, and Bren saw their tormentor—a large black-and-white creature with a dorsal fin, one that happened to be shaped exactly like the submarine.

"A shark?" said Bren.

"An orca," said Nindemann.

"Friend or foe?" said Lady Barrett.

"Only you would ask such a dumb question about a fish kicking us around the ocean floor," said Shveta.

"Actually, it's a whale," said Nindemann, just as the submarine jerked violently to one side, causing all of them to fall over again.

From his back, Bren noticed that one of the oars had nearly been pulled out of its lock. "It's got one of the oars," he said, as they all felt another jerk. "It's trying to pull us now."

"Probably back to its nest to feed us to its babies," said Shveta.

"We need to get upright again," said Nindemann.

"You think we can row away from it?" said Lady Barrett.

"Not a chance," said Nindemann. "But I need to open the hatch. The only way to do that without flooding us with seawater is if the hatch is on the bottom. Air pressure."

He grabbed one of the free oars and instructed Aadesh and Aadarsh to do the same. Lady Barrett grabbed another, and the four of them tried to coordinate enough to rotate the sub another quarter turn. Meanwhile, Bren pitched in by grabbing a free oar next to the one the orca had grabbed and trying to push the whale away. He didn't succeed entirely, but he did distract it enough that it let go of the oar it was biting, giving the others the chance they needed to right the ship.

When the bottom hatch was below them again, Nindemann reached beneath one of the rows of seats and pulled out a harpoon.

"You're going to fight that thing by yourself? With that?" said Bren.

"I hope not," said Nindemann. "I'm hoping a sharp poke to the snout will get rid of him."

Nindemann stripped down to his underclothes and covered every exposed part of his body with lard. Then he crouched, grabbed the hatch wheel with both hands, and turned it counterclockwise a half turn. On the second half turn, there was a great whoosh of air as the seal broke and he pulled the hatch open. They were staring right into the sea, but the water did not rise above the opening.

"Wish me luck," he said, dropping his feet through the hatch and almost immediately withdrawing them. "Colder than I thought," he said, before closing his eyes and forcing his feet back down. He had grabbed a *J*-shaped tube and put it to his mouth.

"What is that?" said Bren.

"Breathing tube," said Nindemann. "I take in a little air, buys me extra time in the water."

"Nice knowing you, bub," said Shveta.

He grabbed the harpoon and slipped all the way through, quickly disappearing from view.

"Should we close the hatch?" said Lady Barrett. "In case that thing turns us over again?"

"No," said Bren. "He'll need to get back in quickly."

They all braced themselves, but for what, they weren't sure. The sounds of a battle? Nindemann's screams, assuming they would carry through the freezing water? Another jolt to the sub? Bren felt helpless and ignorant. He just stood by the hatch, closed his eyes, and tried to pray for the engineer.

Almost immediately, he opened his eyes again. He thought he'd heard something. They all did.

"Was that him or the big fish?" said Aadesh.

"The spy tube!" said Bren. He ran to the front of the ship, where the device Nindemann used to see out of the submarine hung from the top of the craft. Bren put his eye to it and let things come into focus. He saw nothing at first but ice-blue water, so he slowly turned the tube side to side looking for either Nindemann or the orca. What he saw made his stomach leap—the harpoon, falling harm-lessly through the water.

Bren immediately ran back to the hatch. He stripped off his outer clothing, quickly covered himself in lard, and sat down at the edge of the opening.

"What the bloody hell do you think you're doing?" said Lady Barrett, grabbing him by the arm and holding tight.

"He's in trouble," said Bren. "We have to help him."

"He was in trouble the minute he got in the water," said Shveta. "Nothing you can do now."

Ani stood next to Bren. "How can we help?"

"Any of your fancy weapons work underwater?" he said.

She shook her head.

"Just wait here," said Bren, who slipped his greasy arm out of Lady Barrett's grip and jumped through the hatch.

The water was so cold his heart almost stopped. It was so much worse than he had expected, even with the coating of lard. He wouldn't be able to hold his breath for long.

He caught sight of the harpoon below him, still tum-bling toward the darkness of the ocean deep. He swam toward it and managed to catch it before it disappeared for good. He looked back up and saw Nindemann. He had grabbed hold of an oar, but he was bleeding. Bren swam up to him and immediately noticed the gash in his right shoulder; the blood was billowing into the water like red smoke.

Bren grabbed his other arm, to lead him back to the hatch. He was clearly out of air and struggling. But out of the corner of his eye Bren saw the orca coming toward them. Trying not to panic, he pointed Nindemann toward the hatch, and then turned to face the orca, holding the harpoon more like a shield than a weapon. He had no idea what he was doing, really, other than trying to give Nindemann time to escape.

The orca was on him in an instant. The black-and-white face seemed so harmless and round, and then the mouth opened, showing Bren a mile of sharp teeth and an empty gullet. Bren pointed the harpoon straight at his attacker, and then, suddenly, the orca veered away, swimming off and out of sight in a matter of seconds.

Bren didn't have time to think about what had happened. He was just grateful. He walked his way around the hull of the sub using his hands until he neared the hatch. He could see the light from the opening when he felt something tugging him back.

He panicked. The harpoon fell from his hands as he spun around to see what had grabbed him, but there was nothing there. He turned back toward the hatch when he felt the pull again, stronger this time, and suddenly he was ten feet from the hull of the sub.

What was going on?

And then he remembered how the orca had suddenly changed course and swam away. There was something out there in the water . . . something menacing enough to scare away an orca.

Bren tried not to panic. He was almost out of air. He just had to swim harder toward the hatch. He was so close. . . .

But no matter how hard he tried, he couldn't get any closer. In fact, it was as if the sub were pulling away from him, leaving him adrift. Whatever it was wouldn't have time to kill him, though. He was about to drown.

THE BELLY
OF THE BEAST

Something was swimming toward him . . . a fish smok-
ing a pipe. No, it was a seahorse, with legs. No, that
was ridiculous. He was dreaming. *Just enjoy the sleep*, he told
himself. *You need a long rest.*

Ani grabbed his hair and stuck the breathing tube into
his mouth. It was almost too much at first, and he gulped
half the air in the tube at once. Ani grabbed him by the
hand and tried to drag him back to the sub, but something
was still pulling him in the opposite direction. Ani was losing the tug of war.

Bren peered into the murky distance, trying to see what it was. He could just make out a cave opening, as big around as the onderzeeer and ringed with craggy rocks. Maybe it was generating a whirlpool. Then he saw he was wrong—it wasn't a cave, it was a mouth, and the craggy rocks were teeth. He and Ani were literally being inhaled by some gargantuan shark.

The bite on his arm was so painful that he cried out, or tried to. All that came out was a muffled scream and bubbles, and the breathing tube floated away from him. It was Ani, or rather, the grey cat, clamped on his arm and swimming with ferocity back to the sub. When they reached the bottom hatch, she released him and nosed him up through the opening, and then sprung through herself with a powerful kick of her legs.

Lady Barrett had just grabbed hold of Bren and pulled him inside, but when the grey panther leaped into the sub, dripping wet and snarling, everyone except Shveta nearly jumped through the other hatch. Before their eyes, the cat transformed back to Ani, who collapsed to her knees, gasping for air.

"You okay?" said Bren, gasping himself.

Ani nodded. "Cats can swim, but not breathe underwater."

"Neither can we," said Bren. He looked around for Nindemann, finding him sitting upright at the front, bandaging his arm and side. "Is he okay?"

"He will be," said Lady Barrett. "Now what the bloody hell is out there?"

"A shark, I think," said Bren. "Except it's as big as a whale. It scared off the orca."

"Then let's get to rowing," said Shveta, looking at the others.

"Nindemann's hurt," said Lady Barrett. "Bren and Ani are exhausted. How are your rowing skills, Your Highness?"

Bren tried to break it up. They didn't need to be fighting each other. "I'm sure it can swim faster than we can row," he said.

"So we fight it?" said Aadarsh. He was the more bloodthirsty of the two brothers, but even he didn't seem to like their odds against a giant shark.

"No," said Nindemann, his voice drenched with pain. "We row. I've never encountered this shark personally, but I've heard stories. He's slow. Wants you to come to him. Sucks you in, literally. Inhales you."

"Brilliant," said Shveta, who shocked everyone by taking Nindemann's seat next to one of the oars. "What? I'm stronger than you," she added, staring down Lady Barrett, who accepted the challenge and took the seat opposite her.

The brothers took their oars, and so did Bren and Ani, but Bren didn't think he could row another stroke. His whole body was failing him. Still, he tried. He grabbed the oar, forced a stroke, and they went nowhere. He tried again, and again, and it was as if they were going sideways. Then he realized it wasn't just him—everyone had stopped rowing and was looking around. What was going on?

Nindemann struggled to his feet and looked through his spy tube. He must have seen what Bren had seen through the murk, because he came away looking worse than he had a minute before.

"You don't seem pleased," said Lady Barrett. "What now?"

She didn't have to wait long for an answer, and it didn't come from Nindemann. There was a *WHOMP* as the sub jerked to a halt, and then several loud cracking noises. When Bren looked up, he saw teeth coming through the wooden hull.

"What the—" Lady Barrett jumped backward. A tooth had come up from the bottom of the hull and hit her foot.

More cracking, and Bren could see the ring of upper and lower teeth making a giant bite mark around the hull of the onderzeeer.

They were in the mouth of the shark, and it was crushing them.

"What do we do?" said Bren. He looked around at Lady Barrett and Nindemann and Shveta, realizing how desperate he was for one of them to have an answer. They were grown-ups, after all. But they had no answers, because there was nothing they could do.

"If I'm going to die, it's going to be fighting," said Lady Barrett, taking another harpoon and pointing it at the roof of the sub. She drew back . . . and waited. There was another terrifying crack as the shark applied more pressure, and this time, a seam opened between the boards. As water slowly began to seep in, Lady Barrett thrust the harpoon through the crack.

The sub jerked violently upward. Bren flew backward, striking his head so hard a wave of nausea flooded him.

"Well done. You've just made it mad," said Shveta.

And then they were moving. Slowly, but very definitely. Water continued to seep in through the crack, around the harpoon that was still wedged there, apparently in the roof of the shark's mouth, but the crushing had stopped.

"Is it taking us back to its nest? Or lair? Or wherever sharks live?" said Lady Barrett.

"I don't know," said Nindemann. "But we have a bigger problem. We're not just taking on water, we're losing air. The saltpeter machine can't work if the vessel isn't sealed."

Bren knew what was coming next, and he dreaded hearing it.

"We have to abandon ship," said Nindemann. "Swim out, look for holes in the ice. Seals make them, and there's a chance there are some around here."

Bren remembered his vision of the polar bear lying in wait next to one of those holes, and it made him like this plan even less.

"One problem, bub," said Shveta, and she pointed to the floor and ceiling, where the ring of shark's teeth covered both the top and bottom hatches. Nindemann, the engineer, solver of all problems, seemed to deflate right before Bren's eyes.

"I will not be taken into the belly of some heathen beast!" said Aadesh, rushing forward to the harpoon, grabbing the shaft, and shoving with all his might. The harpoon sunk another foot at least into the roof of the shark's mouth, and the curtain of water that was weeping in began to turn red. The shark reacted by biting down even farther, and the crushing resumed, opening cracks along more of the hull. Bren thought Aadesh had made a huge mistake, until he realized this was what he was hoping for. Nindemann realized it too.

"Bundle your furs, shoes, and dry clothes into the oilskin bags," he said. "Cover yourself with lard. When the hull fails, we swim out opposite the shark, and with any luck he'll be too busy chewing wood to notice or care."

"The brothers can't swim," said Shveta, and everyone froze.

"It's not swimming, really," said Lady Barrett. "It's just . . . not drowning. Point yourself straight up, kick your legs, and move your hands like this." She demonstrated for the brothers, who looked scared for the first time Bren could recall. But what choice did they have?

When enough of the hull had split apart that water was now rushing in, they made their escape. Nindemann and the brothers pushed aside the weakened boards, and Bren braced himself again for the shock of the freezing water. Up he went, kicking his legs toward a milky-blue sky.

He had no idea how far below the surface they were. He could hold his breath a long time—he'd had plenty of practice by now—but exposure to water this cold could do him in before a lack of oxygen. He gazed up into the floes of ice far above, drifting by like clouds, looking for an escape. A gap between floes could be dangerous; another sheet of ice might crush him before he made it through. A hole would be better.

And then he saw it—the tail of a seal disappearing from the water. He'd found one!

He continued to swim up but turned to find the others, to tell them he'd found their escape hatch. He got Lady Barrett's attention and hoped she could relay the message; he couldn't hold his breath much longer.

The hole was plenty big, but he had more trouble getting through than he expected. The ice was a foot thick, making it hard for him to get a grip on the rim so he could use it to pull himself up. But he finally did it. For once, being spindly came in handy.

He immediately reached his arms back down into the hole to help the next person. Ani and Shveta came through first, then Lady Barrett. Nindemann had been helping them all up. When Nindemann was out of the water, he helped Aadesh and Aadarsh through. Bren was so cold and so weak he felt sick, but seeing the brothers come through the seal hole made him laugh. It was lucky for them the hole had been made by an animal even bigger than they were.

"Is that our rescuer?" said Lady Barrett.

She was looking now at a large brown seal lounging on the ice, staring with curiosity at the strange creatures that had just popped out of its hole. It twitched its whiskers and opened a mouth full of sharp teeth, but more in a playful than a threatening manner. Then Bren could have sworn it looked directly at him with its glassy black eyes, before turning and lurching off across the ice, to do whatever it was seals did.

CHAPTER
28

PARADISE FOUND

"Change out of your wet clothes and into your dry ones, quickly," said Nindemann, and he didn't have to tell Bren twice. It already felt like his wet underclothes were freezing to his body, and stripping them off was like peeling away his own skin. Fortunately the lard had done its job, both protecting him and making it easier to get undressed and redressed. His "dry" clothes hadn't stayed completely dry in their oilskin bags, but they were better than nothing, and when he wrapped his furs around him again, he just wanted to lie down and get warm.

"Up, up!" said Nindemann. "We start walking now, get the blood flowing. We've all had a shock."

They all had to fight to get their legs moving again after four days of being in the sub, except for Shveta, who seemed to glide along, her furs pooling around her feet. Bren came up to Ani and said, "Why don't you change into the cat? Wouldn't you be warmer? Stronger?"

The question seemed to irritate her, the way Bren had irritated Mouse whenever he suggested she use her gifts.

"You don't know anything about anything," she snapped. "I can't just change into the cat whenever I want. It takes enormous concentration and will. And it . . . it hurts me."

"Hurts you?" said Bren. "What do you mean?"

"I couldn't explain it to a dum-dum like you," she said. "But you're welcome for saving your life underwater."

"Thank you," said Bren. "I thought I had said that."

"You had not," said Ani.

He didn't try to talk to her again after that, until it came time to make camp. They were down to their bare possessions, which meant sleeping without freezing was going to be a far greater challenge—they didn't have the extra furs, or the polar bear hide, to cover themselves. Nindemann had one piece of canvas, cut from an old sail, to cover the ground. Otherwise they had their own furs and body heat to survive.

"Any idea where we are?" Lady Barrett asked.

Nindemann stared out toward the horizon. "I believe we're a great deal farther north than when we began, if I'm reading the sun right," he said.

"What sort of time are we making on foot?" said Bren. There had been no storms since they resurfaced, and even the winds seemed less severe. Maybe they really were close to a warm polar ocean.

"Good time, considering," said Nindemann. "But . . ."

"But what?" said Shveta. She was on a mission and had no time for wavering.

"But say we reach the Pole in a fortnight, or even less. We're approaching the fall solstice. We have no chance to get there and back without overwintering in the Arctic. Permanent darkness. Unimaginable cold."

"Bah!" said Shveta. "There will be no permanent darkness in Paradise. Or cold. There can't be."

"The good Lord made the night and the moon, and winter too," said Nindemann.

"We worship different gods," said Shveta, as if that was supposed to comfort the engineer.

"Do we have a choice?" said Lady Barrett. "Even if we turned back now . . ."

"No one is turning back," said Shveta.

"What do you care what we do?" said Lady Barrett.

"Because we might need to cut you open and use your

carcass for a sleeping bag," said Shveta.

"I hope bickering is keeping you all warm," said Nindemann. "As for me, I'd like a little extra protection, and a decent meal." He turned to the brothers. "You two up for a hunt?"

"With what?" said Aadesh. "We left the harpoon."

Nindemann drew out a large knife. Then Ani surprised them all by producing a katar and three chakram. Aadesh took the push dagger; Aadarsh took the throwing rings.

"Godspeed," said Lady Barrett. "Don't take on a bear."

"You want me to go?" said Ani.

Shveta put her hand on her shoulder. "You stay here and protect us."

Bren didn't want to admit it, but he was relieved to have Shveta and Ani to protect him. He had seen what Ani was capable of. And perhaps Shveta's "magic" was illusion, but surely snakes raining from the sky would scare off a predator? The hunting party came back after only a few hours, dragging something behind them. It appeared to be a very large seal, and Nindemann and the brothers appeared to have attached something to the top of its head in order to drag it. No, it wasn't a seal—it was a narwhal.

Bren's sudden excitement confused the others.

"What's a *nar-wall*, and why are you excited to eat one?" said Shveta.

"It's a type of whale!" said Bren. "With a horn.

Actually, it's a tusk, but that's not the point!"

"It doesn't come and go from holes in the ice, like a seal, does it?" said Lady Barrett.

"No," said Bren. "We must be near open water. Which could mean . . ."

"We didn't catch it," Nindemann said. "We found it on the ice, dead. And no, we didn't see where it came from or how it got there."

Disappointed, no one said anything at first, but Shveta tried to remain confident. "There must be ocean nearby. It didn't just walk to wherever you found it."

"True," said Nindemann. "Doesn't mean it's a warm ocean, like the legends say. The narwhal could've just been unlucky, wandered into a break in the floes. Whales strand themselves all the time. For now, let's just be thankful we have food."

They gutted the narwhal, separated what they could eat, and kept the hide intact for shelter. Before long the ice was a smear of blood and fluids, with steaks and organs stacked to one side and the narwhal's body a sagging, leathery tent.

That night, huddled together inside the carcass, Bren had another dream. He was lying on his stomach on the ice, watching three men approach from the distance. As they came closer, he turned and dragged himself along the ice, away from them. He knew instinctively where he was going, and he found it—water, a gulf of it, off the edge of the ice. And in the distance, two towering mountains of ice, like gateposts to the entrance of a third mountain, farther away and shrouded with fog.

Bren surged forward and plunged into the water. He assumed it was freezing, but he didn't feel cold. He swam effortlessly, with strength and confidence. It felt good. He felt accomplished in a way he had never felt in his life. And there were sounds underwater . . . conversation, and music. He could tell there were walruses a few hundred yards to his right, near the surface. Seals were playing below him, and below the seals were whales.

He dove deeper, where the whale song came to him more clearly, and then an alarm—a pair of orcas had been spotted a few miles away. Schools of fish swept over his head.

Even deeper, there was the pull of something dark and dangerous. Some solitary beast that the others feared.

Bren rose closer to the surface, passing through the two mountains he had seen, then breached for a closer look at the third mountain. It wasn't there. He dove again, looking for it below but finding nothing. When he came back up to look again, everything was dark.

It took him a minute to realize he was awake. He was used to waking to the sharp, clear light of the sun that never set, but it was dark. That's when he remembered he was inside the narwhal.

Nindemann and Lady Barrett were already up. He was stoking a fire of leather and blubber, and she was cooking breakfast. "Are you all right?" she asked when Bren emerged.

"I'm not sure," he said, shivering even next to the fire. "I had another strange dream. I think . . . I think I was the narwhal. I saw something."

They both looked at him expectantly.

"Shveta may want to hear this," he said.

They got everyone else up, and Bren told all of them about his "swim." He could have sworn Shveta's ruby glowed when he told her about the three mountains.

"Just like the mandala," she said. "Was the ocean warm? Was the mountain green?"

"It was covered by fog," said Bren. "And I can't be sure about the ocean. I wasn't cold, but I wasn't me."

"And you alone saw it," said Shveta, ignoring Bren's uncertainty. "Do you wonder still why I had to bring you?"

"Take him, you mean," said Lady Barrett.

"Be smug all you want," said Shveta. "You're no stranger to putting yourself first, from what I understand."

Shveta seemed to have made a direct hit. She turned from Lady Barrett to Bren. "Besides, Bren wants this, too. I can tell."

Bren could tell Lady Barrett was looking at him, and despite his best efforts, he knew the truth was written all over his face. Shveta was right, and Bren was beginning to believe he was meant to help her.

"There's just one problem," said Nindemann. "Assuming this gulf does lie beyond where we found the narwhal, we can't swim it."

"We'll figure it out," said Shveta, who was already gathering her things. "Eat up. The sooner we go, the sooner we get there."

THROUGH THE
GATES OF ICE

Nindemann, Aadesh, and Aadarsh led the way to where they had found the narwhal. Snowfall and windstorms had erased any traces of their previous trek, but they knew how long it had taken them. The problem was, Bren had no idea how far in his dream, or his vision, he had gone from there. They would just have to use what food and supplies they had left as conservatively as possible.

"Have you figured out how to fly yet?" Lady Barrett asked, on the fourth day of their journey.

"I beg your pardon?" said Shveta.

"This gulf of polar sea we're supposed to cross, without a boat, or without all of us becoming marine mammals."

"You could become a fish if you prefer," said Shveta. "You've got the face for it."

"I'd be warmer as a fish," said Nindemann, whose beard was so often covered with ice that it might as well have been grey.

"Did you hear that?" said Bren.

Everyone stopped walking and listened. It was almost impossible to hear anything over the wind, but Bren could have sworn he heard . . . barking?

"I think it's just a seal," said Nindemann, but before he could get the words out, Bren was running away from them. Confused, the others followed, and then they saw what Bren saw—the two huskies, lashed to one of the sleds, barking and barking at nothing they could see.

"It's Caesar!" cried Bren, running toward one of them. He was almost there when he noticed that the sled wasn't piled with supplies, it was a man, curled up and not moving, under a pile of furs.

"Who is it?" said Lady Barrett as Nindemann turned the man over to see if he was still alive.

"Duval," said Nindemann. "He's breathing, barely."

They did what they could to revive the navigator. He seemed to have plenty of supplies with him on the sled, though his fingers and nose and lips showed signs of extreme frostbite. It wasn't until they had examined him more closely that they realized he was wounded. Claw marks on his neck, left arm, and across his body. They gave him water and a little food, and fed the dogs, too, since they could figure no reason for their barking except that Duval had not been able to feed them himself of late.

"It was a bear," he said, when he could finally talk.

"It killed everyone but you?" said Nindemann.

Duval wearily shook his head. "A few. We finally chased it away. A group of us decided there was no hope but to turn back, pray for a miracle. That left me and six others to keep going, hoping to find this open sea. All but me died over the past two weeks; exposure, dysentery, sepsis. May as well count me too. I'm done for."

"Come on, now," said Nindemann, trying to rally him. "We're here now. You're with us."

Duval didn't seem to hear him. "I just lashed the sled to the mutts and told 'em to keep going. Not sure when I passed out."

They tried to get his strength up, and they sheltered him during the night, but Duval died two days later. Nindemann, hard and practical man that he was, wept. Perhaps because he realized he might be the last crew member of the *Sea Lion* still standing. But when he recovered, he tried to remain positive.

"We have two dogs and a sled now," he said. "We can go faster, and all of us don't have to walk."

"We've got a sight more than that, bub," said Shveta.

"She's right," said Lady Barrett, putting one foot against the sled. "I bow to your conviction, Queen Shveta. Assuming we do find this gulf, we now have a raft to cross it."

▲▲▲

Thereafter, Nindemann followed. Shveta was their leader now, driven by a religious determination to find the source of a power she had, up to now, merely tasted. Bren wondered exactly how she planned to remake the world, if she could. Was it just to right a wrong in her home state of Cashmere? Or to defeat the Mogul Empire completely? He found it impossible to believe that anyone with unlimited power would limit themselves. Wasn't that what Mouse had tried to make him understand?

To Bren's surprise, Shveta didn't ride the sled. She walked behind Aadesh and Aadarsh, her bodyguards now taking their jobs literally, guarding her from the winds. Nindemann and Lady Barrett walked, too, leaving just Bren and Ani to ride the sled. Their weight was really all the two dogs could handle, along with the supplies.

Shveta never doubted they would find this open water Bren had seen in his dream, and though it took several more days of trudging through ice and snow, against ungodly winds, with all their joints and fingers and toes swollen with pain, they found it: a bright-blue sea, rimmed with ice, with two mountainous icebergs standing to the left and right of them as they approached, almost like gateposts.

Bren would have dropped to his knees in gratitude if it wouldn't have hurt so much. Instead he just stood there, taking in this vista of his mandala come to life. He glanced at Shveta, whose face was still completely covered but whose eyes said everything.

But as they continued to stare at this dream become reality, they realized there was one problem. There was no third mountain framed by the other two, only clouds and drifting pillars of fog.

"It has to be there," said Shveta, staring into the distance.

"Maybe the clouds are obscuring it," said Nindemann. And as they watched, the clouds floated by and the fog shifted, and Bren thought he saw it. But just as quickly, it was gone.

"You saw it, too," said Shveta, turning to Bren. "I can tell by your face."

"I . . . I thought so," he admitted. He really hadn't been sure. He remembered how they had come upon the Vanishing Island, like a vaporous ghost that became real and solid when they finally got close.

"Arctic light plays tricks," said Nindemann. "We've seen it already . . . mirages, false sunsets . . ."

"No," said Shveta. "Turn the sled into a boat. It's there."

"Did you notice this water is freezing?" said Lady Barrett. "We're hardly in sight of a tropical island."

Shveta wasn't listening. She was instructing Ani and the brothers to make a sail from whatever they had. Nindemann gave up trying to convince her otherwise and did what he did best—solve problems.

"We don't have spare wood for a mast," he said. "Or rigging. And we'd likely get torn apart by the wind anyway."

"So we row?" said Shveta.

"With what?" said Bren.

"This will be tricky," said Nindemann, "but I suggest we fashion one large sail, and we hold it. Human masts. That way we can adjust quickly to wind patterns."

"And hopefully not get carried off into the sky," said Lady Barrett. "Those birds don't look friendly."

Birds. Bren turned to look at the black-and-white birds Lady Barrett had noticed, all flying together toward the same spot—the bank of fog in the distance. Where the third mountain should be.

"It's there," said Bren. "Come on." And he eagerly pitched in on sewing together a large sail they could work manually using the surgeon's kit, spare clothes, and the canvas they had used to keep themselves dry when sleeping on the ground.

When they were finished, they had the worst-looking

sail imaginable, but it caught wind, as they learned when the whole thing nearly blew from their collective grasp. The sled scarcely had room for them all, including the dogs (Bren insisted on taking them), but they got it into the water and all climbed aboard without capsizing. Aadesh and Aadarsh, charged with holding the sail, held it aloft, and off they went.

The sea may not have been warm, but it was remarkably free of floating ice, and as they neared the fog bank, the dogs began barking wildly. Shveta seemed ready to jump off the raft. When a gust of wind caught the brothers off guard, and the raft lurched several feet backward, she wheeled on them as if she were going to cut their throats. They quickly regrouped.

It was all so eerily familiar to Bren—drifting into the fog, surrounded by gauzy mist for several minutes, and then the raft suddenly ground to a halt. Nindemann, who had been standing at the front edge, scouting for land, was nearly thrown off. It wouldn't have mattered. They had found what they were looking for: a mountain, an island, made not of ice but of earth.

Shveta was first off the raft, followed by Ani. Lady Barrett was right behind them.

"Is this the North Pole?" Lady Barrett asked, looking Nindemann's way.

"Your guess is as good as mine what the North Pole

looks like," he said. "It will soon get dark enough that we can find the North Star. That would tell us for sure."

"Maybe this is the North Pole, maybe it's over there," said Shveta. "I don't really care. We've found what was pictured in the mandala. We've found what was drawn on the map taken long ago to the employer of Bren's father. The one he remembered in his feverish state."

"And now that we're here," said Lady Barrett, "what is it you're looking for exactly?"

"A well," said Shveta, and she and Ani were off again.

That's when Bren noticed how haggard Nindemann looked, and depressed. He quite possibly had just led the first successful expedition to the North Pole, the first one that could be documented and verified, that is, and he looked as if he'd lost his best friend.

"What's wrong?" said Bren. "We made it."

"Did we?" said Nindemann. "Does this feel like Paradise to you?"

"Compared to some other places we've been?" said Bren.

"You're still wrapped in furs," Nindemann pointed out. "Touch your hand to the water. Look at the ice and snow covering every inch of that mountain but the bottom."

He was right, and Bren felt all his newfound hope and conviction begin to wobble. This wasn't Paradise. It wasn't the mountain in the mandala. They had gambled on an impossible quest to the ends of the earth and found nothing but more snow and ice. They would never survive the journey back, and there was no one left to rescue them. He would never see home again. It hit him like a sudden punch in the gut that he had seen his father and Mr. Black for the last time.

Anger began to consume him. If he could have known they were splitting up, back at the Caspian Sea . . . but no, Shveta had robbed him of that. He tried to remember the last conversation he had with his father, but his legendary memory failed him.

"This is all your fault!" He charged her. Aadesh stepped in front of him, but Shveta said, "Let him go."

Bren grabbed her by her collar. His swollen, frostbitten hands radiated pain as he clenched his fists around the thick fur. He just stood there, holding her, staring into her eyes, and as he did so, he began to feel . . . warm. His whole body coursed with the kind of pain you feel when you're freezing and put yourself too close to a blazing fire.

He pulled away.

Shveta reached inside her furs and pulled out a sodden piece of fabric and laid it on the ground. It was the mandala. The fabric itself had begun to fade and fray, but the painting was still intact.

"What did we miss?" said Shveta, kneeling before it and gently grasping Bren by the hand, inviting him to take a closer look. He had no strength left to fight her. He knelt down beside her.

The painting was an intricate work, and their attention had been drawn to the mountains in the middle. Bren's eyes went to the edges, where he had dismissed an elaborate border as mere ornament.

"What is this?" he said.

Ani leaned in. "It's writing, I think. Sanskrit?"

She was looking at Shveta.

"What does it say?" said Bren.

"It says nothing important," Shveta replied. "Just typical formal religious language about the greatness of the gods and completeness of the universe."

"Had you noticed it before?" said Lady Barrett.

"No," said Shveta. "Now, if I may point out what you all should really be looking at . . ."

Her finger went to the belly of the mountain, to a tiny image Bren had originally thought was a tree or shrub. But on closer inspection, he saw that he had been wrong. It was a figure, indistinct, barely more than a pair of beady eyes, *inside* the mountain.

"What we came for is in there, in the heart of the mountain." said Shveta. "The Well of Wisdom. We don't find Paradise; we find the power to re-create it."

CHAPTER

30

THE TUNNEL OF
SWORDS AND AXES

They all watched the large grey cat as she ascended the mountain, her panther's paws confidently finding purchase in the snow and ice. She wound around the face of it clockwise, twisting ever higher in search of a way in. They had discovered they were on an island, and the mountain was small by the standards Bren had grown accustomed to traveling across Asia, but Ani still disappeared for hours at a time when she was circling the peak, and each time she did, he felt as if she might not come back.

But finally, she did. One minute a long grey cat was

trotting down the base of the mountain, the next an exhausted, naked girl was on all fours at Shveta's feet.

They camped another night at the foot of the mountain so Ani could recover, and then the next day they climbed to the mouth of the cave she had found halfway up.

It was a treacherous, twisting descent into the mountain, through tunnels of irregular size and inclines sometimes so steep that Bren and the others slipped and slid along the way. But no one was complaining, because for once they were completely sheltered from the unpredictable Arctic weather. Their only light was a weak basket torch Nindemann had fashioned from one of Duval's empty food tins and some blubber, and he and their two huskies led the way.

This was nothing like climbing down into the Pearl Cliffs. Those tunnels had been made by miners and fugitives. This felt to Bren as if he were invading some monstrous anthill or the combs of a wasp's nest. The longer they walked, the longer he had to think about it, and every frightful thing he had ever read, fact or fiction, in Black's Books crossed his mind. And then, thinking about the look Mr. Black would give him if he knew that, the satisfaction his old friend would take . . . it made Bren smile.

They had walked for over an hour when the two dogs took off running through a flat part of the tunnel. Nindemann hesitated, thinking there might be danger ahead, but then he saw the light. They all did, and they moved as quickly as they dared over the uncertain ground to see what was there.

Bren's heart beat painfully against his chest as he recalled the last time he had followed a tunnel to light, on the Vanishing Island. But this time, there was no ancient tomb or catfish man or illustrated bones. It was just a cavern. A floor of mounded rock, surrounded by towering walls that somewhere, out of sight, were letting in a shaft of pale-white overhead light. There were no other ways in or out.

"Are we here?" said Lady Barrett.

Bren didn't think it was wise to bait Shveta in a cavern, but Shveta didn't seem to be listening. She was pacing the floor, as if she were measuring it for a Turkish rug. "In here," she said, stomping her foot once. "It's beneath us."

"What, this Well of Wisdom?" Lady Barrett asked. "You think there's a manmade well in the middle of a mountain at the North Pole?"

"Who said anything about manmade?" said Shveta.

Nindemann, meanwhile, couldn't stop studying the walls. "I think this is volcanic rock," he said, chipping away a piece with a knife, and then kneeling to examine the floor.

Suddenly it made sense—a mountainous island in the middle of a polar sea; the cracks of light; the light seeming to come from high above. They were in the throat of a volcano. The floor must have been pillows of lava that had cooled and filled the center.

"If it makes you feel better, I think it's probably plugged," said Bren.

"Might just be dormant," said Nindemann. "Another eruption could easily move all this rock out of the way."

"It's not that warm in here," said Lady Barrett. "If that's a clue."

"What's the matter with you idiots?" Shveta scowled. "Don't you see? It makes perfect sense. The Well of Wisdom filled deliberately to keep anyone from it!"

"If you think something is buried here," said Nindemann, "how do you propose to get to it? It could be hundreds of feet below us, and we have nothing worthy of digging into rock like this."

"Maybe there are more tunnels," said Ani. "There must be. We just have to find them."

"No!" said Shveta. "We are precisely where we are meant to be. Precisely where Bren has led us. We blast this out, just like the volcano would."

Shveta's words stunned everyone into silence for a moment, and then Aadesh of all people blurted out, "You will not do that! You will not sacrifice us all. And you will not put Ani in harm's way again!"

More silence. "Very well," said Shveta. "You take Ani

out of here. Take them all out. I'll give you time. I don't need you anymore. Just Bren."

Bren had no idea what was going on, and from the looks on the others' faces, no one else did either. Except for Ani and Aadesh.

"Shveta, what do you mean to do?" said Bren.

Shveta slowly removed the bindi from her head, and as she held it with one hand, she loosed the ruby from the center with the other.

"Come on," said Aadesh, grabbing Ani by the hand. Aadarsh nodded to Nindemann and Lady Barrett, encouraging them to come with him.

"I'm not leaving without Bren," said Lady Barrett.

"You will, unless you want everyone here to die," said Shveta.

Lady Barrett stood there, as if trying to decide whether to call her bluff. Assuming she was bluffing.

"Go on," said Bren. "I'll be fine."

"No," Lady Barrett replied, her voice breaking. "You won't be. I promised your father and Archibald that I would bring you home."

"You tried," said Bren feebly.

Lady Barrett slowly shook her head. "Not hard enough. Not nearly. When you told me what you told me, Bren, back in Murmansk, well . . . I thought about it long and hard that night. Searched my barren soul. I could have given you no choice but to come with me. Instead, I chose to let you go, so I could come too." She turned to Shveta. "You're right, I have a reputation of putting myself first, regardless of who gets hurt. I just didn't think . . . oh, Bren, I am so sorry. . . ."

"It's okay," said Bren, barely loud enough to hear. "I mean it. Just go. Look where we are. You can't make good on your promise even if I follow you out."

He could see Lady Barrett's eyes filling with tears. It was all he could do not to break down.

"Let's go," said Aadarsh, pulling Lady Barrett away. Nindemann grabbed the huskies and led them back toward the tunnel. Aadesh was following with Ani when Ani suddenly broke free of him and ran back to Bren. She grabbed the front of his furs, pulling his ear to her mouth.

"Listen," she whispered. "Did you get a good look at the Sanskrit written around the mandala?" Bren nodded. "It begins in the top left, above the mountains," she continued. "Left to right, just like your language."

"Okay," said Bren as she released him and walked back to Aadesh.

"Go!" Shveta shouted. "Enough with this pitiful sentiment! This is not the end of the world, but the beginning!"

Bren felt numb as he watched Lady Barrett and the others disappear into the tunnel. He knew it didn't matter, but he asked anyway. "Why don't you want me to leave? Haven't I done all I can?"

"To be perfectly honest, I don't know," said Shveta. "But you have brought me to this place, as if you were meant to be here. And therefore I can't let you go until it's over."

She was on her knees now and had placed the ruby on the ground between them. She held up the palms of her hands to Bren, her index fingers and thumbs touching.

"There is an Apocryphal book of the Veda, our most sacred scripture, that tells of a single powerful point of energy at the center of everything, a force of immense creation or destruction, depending on how we harness it."

Keeping her hands in the same position, she lay them flat on the ground so that the diamond-shaped space between them surrounded the ruby. She closed her eyes and began to speak, words Bren couldn't understand.

The ruby began to glow. At first, only as if it were catching light from a distant sun, but then, more hotly, as if the jewel itself contained a furnace and Shveta was stoking the fire.

"It's working!" she said, opening her eyes and lifting her gaze to meet Bren's. "Watch."

She scooped up the glowing ruby, cupping it in her hands, and stood. The light from it was growing so intense that Bren had to shield his eyes, and he felt heat against the palm of his hand. Shveta was staring at the blazing jewel, which reflected in her wide brown eyes like fiery pupils.

Her hands began to shimmer. At first Bren thought it was just the halo of light from the ruby, but then her arms began to turn red, and then her entire body, until she was surrounded by a nimbus of bright hot light.

And then the cloud of light ignited, engulfing Shveta in a pillar of fire. She began to laugh at first, but her laughter became cries of pain as the ruby turned to a pile of ash in her hands.

The whole cavern began to shake, and Bren realized the floor was moving, bulging and buckling as a terrifying rumble came from the bowels of the mountain. He turned and ran toward the tunnel, looking back over his shoulder one more time at Shveta as the fire incinerated her. He was perhaps a hundred yards into the tunnel when the floor began to give way, and he fell, rolling uncontrollably backward as the floor of the cavern opened.

The last thing he remembered was plunging weightless into complete darkness, while far above him a ball of fire burned to a bright-white point of light, like a collapsing star.

▲ ▲ ▲

He counted the seconds as he fell . . . one, two, three . . . but when he grew bored with that, he tried to remember the title of every book he'd ever read: *The Throat-Cutters of Carib; The Isle of Dread; Adventures in Amazonia* . . .

That would take forever. He didn't have forever. He stopped counting and realized he had stopped falling. He was at the bottom of a chasm . . . a well? No, he was inside a mountain . . . a volcano. He was able to see, sort of, which surprised him. Angles of light had wedged through cracks in the mountainside, and across from where he lay was an opening to a wide tunnel. Perhaps he would get out of here after all.

Bren went to the opening and peered in, and what he saw struck him like a blast of polar wind: the entire tunnel, floor, sides, and roof, was toothed with swords and axes, daggers and knives, pikes, polearms, lances, and more.

He backed away and circled the cavern, looking for another way, but he found none. Of course not—this wasn't some random, natural formation. This was deliberate. A test. Through this tunnel of swords and axes were the Lost Words of Magic. Even after everything Shveta had done, he wished she was here to see it, and to help him figure out how to get through.

What if he just declined? He looked up to see if there was any way he could climb out, but the walls seemed to rise for miles.

This was the only way. Maybe Shveta was right. He, Bren Owen, had been chosen for this. But he had to be willing to suffer to find out what he was meant to do.

He stepped into the tunnel. The blades cut through the thick, fur-covered leather boots he had worn since boarding the *Sea Lion*. He could feel the blood pooling under his feet. In agony, he stumbled and put out his hand to brace himself against the tunnel wall, and a lance pierced the palm of his hand. It was all he could do to keep from falling to his knees in pain.

On he trudged, looking for any sign of light, an end to the cruel passage. And then, the pain began to recede. His wounds still hurt, but each and every step no longer cut him, and finally he staggered into a chamber where one enormous book lay open upon a massive stone pedestal.

He went to it, and looked at the open pages. He couldn't read what was written there, but he knew what it was. He turned page after page . . . the language changed again and again . . . wedges, runes, hieroglyphs, pictograms, alphabets of infinite shape and form . . . the book was a polyglot of ancient, lost magic.

And it was he who had found it.

He closed the book and studied the cover, a thick leather hide embossed with a serpent swallowing its own tail. He picked it up, weighed it in his arms, thinking about carrying such a large book all the way home. It was priceless. He could sell it, and his and his father's troubles would be over. But what responsibility would he bear putting such a powerful book back into the world?

He returned it to the pedestal. He could just leave it here. No one would find it again. But *he* found it. Bren Owen, a fourteen-year-old boy from a small town in Britannia. Or was he fifteen now?

He could bring the book back into the world but guard its secrets. If he was one of these Nine Unknown (which still seemed ridiculous to him), perhaps that was what he was meant to do. Power like this couldn't be destroyed, but it could be kept out of the hands of the wrong people.

Shveta had said she wanted to remake the world. Didn't it need remaking? Was there anything about it that seemed good and just? Admiral Bowman had been mad, but he hadn't been wrong when he explained to Bren the cruelties of colonialism and the corruption of the company system. No doubt Shveta nursed legitimate anger against those people from Bren's own country who had taken over her homeland.

Bren could hear Archibald Black scoffing at him. *Do you see a pattern there? People righting wrongs with more and more wrongs?*

He heard Mouse speaking to him again, on another mountain in another place: *Whoever comes to power, there will no doubt be a prophecy about their downfall, and another child stolen from a family, or some other atrocity by those hoping to make it so.* He and anyone else would just have to make a better world for themselves with their own mortal powers.

Had it been Mouse at the Leopard's Nest? The deep and silent way the monk looked at him? Knowing all about navy signal flags—and knowing that Bren would under-stand them? If so, then she had given him the tangka, the mandala, and the instructions for where to find the Lost Words of Magic for a reason. And he thought he knew why. Ani had understood, too.

Bren knelt in front of the pedestal and began to write in the dirt with his finger. He had no understanding of the words, he had only memorized the images, running left to right around the border of the mandala. When he had finished, he stood up and waited.

The rumbling began again in the belly of the volcano, and this time Bren suspected the damage would be far more catastrophic. He hoped that Lady Barrett and Nindemann and Ani and the brothers were far enough away, but even if they were, they had hundreds of miles to go with precious few resources.

There was an explosion. Rocks began tumbling down from above, crashing all around Bren. One hit the pedestal, splitting the book in two and rending the binding, and to Bren's astonishment, the words fell from the loosed pages until he was standing in a litter of broken spells and scat-tered letters.

The floor began to give, and when it did, Bren fell

deeper into the mountain, expecting to land in a lake of boiling magma. Instead he kept falling, and falling, until the rumble and roar of the volcano faded from earshot, and all he could hear was the whistling of cold air past his ears and the echo of his own beating heart.

CHAPTER
31

THE IMPOSSIBLE
BLACK TULIP

The *tap, tap, tap* sounded like it was inside his own head.
And it was annoying. His head hurt enough as it was.

It was pitch-black, wherever he was. He couldn't
remember, actually, and when he fumbled for a light all he
managed to do was ram his knuckles against rock.

"Ow!" Bren screamed.

As he nursed his hand, he heard, *Did you hear that?*

Aye. Behind there.

Bren tried to stand up and hit his head on more rock,
letting out an even louder howl of pain.

Over here!

There were a pair of taps now, *tap, tap, tap-tap, tap-tap-tap*, which grew louder and louder, until Bren heard rock tumble from a wall and a small beam of light showed him that he was in a tunnel. Again. At least, though, it wasn't made of weapons.

The hole grew bigger, and the light brighter, until soon Bren was staring into the smutty faces of two miners. "Dear God!" said one. "There's a boy down here!"

▲▲▲

Before Rand McNally had transformed Map into the mapmaking capital of the Western world, this part of the Cornish Peninsula had been known mainly for its tin mines, and mine shafts and tunnels still honeycombed the ground below the town. Most of the tin was gone, but a few enterprising men and women still occasionally went treasure hunting, usually with a map they had bought from Rand McNally.

Bren crawled through the hole, past the stunned miners, up and out of the tunnel and into what felt like an early spring evening with a bright full moon. All the mine entrances were north of town, and so Bren walked through the neighborhoods of the tradesmen, relishing the yeasty smell from the Belgians and their beer vats, and the strong scent of soap from the Italian garment makers, until he came to a familiar storefront in a narrow lane of Map's

Merchant Quarter. Bren wasn't sure what time it was; it didn't matter. There was a light burning inside, and Archibald Black sat at his counter, hunched over his chess board.

Bren quietly opened the door and shut it just as silently. "You're going to have to get a lot better if you want to beat Aadesh," he said.

Black looked up at Bren, then back at the board, and he began to weep. They embraced, and when both had regained a measure of their composure, Black told him how it was indeed spring 1602, and Sean had gotten them back to Britannia months ago. Sean had stayed with Black for a few days but finally decided it was time to go see his own family back in Eire.

"Oh, Bren, you must know we didn't want to leave you. If there's anything we could have done differently . . ."

"I know," said Bren. "You didn't leave, you were taken. So was I. You did the right thing. Lady Barrett told me everything."

"So she did find you!" said Black. "Did she bring you all the way back here?"

"No," said Bren. "And I don't know if she's okay. If I were to guess . . ." He stopped and said, "It will take a while to tell you everything. What about my father?"

"He sits up all night, getting drunk on cabbage wine," said Black. "Go see him."

When Bren reached the shabby clapboard house with the leaky thatched roof, now looking shabbier and leakier than ever, he was afraid to go inside. He wasn't sure why it was so hard, but he had to remind himself how much his father needed to know Bren was alive.

Bren never told his father he went to see Black first. They sat up until dawn with each other, talking until David Owen had to leave for work, and then Bren climbed to his sleeping loft, determined to sleep for days.

He arrived on the landing to an astonishing sight—on his narrow windowsill sat the neglected clay pot where he had planted his tulip bulb so many years ago, and blooming there was a perfect black tulip. Bren went to the window, looking at the tulip from every angle in the light, convinced it must really be a deep purple. But it wasn't. It was solid black.

He smiled and turned to the wall across from his bed, where as a child he had drawn his large map of the world's most fantastical places: the Orient; the East Netherlands; China. Improbably, he had been to all these places. But the map was different now, as if someone had been revising it while Bren was gone. There was the Vanishing Island in the southern Indian Sea. And there was the island where Bung Ananda had tried to build his own Paradise. The Pearl Cliffs, Qin's tomb; Khotan and the Dragon's Gate and the Leopard's Nest. The Arctic

Islands no one had thought existed.

Only one thing was the same. There was Fortune, the place his mother had told him about as a child. An enchanted island that hovered between sea and sky, appearing unpredictably.

"I'd like to think it's real," his mother had said, and so Bren had mapped the imaginary island in detail, hoping, as a child would, that mapping Fortune would somehow make it real.

Except he had kept that map, that childish wish, hidden inside his small writing desk. And yet here it was, tacked to his wall.

Something startled him. Mr. Grey hopped through the window, knocking the black tulip sideways, causing Bren to jump toward the window to try and rescue his priceless botanical, nearly pushing it entirely off the sill instead.

"Where on earth did you come from?" said Bren. "Have you been coming here this whole time? Who's been feeding you?"

Mr. Grey just sat there staring at him, then ignored him completely and began grooming himself. Then, as if it had been his idea, he walked toward Bren, pausing within arm's reach to stretch and invite Bren to pet him.

As he bent down to stroke Mr. Grey, Bren noticed grains of sand on the floor. Probably just dirt—it would be just like his father never to have cleaned up here—but then he noticed sand all over the floor under the map of Fortune as well.

His mother had told him something else about their enchanted island: that she imagined it as "a place of peace, where only the people you love can find you."

He stood up and reached into his pocket, feeling around until his fingers found the cool, smooth surface of the black jade stone. He had taken it out of his pocket long ago, convinced it was worthless, and had no memory of replacing it. And yet he knew it would be there. He took it out and held it on his palm. "Let's pretend this is a piece of Fortune," his mother had said when she gave it to him.

No, it couldn't be. But then Bren looked at the blooming black tulip and reminded himself that nothing is impossible. He placed the stone back in his pocket, scooped up Mr. Grey, and closed his eyes. He cautiously stepped forward, imagining all the time that instead of a wall, he would feel a warm wind against his face and hear the thunder of ocean waves. It was only when Mr. Grey squirmed out of his arms that he opened his eyes, and kneeling on a vast beach under a pure blue sky, he grabbed a handful of brilliant white sand and let it slip gently through his fingers.

ACKNOWLEDGMENTS

Shortly before this book went to print, I lost a dear friend, Dale Mackenzie Brown. Dale gave me my first writing assignment for publication, and he continued to encourage and advise me through the years. I am deeply saddened that he won't read this. The book is dedicated to my agent, Jen Rofé, but I would be remiss if I didn't thank the Andrea Brown Literary Agency for allowing Jen to take a shot on me way back when I submitted a peculiar book about a puffin. And to Jordan Brown and Walden Pond Press, who gave me a chance, I will forever be grateful.